# Sunshine Alley

*Sunshine Alley*, by Gail Kittleson, pulled me in from the start with Kin's heart-wrenching journey surrounding the separation of her son, Jesse. Told in prose as measured as a mother's heartbeat, this WWII story unfolds with experience rendered with quiet truth. The author's judicious research is compelling along with her unique literary style. In an age of instant news and gratification, which has dulled our sense of longing, this story reminds me what it means to wait—to love across oceans, war, and through silence.

~Becky Van Vleet
award-winning author of *Her Strength Within*

After reading Gail Kittleson's newest book, *Sunshine Alley*, I felt like a missing part of my childhood was "filled in." My dad served in World War 2. He treasured his connection with his "war buddies" and stayed in touch with the war survivors right up till he died. I asked him many times to explain what it was like … but he refused to talk about it.

I finally found a book that described the mindset and courage of the people who lived through this terrible time in our country. Gail captured the spirit of a country that fought together and supported each other in brave patriotism.

She has a beautiful way to share her faith in her stories, an honest and clear way of bringing her characters through trauma and healing. I was actually sad when the story ended. I wanted more!

~Kay Hiscox

This is Gail Kittleson at her best: dark secrets, redemption, an impossible romance, relatives lost and found, absolutely stellar writing. When you read it, you won't be disappointed!

~Cathy Fiorello
Amazon.com bestselling author of *Dreamreader*

In Gail Kittleson's latest novel, *Sunshine Alley*, the author uses history as the foundation for an engaging story about faith, hope, love, redemption and belonging. She takes us on a spiritual journey with a strong but troubled woman named Kindred who comes to grips with personal demons while trying to reconnect with her son, a soldier in World War II. As in many of the author's stories, two themes emerge: 1. We all have a place in the world, and we are never completely happy until we find it. 2. Love is a bond that transcends time and space.

~Michael Barr

I don't read a lot of historical fiction, but [*Land That I Love*] compares to the best of all literature from throughout the ages…not simply a specific genre. Kittleson has woven words reminiscent of lyric poetry throughout and poured bits of historical information into a touching and tender personal story of a father, a son, and a faithful retainer as they settle into the Texas Hill Country prior to World War II. Watching the characters' lives grow and change as the world around them copes with war presents a fascinating picture of human dynamics, while the words that tie the history to the story of real people is one of the best jobs I've seen. This is a novel you don't want to miss. Even if you don't particularly like historical fiction, I think I can guarantee you will consider this novel an enriching and enchanting experience. Kudos of the highest order!

~D.A. Featherling
author *Conventional Murder*

Kittleson deftly writes strong female characters facing heart-breaking tragedies. *Until Then* features two: Marian, caught in the Blitz, and Dorothy, a surgical nurse whose work with the 11th Evacuation Hospital has taken her to North Africa, through Sicily and into France. Their stories intertwine in a narrative that touches then heals the soul. Highly, highly recommended!

~Literary Soirée

Also by Gail Kittleson

# Women of the Heartland Series
In Times Like These
With Each New Dawn
A Purpose True
All for the Cause
Until Then
&
Kiss Me Once Again
*a Women of the Heartland story*

In This Together
Catching Up With Daylight
Land That I Love
Secondhand Sunsets
The Winds of Change
A Mystery on Church Street
Love at the Lavender Farm
Providence

*with Billy Rae Stewart*
Country Music's Hidden Gem

*with Cleo Lampos*
The Food That Held the World Together
A World War II Holiday Scrapbook

# Sunshine Alley

*a novel*

# GAIL KITTLESON

WordCrafts Press

To authors, famous and seemingly insignificant,
whose writing lives on after them
to inspire and challenge us all.

Never watched someone die before. Didn't mean to send a man to perdition. Certainly never shot anyone and had no such intention. Not to say my imagination had never laid a fellow low. Notions like this had brought me to this moment, alone in the country, lifting a green glass bottle to my lips. Such an elemental scent, like lilacs way back in the Kentucky hills just before their buds fully burst. Or not-quite-ripe grapes, stark against the palate, yet full of promise.

But I knew none with a hint of … *Hmm.* What *was* this tang?

In a sheltering cottonwood's shade, this bottle called to me. Mere inches away, a flicker of sunlight made all the difference. This shift between shade and shadow would slake my thirst.

Thick emerald glass had brushed cool against my burning skin. With slight effort, I released the cork, liberating a mere suggestion of scent.

The bottle's lip touching mine, I considered. What if the liquid had been tainted? But my craving won out and banished all catastrophic possibilities. With the first tiny sip, relief went sliding down my throat. Like a dip in the creek on a sweltering childhood day, another refreshing drink eased the tight wire strung through my being.

Before my eyes passed images from yesterday with its typical chores—washing, cleaning, cooking. Thank goodness I'd set the chicken coop to rights before sunset and toted plenty of water for my hens.

Here in the shade, another set of hens from decades ago came to mind…Mama's. She always called them her girls, and so did I.

Pondering their persnickety natures, I drew a solid breath for the first time since leaving them all behind. Mama had left hers, too, when she and my sister Annie pulled me in a rickety wagon down a hazy path one moonlit night. I only knew we were fleeing Papa's wrath.

Somewhere above me, leaves brushed in a whisper. All would be well. Mama had survived, and so would I.

And then came clarity, like a waylaid phantom. Here on this slab of grey limestone boulder, warm in spite of the shade, the covert taste made itself known.

Tears.

Tears of regret, and so much shame, a choking realization. Heat enveloped my eyes as my thoughts returned to the event that had urged me away. An inner alteration transpired. No surprise, as I had already lived two lives—one forever ensconced in this hardscrabble ranchland, another in the university's scholarly halls.

Ah, such a difference—cold and heat, North and South, scorching sun and the midnight impenetrability of Texas range. I scarcely recalled those months of learning, teaching—golden hours immersed in books, doing what I loved, knowing my passion had found a home.

And so much more to come! One day I would become a professor—Mama's pride would know no end. I would show students essential literary truths for living one's best. And one day, perhaps, I too would write, creating poetry and stories for hungry souls.

How could I possibly have forsaken all of this when Clyde launched his pursuit? All I can say is that losing Mama so unexpectedly devastated me. I couldn't sleep and had no appetite. I lost my bearings.

Years before, Annie had married and moved to Kentucky. When word came that Mama had passed, I know she grieved too but had her own family to tend.

After the funeral, each day I awakened to an emptiness nothing could fill. Mama had been my benchmark, my confidante, my best friend. How could I possibly go on without her?

Way back in elementary school, soon after the three of us arrived from Kentucky, Clyde, an unruly, unwelcome menace in our classroom, had staked his claim. I kept my distance, but he vowed to make me his wife one day.

Dear Mama *pooh-poohed* his attentions and laid a strong foundation for my future—a future without a crude man like Clyde. My education would be secured before she left this world. She saw to this with her fingers, cleaning and sewing for others.

But now she had passed, and with her, my inspiration. How might a body manage such pangs, or a mind, for that matter? Scattered and wind-whipped, beleaguered thoughts often betrayed me, hindering actions that might have changed everything.

But yesterday, leaving the ranch Clyde called home, I could only swallow my distress. Regret, that vast, despairing wilderness, an utter wasteland. Heaven only knows how deep this chasm, how full of remorse. Virtual mountains of it loomed beneath my breastbone.

Near the point of collapse, this pause beneath sheltering branches, most likely the result of an early settler's foresight, staved off despair. The bottle awaited discovery. Perhaps some recent wayfarer had left it by mistake. Or maybe on purpose, to help another traveler on their way. At any rate, it waited where I would find it. And full.

This unique essence brought a gush of pilfered tears, for on such a day, who could sense no compunction? After the deed I had just carried out, however unplanned, I hurried to the cabin to pack a quick carpetbag. Eyeing each corner that had been our home, I weighed what might be most needful.

Strange, though I'd thought of leaving hundreds of times, I never considered what to take. But first, 'twas easy enough to drop Clyde's belt and boots down the well's deep chasm. To write a note for our closest neighbor, Mrs. Willard.

An eighth of a mile down the dirt road, I left it in her mailbox, asking her to care for my girls—my cackling friends. Like everyone within twenty miles, Sophie Willard knew my husband. She would stay clear of the house and other buildings when she came for the hens.

Old Drake aided me with Clyde's body, too large for the well and too heavy to lift. Such a faithful work horse all these years—had Drake any idea of his mission? In effect, he would deliver his longtime master to a final resting place out in the cornfield.

No need even to touch this fine animal, for noting my nod and the slump in the makeshift sling attached to the cinch, he pulled the ropes. Perhaps he knew scavengers would make light work of this load.

Heat and wind would soon dissipate Clyde's clothes. Buzzards would do their part, vanquishing his earthly form. The sun would bleach beyond recognition whatever they failed to ingest, and at night, wild hogs would complete the work.

Once I left, Old Drake would fare just fine. Pete, our derelict hired man who showed up when the mood struck him, would not neglect Old Drake, his one pal in this world. He would wonder about us, but summoning the Sheriff meant a three-mile trip into town—too much effort.

Instead, finding the cabin empty, he would help himself to a swig of whatever sat on the table. He might actually move in, a far sight better quarters than he'd ever known.

The scene unfolded now as I rested on this accommodating limestone. Mama used to tell stories as we traveled further from Papa, and oh, the irony of this one I was living! Someone else would take over the cabin so rudely vacated. As if he'd worked hard for this place, Pete would take charge of Clyde's ranch.

My own chuckle startled me. At this juncture, others might have panicked, but another irony struck. 'Twas the Law that first planted in me the seed to leave.

Those times I sneaked into town to talk with the Sheriff, he took one look at my bruises and declared striking out from the ranch "…the only way, Ma'am. Meanest sort I ever did see. Men like Clyde Lovelace never change, not in this lifetime."

But I never truly thought to go, for fear's invisible fetters arrest the soul. They render us incapable of advance, tie us to an idea that scarce exists in reality even though its deceptiveness threatens our very lives.

No matter how I may have cursed my decision to marry Clyde, and though I knew grief over Mama's death had nearly rendered me daft at that time, I could not forgive myself, nor bring myself to leave.

My soul harbored one grave mistake, but to hurt Mama again by breaking my marriage vows…I simply could not face the inward condemnation. Certain about what needed to happen, I had been helpless to act.

Grateful for the shade, I relished another swallow. A second, much more powerful taste made me wonder. Even as I sipped, a wayward sun shard revealed a tinge of gold in the bottle, like the harvest moon that shone on recent nights. Recollection took me back once again to the ranch.

Clyde always said, "Them's yer hens, you take care of 'em. Them Appalachian cedar cutters kin steal y' blind, but I ain't 'bout t' git that chicken stink on me."

So I watched my flock day and night, like youngsters. Chattered to them from the time they emerged from their eggs as if they could understand.

Yesterday was no exception. Last night on my final turn about the ranch, the moon shone day-bright, so I stayed out a bit longer than usual. But then, a foreign sound echoed—*could that be a footfall?* Cloth ripping on the fence—*only a stranger would venture so close to those barbs.*

My heart skittered as I spied someone. In the shadows on the southwest side of the coop, he leaned over my prize hens. Something came over me, like a spell sent by ancient Miz Tierney down the road a piece. When she set a spell on you, you'd know it for sure, folks said.

These hens comprised my lot, all I had in this world. And someone had stolen way out here, fixing to confiscate my biddies?

Well then.

Quick as a lizard, quiet as one too, I raced to the milk house, where just inside the door leaned Clyde's shotgun. Nary a telltale squeak as I edged that decrepit door open to the lingering richness of yellow cream awaiting my churn.

Without a peep, I slipped back to my watching spot.

Short *scrapings* then, like the hesitant steps of a wee one learning to walk. The intruder moved along to the next hen, checking the wire I'd placed to ward off foxes and coyotes.

*My* wire.

Upraised, the twelve-gauge pained my shoulder. But I held her secure.

"Mister." My voice seemed remote, riding a night breeze, except no such thing existed on this blistering Texas night.

He jerked up, poised motionless as a beetle in a sudden frost.

"Those hens are mine. Now you *git!*" He half-turned, but before I could make out his face in the moonlight, gunshot nearly split my eardrum. Knocked me on my backside. I'd learned long ago to lay my finger flat against the barrel until ready to shoot, lest an inadvertent quiver set off the action. Besides, Clyde always warned that this gun had a hard pull.

The cicadas continued their chorus and moths stirred from their hiding as my hens took flight. My mind recounts the scene over and over. I never did pull the trigger.

Guns sometimes do simply *go off*. Accidents happen—*don't they?*

After the shock of the explosion, I roused myself from

the rocky earth outside the chicken coop in a maelstrom of feathers. That thieving rascal still swayed like a wormy post listing in the wind.

Any second, Clyde would surely run out across the yard—though liquored-up, he could still hear. Yet the whole ranch echoed a peculiar stillness.

*Thud.* That smack of flesh on harsh Texas soil, I shan't likely forget.

One step closer, something shiny stole my breath away.

Clyde's belt—the buckle he'd bought himself at the county fair a few years back. Chiseled and mighty fine, he declared. Cost a pretty penny, too.

What had he been doing out here? Other questions I asked years ago came forth, from when I sprawled broken-ribbed in a corner, or when my babies died before their time.

What had Clyde done?

Oh, my babies…the times he…

On my way to the cabin, step-by-step, their three bitty graves against the fence lanced a mighty shiver through me. Some things stay with a body forever.

Sweet newborn faces. Recollecting how they passed before they had a chance still set me to quaking. Even worse, how they received no wrapping, slung into the earth like so much chattel.

Forgiveness, redemption, humility, justice, reconciliation—when I consider those three Innocents, these words find no settling place. But I remember their names.

Magnolia, Violet, and Charles—in spite of Clyde, I gave them their birthrights. Three times, he whisked them away. Three times I believed they might have lived, had they known their mother's care.

But I had bled too much and could only lie there. Outside the cabin, Clyde's relentless shovel struggled against hardscrabble rock.

The fourth time, he softened a twinge and fetched the midwife. She took such gentle care with our baby, and people hailed that tiny boy as our firstborn.

Jesse. For his life I shall ever render thanks.

Entering the cabin last night, something in me wakened. As I gathered the needed tools and headed out to find Old Drake, one instruction propelled me. I must leave. Soon.

Hours after the limestone boulder and the shade, famished and, as Mama often muttered, "all done in," I leaned against a rickety corncrib. Still a distance from the turn onto a main road, the structure's wooden slats creaked and moaned, mimicking my exhaustion. Which way—East or West?

Unable to decide, and despite the heat bearing down, I dozed off. By the time I roused, day's end ushered in twilight, and shadows masqueraded as evening silhouettes.

In the Northwest, a steely cloud bank hovered. No farmhouse in sight, only this reeking old crib full of rats and who-knew-what-else. I pressed on, and five minutes later, two lights shone in the distance, side-by-side, conquering a hill.

On the country paths, only ramshackle trucks had meandered between fields spattered with lazy-eyed cattle or sheep. In contrast, this first-rate, graded route boasted plots of sorghum, wheat, and corn. On either side, cattle pastures, and between them a *bona-fide* automobile bore down.

As it neared, its size loomed, like an ambulance of sorts, chugging toward me just as the first wet splotch fell from the sky. I halted and wiped my face.

The driver slowed to a crawl, peered out and opened his window. A weary-looking, mustached man, his voice came placid as a spring breeze.

"Need a ride? Going to Waco?"

Was I?

I managed to mumble something. As raindrops increased, the dust covering my arms turned into muddy trails.

"Get in. I'm a doctor. Work over at the Vets' Hospital. It's not far back, and I can see you to where you need to go."

Truly? And where could that be?

The shower commenced in earnest as he set the brake and hurried 'round. He ushered me into the front seat and shut the door. Oh, what soft leather to languish against! Gradually, my fingers relaxed from clutching my carpet bag as he wheeled 'round and headed eastward.

I hardly noticed that he changed his direction for me. Something about this leather spelled safety, refuge…hope.

At his second query about my destination, my reflections turned to mush. Against my will, a hopeless jumble issued forth.

"Going to…I…started out quite… Not sure where…oh, do forgive me."

The driver's composure made room for my trembling, endowing a measure of dignity. He seemed to know what to say to one bewildered—or perhaps simply how to keep silence.

Do I recollect what he did say? Not precisely, but his demeanor somehow quieted my jittery spirit.

How else can I explain the quiet that descended? I felt sure this kind man would do right by me. Images of a brighter future paraded before my mind's eye in sync with the motor's loud drone and the growl of the clutch.

Though I could not have put these visions into words, a visceral serenity engulfed me. There would be bumps along this new path, of course. But something about the set of the driver's shoulders, even the drips falling from the brim of the worn brown Fedora he tossed into the back seat, dispelled all trepidation.

I had been bound to meet someone eventually, right? Bound to fall into a semblance of design. Some of us seem incapable of creating these plans on our own initiative but react to circumstances instead.

How do we meet just the right people when we need them? Does guidance arrive in human form, so that with the help of another's presence, our thoughts about what may come to be take shape?

Pondering all of this, I rested in the rider's seat, stroking much-used upholstery. Marred with age but comfortable and inviting, the thick covering spoke of endurance. It was then I apprehended the second taste: a savor of hope.

By the time a sprinkling of lights appeared in the distance, my rescuer understood my lack of destination, that I could not return to my starting point, but could work. Little-by-little, he amassed this information and laid out a course of action.

"I know someone." His tone turned cheerful as the dawn. "She runs a boarding house, and just the other day when I visited a patient there, she said with so many excess workers moving in for the war effort, she must find more help. Perhaps you…"

He glanced my way while navigating the city's perimeter. Down a street with measured blocks on either side, he made a narrow turn and passed a wide grassy area to a private drive before a mammoth frame house set back by itself.

"Perhaps you and Miss Millicent will be able to strike a deal." His mustache scrunched up as he grinned, and his heavy dark eyebrows lifted like retreating storm clouds.

With that, he grabbed my valise, led me to the side entrance, and knocked. Beside him, I stared upward—two stories above the ground floor, this residence stretched beyond my sight. The structure must be twenty times our cabin's size.

No rain here, only the beginnings of a cool breeze. Some bushes separated the distance to a building set in a deep back yard among several shade trees. I returned my gaze to our spot beside the door, to a bush with yellow roses.

Something about that bush whispered what my soul required. *All will be well.*

How many times since then have I traversed that particular threshold? Upwards of a thousand, surely. Out to fetch the milk in the mornings. Out to gather eggs, out to volunteer at the hospital, back in with aching feet after a long shift. To the garden to fetch last-minute dinner vegetables or to weed for a while in the long rows.

Grateful, always grateful.

The doctor? Once a week, he stops here after his morning rounds—sometimes on Wednesday, sometimes Thursday. It wasn't until yesterday I realized he isn't actually *Doctor Graham*, but Doctor something else. People use his first name as his last.

No need to know your deliverer's formal moniker, and no one here has the slightest inkling of mine. For them, I answer to Kindred. Miss Millicent once asked my surname, and I blurted, "Fresh."

Kindred Fresh. I like that. Fresh from another life, fresh like the snap peas I prepare for dinner, fresh each morning, rising to work and seek the day's beauty.

Before my arrival here, life had turned stale. Ever-dusty air, the same old door creaking on rusty hinges, same ancient floorboards thrusting a nail here or there to trip you up, same piercing eyes following your every move.

But I had rounded a curve, hurtled through an opening—a once-in-a-lifetime shift from one world to another. Yes, and just when I'd become convinced my life had reached the very end.

Chapter One

*Waco, Texas, July 1, 1941*

In exchange for room and meals, this boarding house—every stairwell creak, every ceiling crack, each droop and inadvertent fold in the dining room's flowered wallpaper—has entered my being. An inanimate object, this house where I live and work, and yet she breathes.

Water stains from the beleaguered roof remind me that despite imperfections, this building shelters workers for the coming war—too many, fears Miss Millicent. But Judson, one of the boarders who hailed from the Deep South, replies.

"If some inspector shows up, I'll take care of 'im."

Miss Millicent adds, "He will surely convince them of its safety, if anyone can."

Miss Millicent, a willowy remembrance of days gone by, inherited this property when her parents perished from the influenza. "I rely on Judson's judgment, for without our establishment, what would we do?"

By *we* she means she and Elwyn, her husband who resides upstairs, second floor, far northeast corner. And such a sight I never did see.

At nineteen, Miss Millicent received Elwyn back from the Great War, a mere ghost of the young soldier to whom she'd bidden farewell. He arrived in France with plenty of time left to fight—time to be wounded and gassed.

Mustard gas, they say, burns the skin and lungs. Sends the

eyes astray, so much so that if you happened to wander into Elwyn's quarters for the first time, you'd back right out.

But Miss M had promised herself to him in matrimony, and his condition only fueled her devotion. As she quips, "Love is love, don't you know?"

On my first day here, she introduced me to Elwyn as if bringing her finest guest to their obscure room at the end of the long oaken hallway, around a surprise turn. Laying a gentle hand alongside his face, she gestured my way. Her other arm extended toward me like a branch.

"Elwyn, I want you to meet Kindred. Touch her hand for a sense of her. She'll be bringing your breakfast from now on and cleaning up in the mornings."

"Nyea, Mul." This response passed through lips marred and nearly sealed by white scars as Elwyn fingered the edge of my sleeve.

From his wooden chair on wheels, for his left leg had shriveled to nothing, he provided my first language lesson. Reduced by the mustard gas searing his larynx, his voice sheared like knives being sharpened.

And his cough, oh my! To think Miss Millicent cared for him all these years here in this obscure corner of the world. Seeking for words, I waited for this spell to end as she held him through the worst of it.

*Reduced* covered nearly everything about this man. Frayed eyebrows, bushy in one spot and burned off in others, sunken chest, stick arms that coursed from shoulder bones crushed inward— everything about him had been diminished.

"Kindred will bring you the paper, too." Miss Millicent turned to me. "My Elwyn thinks as sharp as the day he left for the war. If you read him a section, he will take in the information and ruminate. Later he may have a question or an insight and will look it up.

"He *can* see somewhat, just so you're aware. Circle what you read and during the day, he'll re-think it." She held up a magnifying glass on his bedside table. "You'll see."

Indeed I would.

Outside his door she mouthed, "Did you understand what he said?"

"*Yes, Mil?*"

"Exactly! You have a way, Kin. Somehow, I knew you would." Her skirt brushed against the wall as she turned. At the same time, the window at the end of the hallway, awash with stained glass, spread gilded lilac and rose medallions over us.

"He suffered other wounds, as well, but I take care of everything having to do with…" She pressed her lips together. The stairs sighed, cushioning her descent.

"But to have someone bring him his breakfast while it's still hot and take time to read to him a bit, oh my goodness! I cannot tell you…"

A shallow breeze conveyed the subtle scent of lavender, Pausing mid-step, she breathed in through her ultra-slim nose. "Why, no one but me has ever…" She hesitated. "…except Doctor Graham, of course, and Judson. Most evenings, he takes a notion to get Elwyn some fresh air.

"That wonder of a man! He hauls Elwyn downstairs, out to the porch after most of the boarders have gone to their rooms. Often, he pushes the chair, and the two of them go for a walk." The floorboards on the first landing breathed a welcoming sigh as she passed the worn banister.

"It gets harder and harder. Judson…" Her tender brown eyes found a spot in the wainscoting and rested there. "He brought Elwyn back to me—he had been wounded and suffered shell-shock, too, but still found me. He knew Elwyn belonged here."

As if pondering whether to continue, she stalled. This old house seemed almost alive. Were the walls listening, awaiting her next word?

"Somehow, Judson got himself over to France in the first place. They weren't looking for men of his origins—darker-skinned, you know. But if Judson decided on an action it would be mighty hard to hinder him.

"Way back in the Deep South, his people were warriors and

earlier, in the wilds of Africa. Elwyn told me when news of the Great War filtered to Judson, he yearned to fight. He's one of those who doesn't quite fit anywhere, but he found a way…"

The clock's tick became loud in my ears. The golden-bronze of Judson's skin reminded me of a statue I'd seen once in a town square, weathered but burnished. A mulatto, some would say. Not quite one, not quite the other.

"And he fits here, too. Once we settled Elwyn, Judson simply stayed on. People around here highly value his work—he's never without something to fix or build. Especially now, with the Bluebonnet factory going up over in McGregor and a new warehouse or airplane hangar on every corner."

"He's found a place to belong."

"You are so right." We proceeded down a few more steps before she turned to me.

"There will be a war, he says, no doubt about it. He watches everything and has met with some of the soldiers here. Besides, Judson…has a way of simply *knowing* things."

This hallway, adjacent to the dining room, revealed another sort of knowing…the skill of the woodworkers who set these boards in place, sanded and varnished them to a luster, and the window makers who gave such attention to each detail, creating this unique beauty.

An aromatic remembrance from tonight's meal—cornbread, scalloped potatoes and ham, homemade pie—lingered too. Another brand of beauty.

Probably most boarders were none the wiser, but the door to Judson's room, just down from Miss Millicent and Elwyn's, harbored a distinct squeak. Often in the darkness between midnight and the first thought of morning, Elwyn would cry out and Judson's door would jerk open.

Footsteps sounded in the hall, shushed voices… My tiny room, once a third-floor storage space, sat right above them and echoed each break in the silence.

On those nights, a puzzle piece slipped into place for me. Judson still carried out his warriorhood. Seminole, perhaps, mixed with the blood of slavery, his step stayed light for such a large fellow. I imagined him in the dark, gaze focused, back straight as a telephone pole, his mission clear—to care for his buddy.

"When he lifts Elwyn to his rocking chair on the porch and they begin to discuss the day, I relax." Miss Millicent added, "Do you understand?"

"Ma'am, I…I think I might. Someone else takes over for a while. Is that what you mean?"

"Exactly. How insightful you are—a godsend to us in these dire times. And do please call me Miss M, like everyone else." She stopped and faced me, awaiting a response.

"I do hope to be of help, Ma'am…Miss M. We all have to support each other, right?"

There in the lower hallway, near a grandfather clock forever casting time aside, we caught our breath. An east window looked down at the back yard and on a path overshadowed by a tall cottonwood and dappled in sunlight. Was it part of this property, and if so, where did it lead? For just a moment, I glanced out to see the sunshine play on the branches, and before I knew it, Miss M had disappeared. Had she gone into the kitchen through the door on the left or further down, to the dining room?

I couldn't say, most likely because Elwyn's form…the way his eyes scattered as they tried to focus, the trace of ammonia and aftershave in his room, how he jerked in his chair, that shriveled leg… The entire scene had penetrated me.

Similar sights played out with patients when I volunteered over at the V.A. hospital three days a week. Plenty of older men who had lost their way out in society and would remain in the V.A. until they passed from this world.

Then there were boys learning to walk again, to find words

to converse, to discover how to use an arm or leg shattered in a pilot-training crash. They struggled to move beyond the boundaries of their wounds.

Miss M was right to use the word *dire*. Regardless of our country's official status, the war had already begun. Pilot training, with its share of accidents, kept our wards nearly full, since this dry, flat countryside made a perfect setting for aerial instruction.

Outside of town, near the site of the original Lake Waco Dam, workers were constructing an airfield. An airport for the city, word had it, a municipal airport. But Judson claims the U.S. Air Force will soon use the facility for recruiting and training.

In the last war, Elwyn and Judson led the way. Now, they observed young fellows flooding to Waco, ready to offer their all. And night-by-night, with gusto, they shared front-porch speculations. For a man otherwise so silent, Judson wakened his tongue to speak with his war buddy. And after days spent mostly in solitude, Elwyn came alive.

Mama had such high hopes for me. As long as I can recall, she asserted that my intelligence exceeded all expectation. Now I have learned through hard experience, with fearsome war news from Europe and betrayal on every hand, common sense holds far more sway than mere intellect.

With the hospital patients and right here at home, faithful service wins over brilliance every time. Where had my intellect gotten me, anyhow? When I ponder this, the ever-fading image of my years with Clyde spring up again to mock me.

Judson, his days filled with hard labor and his nights encumbered by cries from the darkness, instructs me. We've barely shared two words, but his steadfast behavior communicates more than can be verbalized. It's not simply his actions, but his bearing, like a ship set on its course once and for all.

His brand of wisdom cannot be learned from books or even honed through practice. His insight comes as sheer gift—as Miss M says, "He just *knows*—he said Doctor Graham was the one who could help Elwyn, and here we are years later, with the good doctor still coming to care for him."

She speaks like this in a tone of wonder. "Judson is our special gift from heaven, that's all I can say. And I am so very grateful."

Judson's cavernous facial lines tell their own story, along with a luminous glimmer in his black eyes. Who knows what he experienced in the Great War, in addition to seeing his comrades slaughtered or rendered senseless by gas attacks?

And who can tell what he endured before that, during his childhood? I can only imagine, as Mama's people hailed from deeper in the South. Many of the tales she told in my childhood claim a violence all their own.

Case in point, her Uncle Rand, who struck out from his rural home to seek his fortune when he turned fifteen. But his older brother, Hoke, wanted Rand to farm with him for the rest of their lives.

Having taken over the family farm when their Papa died, Hoke followed his wayward sibling and summarily brought Rand home in a hastily-constructed wooden box. Come Hell or high water, this young'un *would* submit to his will.

True story. Hoke saw himself as the family boss. So, for the rest of his days, he farmed alone.

Senseless, this saga, like the Great War. And like this developing one, except that evil seems so much more powerful today. At least last time, military mechanization had not progressed so far.

But come what may, England must win, even though some side with Neville Chamberlain and believe in appeasing Herr Hitler. Right here in Texas, plenty of folks agree. They call themselves isolationists, as opposed to interventionists, who want the U.S. to get involved. President Roosevelt, the isolationists say, will lead us from wise neutrality straight into destruction.

In one of his Fireside Chats, the President told us America should be the "Arsenal of Democracy." On September second last year, he openly defied the Neutrality Acts by passing the Destroyers for Bases Agreement. In exchange for military base rights in the British Caribbean Islands, this deal gave fifty WWI American destroyers to Great Britain. And as isolationists are quick to point out, Hitler and Mussolini responded by joining with Japan in the Tripartite Pact. For every move we make, the enemy makes another.

Until now, this ongoing debate had been largely lost on me, for Clyde preferred seclusion—total isolation. Nary a newspaper or town meeting or political campaign reached us on the ranch.

But thanks to Judson, I hear all the details now and have gained new understanding of the tensions that existed during those years. Of an evening when I occupy a rocker at the far end of the porch, the specifics gradually fill in. It's as if I've finally come out of infancy and can take adult food.

Judson makes clear that while some of our citizens still debate, for all practical purposes, we have already entered what he believes will become a full-blown war. Over at the V.A., support for his view—admissions and death tolls—keep mounting.

We have been supplementing England with our Merchant Marine. Already, we have lost plenty of ships and men.

At every turn, another need sprouts. Then another, and another. These doctors, some who served during the Great War, devote their lives all over again. Many have taken to bunking at the hospital on the heaviest days.

Because of Doctor Graham, I feel a part of that group, too. A very small fragment, but still a minute measure of the healing.

Chapter Two

*January 1942*

Minnie Louise Haskins—such a simple, straightforward name. I don't know what else she wrote in her lifetime, but this evening when Judson and Elwyn discussed the goings-on in Europe between Great Britain, France, Serbia, Russia and Germany, they mentioned King George VI's Christmas broadcast of 1939.

Having inherited the throne when his brother Edward abdicated in '36, this British monarch never planned on being King, but has grown into his role. His much-awaited Christmas address encouraged British citizens and others around the world.

Why did he choose a woman's poem for the broadcast? In the library, I discovered that his decision centered around thresholds. He encouraged his people to move through doors into unknown places, urged them to take one step at a time to alter their circumstances.

On the eve of 1940, nothing could have described England's position better. With Hitler's monstrous beast of an army lurking just across the English Channel, vastly significant decisions lay ahead.

Of course, I did not hear the King's speech, but the copy I pored over satisfied a profound need. The poem he used, written by an obscure woman who had worked both in India and in London's poor East End, someone largely unknown to the King's listeners, struck a chord.

Reading more about Minnie, a professor who penned these thoughts in 1908, made her phrases simmer inside me for weeks.

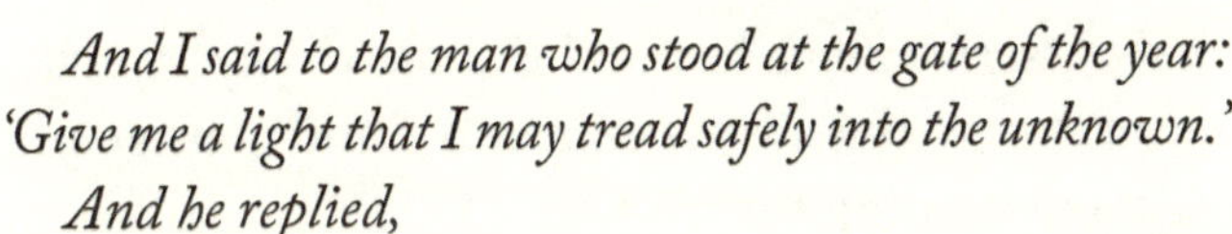

*And I said to the man who stood at the gate of the year:*
*'Give me a light that I may tread safely into the unknown.'*
*And he replied,*
*'Go out into the darkness and put your hand into the*
*Hand of God. That shall be to you better than light and safer*
*than a known way.'*
*So I went forth, and finding the Hand of God, I trod*
*gladly into the night. And He led me towards the hills and*
*the breaking of day in the lone East.*

Minnie Louise titled her work, "God Knows," but the powers that be altered it to "The Gate of the Year." A gate stands for an area to cross, a liminal space, a gap of unknowing where one steps out or through, unaware of the results.

Another two years have passed, but Ms. Haskins' sentiments also describe our world at present, scarcely three weeks since the Japanese attacked our Navy at Pearl Harbor. What had seemed like growing chaos as folks from all over came here for factory work has now turned into full-fledged pandemonium.

Nights have become like day. People work all hours in shifts that go on and on. Increased traffic from so many Army vehicles gluts the streets, and even the earliest morning now echoes the noise of people at work.

But not at Miss M's. Oh no! Here, a haven awaits boarders. Entering by any door, walking the hallways, climbing the stairs, one senses peacefulness. Even the wall hangings create serenity— hand-stitched prose or poetry, pastoral landscapes against faded wallpaper, long-cherished portraits.

Perhaps Miss Haskins' poem describes my journey to this abode. So much upheaval, yet I could not have traveled through the hill country at a more opportune juncture. Even then, from all over the country, men and women were being drawn to the perfect flying weather here.

Now, other businesses have begun to flourish. Recent word

has it that the General Tire and Rubber Company will soon build here to support the airplane industry, and contractors are developing more housing for workers.

From the time of the black blizzards, great clouds of dust sweeping over the Midwest and South, nonexistent wages have greatly increased, with jobs springing up out of nowhere. From aircraft manufacturers to creameries, nearly every company requires more workers.

But back to this house… Doctor Graham brought me here as by divine appointment. That very night, in a cubbyhole off the kitchen with the water pipes for company, my heart found its ease.

Miss M apologized for the cramped space and the sounds coming from her recently purchased Frigidaire, assuring me that she would ready a room for me the next morning. But just as that friendly shade tree over grey limestone guided me to the sunlit bottle on the first day of my trek, so did this happenstance.

The Frigidaire's gurgles and groans produced an odd sense of hominess. Their rhythm muted the clock's ticking, which would have kept me awake.

If only I had known when I started out, as Miss Minnie wrote, that I could put my hand into the Hand of God. But despite Mama reading the Bible aloud and having me memorize verses by the bucket load, life with Clyde had drained all spiritual sense from me.

Except for one truth. *I must leave.* I had known this for months but seeing someone after my hens nudged me. And then, Clyde's passing that fateful night spurred me to act. The moment I did, everything changed.

Oh, a deep ache still holds my heart—a longing for my son, Jesse. To touch him, to see him and hear his voice. I can scarcely imagine this. The other throbbing, to be near my sister Annie once more, has haunted me since Mama passed.

But Miss Minnie used the word *finding*. Perhaps that Hand held mine far before I realized it. Something is to be said for initiating a passage with nothing but need, devoid of all except yearning. Yearning for family, yearning for life during all those lost days that ran together like mist.

Perhaps we simply lift a foot in a direction and take a step forward, or a step away. Is that all it takes to start again? Isn't this what the great men and women did?

Wasn't it Sam Houston, the father of the Texas Revolution, who said, "Texas has yet to learn submission to any oppression, come from what source it may." Unlike Texas, I submitted to Clyde far too thoroughly. Yet still today, our people as a whole have not learned that submission—hopefully never will. Every morning, a line forms at the recruiting station, filled with young men their mothers would call *boys*.

With over two thousand like them dead in the waters of a Hawaiian harbor we'd never heard of before December seventh, revenge rules. The streets overflow with hatred for this enemy.

I wonder, did Judson and Elwyn entertain the same level of fury back in their day? The correct term may be *fervor*. Once again, I wonder how Judson managed to gain entrance to a military that blocked his race from serving? So many questions I'd like to ask.

One day Doctor Graham remarked on the recruiting lines to Miss M when she took him up to check on Elwyn. "Those boys look so proud, don't they? I recall feeling the same during the Great War. We believed in the cause. We wanted to do our duty."

"Yes. Duty first. About that—I heard they brought in more pilots from a crash again last night."

No reply from the doctor except this: "Just so you know, Elwyn will never be forgotten. No matter how tight things get at the hospital, he will always be on my mind."

"Thank you, Doctor." After a long silence, with their footsteps the only framework, "How long do you think…?"

Merely a snitch of conversation wafting through the stair-well. I heard no more but assume Miss M referred to Elwyn's prognosis. In recent weeks his energy has dwindled, yet his spirit remains so strong.

What a powerful promise. Doctor Graham will remember him no matter what. Does he make home visits to other veterans, or to Elwyn alone? If so, what stirred him to extend this extra service to one victim of his war?

At any rate, he means what he said. We all live on such vows, and to analyze his would be to scrutinize love.

After dusting the dining room, I fetch water and another rag for the wooden bannister, a lovely piece that must have taken the builder a great deal of time. All the while, ponderings fill my mind.

So many unknown facts, so much behind choices we glibly judge. Running my rag between each opening in the bannister, my view includes the floor above and the one below, depending upon the angle.

My present location on my knees between the two is only temporary. Each time I gather my scrub water and step down, regaining my footing takes a moment. Nothing against either below or above, past or future, but always a need for stability wherever we find ourselves.

To know this is to seek solid ground.

Chapter Three

Some mornings when I collect the eggs, I lollygag a bit in the back yard. Often, the sun has just begun to spill light through our crepe myrtle trees, and I take time to breathe deep of the cool air. On my days at the hospital, a world of not-so-pleasant odors awaits, so I take advantage of this path through the property. The whole grassy expanse belongs to Miss M and Elwyn—what a delight!

As promised, the first day after I arrived Miss M arranged my own small room on the third floor. What a luxury, a place of my own, and even with a window. Still, with so many of us in the house, I relish the idea of this outdoor space being available if I need a walk. Of course, the grass will turn brown, and the leaves will fall, but most of the year sunlight winks through green leaves, with faint breezes astir. Just past the carriage house, this track offers solitude and serenity.

The short trek to the Vets' hospital always energizes me, too. Just two blocks left on Kendrick Lane, one long and four short blocks on Bagby, then right on New Road. Soon, the front gate of the great building announces government property.

When I first arrived, I'd forgotten what it was to cover territory marked into smaller chunks, quite different from country miles. I expect in all these blocks, there might be a mile or so, then a mile back home. After the midday meal, the short walk provides a constitutional of sorts as I return to a menagerie of complicated situations.

Not to discount Elwyn's terrible coughing, adhesions, his constant pain and Miss M's heartfelt concern, but entering the hospital wards magnifies such troubles. Everything here looms larger, for one thing—the structure itself, an impressive entrance, the distance from floors to ceilings, high windows letting in the light.

Hallways branch off like roads, units seem to go on and on. Deep in the maze of these walls, one might forget an outside world exists, lose oneself in the hurry and bustle, the odors and urgent cries.

On the way home, sometimes what I've seen inside, the suffering, the fears, and at times open terror, catches me up in a knot. In a sense, my walk stalls time; gives me space to process what I've seen, a knot that unravels step after step.

The name, New Road, for this street seems no coincidence. I wonder why someone named it this, but the answer may be obvious. Workers forging a new road—not much pause for creativity.

This area has started to grow with the war training, Miss M says, and the little town of Beverly Hills, a few miles south of Waco proper, has begun to grow. So many workers make their homes here, a village bustling with beautiful children.

Some of them must take care of themselves after school. The older ones watch younger brothers and sisters till their mothers and grandparents arrive from working for the war effort.

So different from the ranch. In the vast stretches I walked from there, a label for the path never crossed my mind. Had I thought to name that first track before discovering my grey limestone bench, I might have called it *Hell's Highway*.

From that point on, where I turned north, I might have chosen *The Second Stretch*. From the first farmhouse where I spent the night, *Reinforcement Road*. The next day's journey could answer to *Decision Drive*.

But of course, none of this passed through my mind, so intent was I on the act of leaving. The goal of getting as far away as we can negates most anything else.

What did occur to me during those long hours? Honestly, not much. I thought of Jesse, and of the graves left behind. Ah, dear Jesse! I pondered how he must have grown by now, what he must look like, how tall he might be, how manly, even.

Yes, manly, for he had turned sixteen. Eight years gone from us…from me. The summer he left had tried Clyde to the core. With vast reams of dust darkening the sky like rain clouds, he refused to leave.

Refused, even though we came close to starving. Potatoes saw us through. At one point, we went for three weeks eating only those shriveled brown specimens.

The winds began early in the '30s, whipping into black blizzards. Clyde would come home from town and tell how not far away, those gales had destroyed a whole house, and the *Texies* there had absconded for greener pastures in California.

One of those times, he said stores had started closing up in town. Jesse asked, "Are we gonna leave too, Papa?" An innocent question, but it brought forth a palpable evil horde.

I'd seen a lot already but had never witnessed Clyde utterly consumed with rage. Whatever came upon him must have caught him by the throat, because that's what he did with Jesse. Like a burlap bag of onions, our son, held by the neck, suddenly dangled against the wall.

"How dare you think them thoughts, boy! Al'ays too smart fer y'r britches. Now you hear me good! We ain't leavin' this place no how!"

He held Jesse against the wall boards, my dishpan clattering on its nail inches from his small head. Clyde planted his boots, the biting blue of his eyes darkened into iron, his sharp nose nearly touching the lad's face.

My heart beat out of my chest, but my feet still functioned. I slapped Clyde's arm, hard. Shook him, and that made way for my voice.

"Leave him alone! He only asked a question."

At first I thought Clyde would turn on me, but he loosened his grip. White-faced as rain lilies against a watered field, little

Jesse, always a thin boy, sagged against a chair and attempted to gather breath.

Despite Clyde's glare, I hugged Jesse close. "You're all right now. I won't let him hurt you."

Finally, Clyde took a few steps backward. Then he tramped outside, slamming his boots on the porch steps. Stunned, Jesse and I blinked at each other.

At such times, clarity sometimes makes an entrance. For me, it lay in one severe question: *Why had I ever agreed to marry Clyde?* But no matter. Right now, I had to protect Jesse. Faster than lizards a-scampering, a plan took shape.

I would send Jesse to Annie, who had married Winn Kline, a friend of our family from Kentucky. His parents had brought him out here years ago when they were considering a move to Texas but decided against it.

On that visit, Annie and Winn hit it off and started writing each other. A couple of years later, Annie headed back East to wed.

She'd written me every month as her family increased in size. Now three children still lived at home. Had she been with me when Mama died, Clyde's appearance might still have startled me, but I might have found my backbone.

With the back door still screeching on its useless hinges and Jesse in shock, I shook away these conjectures. Suddenly, my mission shone as distinct as the sinking sun in the distance.

"You must go to Aunt Annie and Uncle Winn, Jesse." The solution poured from my lips as I stared into my son's terrified eyes.

Oh, what a change there! I saw the same mix of trepidation and eagerness as on his first day of country school, but as I talked more about Annie and her family, excitement gradually won out. At her house there would be three cousins to play with, two boys and a girl, a farm with a hay mow, and a large school a few miles off—a school in a real town.

This way, he could further his education—could even attend college some day and become a professor, a doctor…whatever he wanted to be. What remained here for him but more of Clyde's belt on his backside and more scenes like tonight's?

Nothing at all. The shudder that took me as I considered what might have happened if I hadn't been in the kitchen nearly threw me to my knees.

"This will turn out all right, I know it will." At my whisper, Jesse took another feeble breath. Staring at the red marks on his neck—my only son's neck—I vowed this would never happen again.

That night, Clyde stayed out in the barn. No need to check on his state. Drunken, he would sling himself into a pile of straw like a forkful of rancid manure. Predicting tomorrow came easily—he'd be long in getting up. The cow would be mooing for attention like crazy before he stirred.

Plenty of time to get into town early and put Jesse on the train. I might pay the price when I came home, but only one thing mattered.

Though fear assailed, I knew my son had a good head on his shoulders. He'd won every mathematics and spelling contest in our country school district for three years straight, and his teacher bewailed the lack of opportunities for him.

Once he knew the plan, Jesse quickly memorized Annie's address. Next I drew a map complete with towns along the route, which he pocketed.

I cached my egg money in my bodice and helped him pack a bag. So few belongings—a couple of shirts, some jeans, his favorite books.

"We'll leave at first light. As soon as we get to the station, I'll send Aunt Annie a telegram that you're on your way, and she'll be at the depot to meet you."

Jesse licked his lips. "Mama…" He swallowed and fought back a surge of emotion.

"I know, son. I'll miss you so much, but this is the only thing to do. You understand, don't you? I must keep you safe."

"When will I see you again?"

"That, I cannot say. But Annie knows where I am, and if you need me, she can…"

His somber eyes told me he knew better. Annie would never ask, and I would never come. But he'd seen other families torn apart in past years by those horrific black clouds, the plowed-out earth, the relentless wind, the times.

"Having you safe is all I care about, Jesse. Aunt Annie and her husband are kind folks, and your papa will never have a chance to lay hands on you again."

Two ruddy splotches rode below his cheekbones, splashes of heat and desire. Jesse, my firstborn, my only. I explained the sketchy map again and sat by his side until he fell asleep. The song I sang sprang from somewhere in the past, about Kentucky hills, about green grass and hope.

When his breathing came regular, I slipped down beside him, holding him close until dawn. Looking back, I forgive myself for sending him off, for my motive sprang from love, just as surely as my motive for marrying Clyde issued from grief.

In town, I spoke with the station master and the conductor, a gentle sort who held his hand on Jesse's shoulder. With each conversation, Jesse grew calmer.

"You'll be on the train about seventeen hours." I handed him enough coins to fill his pockets. "Don't be afraid to buy something to eat and drink, all right? You need to keep up your strength to play with your cousins when you get to Kentucky."

Finally, the conductor shooed me off, and Jesse waved good-bye through the window. With such pure motives, why did I feel so like a criminal?

With the platform emptied of well-wishers and the train a far-away speck, I walked to the Sheriff's office. A good man, an honest man.

"You know our son, Jesse? Clyde's been after him, and I'm afraid for his life. So I sent him off just now to my sister in Kentucky."

"Long trip on a train." Sheriff Stringham scratched

underneath his hat. "But Jesse has more common sense than some far older. He'll be all right, I reckon."

"Could my sister send a telegraph to you when he gets there? Her name's Annie Kline."

"Sure. I'll find a way to get word to you." Sheriff Stringham stroked his chin. "My Effie has remarked more than once that your Jesse's the brightest boy she's ever taught."

He stared after the train. "The brightest ever, she said—catches on without any help a'tall—and you know she's taught young'uns many a year."

Everyone knew this man, whose first wife had died of a fever, was stuck on Miss Effie but wondered if he would ever make a move. With the backs of my eyes burning, I looked away, but I knew the Sheriff meant well.

As if to prove that, he patted my shoulder. "Your boy'll make out all right, I'm sure of it."

What a ceaseless two days, with Clyde at me like a shrew. His fury knew no bounds—but somehow, nothing he said or did touched me. He swore he'd go to town, get on a train himself, and find Jesse.

"I'll drag that boy back here, I will. Although with his nose always in a book, he ain't much earthly good."

Finally, I threatened to go stay with Sophie and her husband, Holland, if he kept at it. He quieted down then.

What relief when Sophie herself brought me word. The Sheriff's messenger asked her to, since he was needed back in town, and this would save time.

"You sent him to your sister?"

"I had no choice."

Sophie mistook my sobs for a torrent of regret. "Well, you can get him back, surely."

"No. He can't stay here…" She peered closer at me. Only friendship there, and trust, hard-won through long years. "Clyde almost killed him, Sophie. Next time he will."

She gritted her teeth. "Like them babies a' yours. I might could do in that monster m'self. Don't deserve the ground he's standin' on." She knew it, and so did I.

But Clyde owned that ground. His land, and there he would stay.

My goodness. I have already reached the last block on New Road before the hospital's front entrance. All brick and mortar, the edifice stands to my left, and everything to the east, technically, remains outside the city limits.

That includes Miss M's property, but it still seems like we're residents. Things change in a city—inclusion becomes technical, a matter of maps and streets and regulations.

Before entering the hospital, I lift up Jesse. Lift him up to the Deliverer who put me on the path to this dear place and set my spirit aright.

Why didn't I take Jesse away years before? And why didn't I board that train with him? What had been wrong with my thinking back then, to continue on in such a woeful way? Unanswerable questions.

Dried grass crunches as I pass an Army truck lumbering toward the back entrance. They'll deliver sheets and towels, bandages and cloths for dipping into cool water. Cool water for feverish heads…young soldiers taken with all sorts of infections and delirium.

And then Jesse suddenly seems so near, as if he materialized from the bricks. This has happened over and over during the years since I put him on the train, but today he seems even more tangible—as if he is reaching out.

He climbs the front stairs with me. Only a mother who has had to send off her child knows what I mean. By now, I surely hope he understands my reasoning, faulty as it was. I'd made a vow, and Mama would never countenance divorce.

"But your Mama had passed years before then!" Someone might say this, and they'd be right. In my thinking, though, she still reigned. I had failed her by leaving college—I must not fail her again by leaving Clyde.

Maybe one day when he has children of his own, Jesse can fathom how settling him on that noisy train with his skimpy bag and six quarters for food nearly destroyed me. Does he realize how I've longed for him all these years?

Whether he comprehends why I could not go with him, I cannot conjure. But do I even understand fully? What I cling to comes in letters. Faithful as always, Annie responded right away when I sent her my new address. She included a quite grown-up letter from Jesse.

*We had a debate, and my team won so we get to go to State now, and I'm a running back on the football team. In winter, I'll play basketball, too, because Coach says I'm quicker than most.*

*If you're wondering about my schoolwork, it's all pretty easy. I've learned to type forty words a minute, which everyone thinks is super, but really, there's nothing to it.*

Annie used to enclose notes and drawings from him each time, but he had become a young man now, and those missals had ended. "He's itching to sign up," her last letter said, although he was underage for the draft.

"Shall I sign for him?" Legally she could, for he went by *Kline*, her married name. I had sent no reply as yet. How could I find the words, and besides, what right did I have to an opinion?

A set of double doors leads into the dressing room where I wash up, put on my uniform and an apron. Beyond the door, down the hallway, lie boys not much older than Jesse. Here, I have discovered the incredible gift of meeting their needs as much as possible.

Down a hall smelling of antiseptic and ether, I step into the ward. Crossing this transcept, one enters another world, leaving behind all else. Even Jesse. These boys, consumed with pain, long for their mamas. War has turned out differently than they had imagined.

Doctor Graham gestures me to the worst of them, just out of surgery yesterday. Some of them already passed from this world during the night hours. They will have been taken somewhere cold, somewhere austere and heartless.

No one speaks much of the morgue, reached through a conglomeration of hallways and descending stairwells. Our young soldiers' effects accompany them as they await burial here or families to fetch them for their last ride home.

Recently, a father toted one such precious load out into the country, a stricken parent with a team hitched to the wagon he and his son once filled with hay. Sent off to war with pride and high hopes, his son came home all too early. There, the boy's mother waited.

In this ward, some patients on narrow mattresses beneath white iron steads have skin matching the sheets. Will they make it? No one knows. Others exude a certain radiance, a tinge of life—they have begun to heal.

Doctor Graham's glance of welcome and gratitude warms me as I slip into my duties, centered around twenty young men traumatized by wounds and surgeries. They need sips of water, a cool touch, a tender word, a listening ear.

Some have fallen from the sky in fiery crashes. So far, not many have reached this facility from faraway places, but I can almost visualize them streaming in.

Traveling the aisle from one to the next, I try not to hurry. Here a young man sobs. There one cries out and another moans in pain. A little further, a stoic fellow stares at the ceiling.

Along the way, two objects stand out. A vial on a central table and a small medicine bottle, fashioned from green glass. These simple items take me back to the bottle that waited for me under my shade tree, green with sunlit glints of gold.

My woundedness, invisible from the outside, found solace

in that temporary refuge. My inner darkness cried out for light, and sunshine on that bottle called to me.

For these patients, let me be that bottle, that light. Make me a part of the elixir that strengthens them to go on.

Later, Doctor Graham pauses to say, "Be sure and stop at the kitchen. Say hello to Rosita before you leave, all right? She asks about you nearly every day."

Rosita, the main cook here, Dr. Graham's wife, must be the kindest woman in the world. Someone said they married just last year, Rosita for the second time, Doctor Graham for the first.

An unlikely pair, some might note, for marriages between Hispanics and Whites are rare. But Dr. Graham is honing his Spanish, and they go together so well.

Every day, trucks deliver food and supplies, administrative offices run full tilt, and Army vehicles come and go. A bevy of stretcher-bearers pass in and out of this hospital. At any time of day or night, military police enter or leave.

Something's always astir here, but it's love like Dr. Graham and Rosita's that keeps this place working. Here early every morning, here all day long, not just in body but pouring themselves out for all in need. If I provide an encouraging swig of hope to some of the wounded, it's their steady love that holds everything together.

Chapter Four

*February 1942*

"**H**ey! I'm gonna be bruised for weeks!"

"Yeah. Me, too." Rubbing his backside, Jesse Kline grinned at his best friend, Willie.

"Remember this when we're groaning about Army training, okay?"

"Yep. Bound to get worse'n bruised, but we'll do far more to them Japs. They'll be more'n sorry the U.S. got in the war!" Willie dragged himself to shore. "Never thought I'd slide down that waterfall, but I might just try it again."

"Beat you to it." Jesse scampered clear of the stream and raced to the top again. "Whoo-ee! Japs, here we come!"

As sunshine filtered lower and lower through branches barren of their colorful fall leaves, his sigh spoke for both of them. "S'pose we'd better be gettin' home, Will. Don't want Aunt Annie to worry. But I'm sure glad Beau stepped up to do my chores today. Always wanted to see the Red River Gorge."

"Nothin' so beautiful anywheres, they say. And since we're leavin' for the induction center next week, Pop didn't mind me takin' a day off. He's so proud of us joinin' up, he can hardly stand it."

"And your mama?"

"Well, that's a different story. Sure do hate to think of her cryin' when we leave."

*He's so proud of us…when we leave…* Willie had been including him in the family ever since Uncle Winn passed last fall. Willie's dad took Jesse in, too, just like Aunt Annie and Uncle Winn did eight years ago.

As they rode their horses across the hills toward home, melancholy enveloped Jesse. He'd inherited this tendency from Mama, Aunt Annie said—she was always pondering words and phrases, meanings and life in general. Usually he could shake it off, but today proved an exception.

A few days ago, he and Willie joined hundreds of other Kentucky recruits to register, in a line as long as a football field. Next, they'd head to the induction center and then be sent off for basic training.

Early January air carried a chill. Willie turned to Jesse. "Ever think we'd be goin' off t' war? If them Japs hadn't attacked us at Pearl Harbor, we'd be…"

*Pearl Harbor.* Even hearing those two words produced a chill. That place must be cursed.

"Damnation! Just wait till we get at 'em!" Better voice his feelings here, where no one but Willie could hear him. Aunt Annie would never countenance him using the "D" word—but Uncle Winn had let it slip when they were out hunting on rare occasions. It wasn't often he missed a shot.

This morning, taking a skip day from high school felt so grown-up. But for a moment astride his pony, Willie looked like he had eight years ago when Jesse first arrived here, a freckle-faced kid with dimples as deep as China.

Jesse's thoughts went back to his visit with Mr. Somerset, his favorite teacher. He'd gone to see him after registering, before telling Aunt Annie.

"You already signed up?" The tall teacher finished erasing today's lesson from the blackboard, spreading chalk dust everywhere when he released the eraser. Jesse's sneeze made him glance up.

"Yes sir, Willie and I went together. We head out in a couple of weeks."

"Guess I'm not surprised. Fort Thomas Induction Center?"

"Mm hum."

"Been there." Usually short on words, Mr. Somerset seemed especially conversational today.

"Great War?"

"Yep. Still remember it all like it was yesterday." He tapped his fingertips on the desk. "I signed up early, too, like you and Willie. Couldn't wait to get my hands on a rifle and shoot some Huns."

"What's the Fort like? They said we'd have physicals, be fingerprinted, and have a criminal background check."

"Right. There's an interview, too, before they assign you a job. Probably a classification test these days. If you want to fight, don't let it slip that you can type so well or you'll end up behind an Army desk somewhere. Never did see a student learn as fast as you, Jesse."

"Magic fingers, I guess."

"Let's see. You'll get your serial numbers and have a swearing-in ceremony." Mr. Somerset squinted out over the schoolyard. "Eventually, you'll go to another fort for basic training. Sure you're ready for this, son?"

"As ready as I'll ever be, and *now* is when they need me. We get a two-week furlough before reporting to a reception center, so I'll stop in to see you again."

"Hmm. We'd better say good-bye, just in case. You'll find out soon enough that the Army changes its mind at least half the time, and a promise isn't always a promise."

Lest he end on this note, Mr. Somerset gave Jesse's shoulder a fatherly pat. "You'll do well, in spite of it all. I know you will—you and Willie both."

"You bet. We'll be the best—that recruiter said so, and we'll prove him right!"

Following Willie down the last stretch toward home, Jesse breathed deep. Life had already taught him to say good-bye, first to Mama one long-ago morning, then when Uncle Winn died way before his time. But it didn't seem to get easier with practice.

All around him and Willie, rich shades of Kentucky green colored the hills. Better memorize this scene—might be the last time he'd see it.

On the appointed day, Jesse and Willie climbed aboard a train car. Willie took the aisle seat, trying hard not to look out at his parents. As he predicted, his mother sobbed, but Aunt Annie kept her composure, with Pearl and Beau standing beside her near the depot.

She promised as much before they left home. "Let's say good-bye here. I don't want to make this any harder than it already is. Your mama's never been much of a crier, but she would cry today, I can tell you that."

Her eyes, as green as Mama's, took on a far-away look. "I thought she never would get over sending you to me."

"How did you know?"

"Her letters…she put her tears into words on paper."

Her deep breath tore at Jesse's heart. "I just wish Winn were here. You know he'd be more than proud of you."

Nodding was all Jesse could do. His throat had one of those pink rubber balls stuffed down it and noting other families around them didn't help. Most weren't even trying to hold back their emotions.

Then suddenly the conductor called, and the leave taking ended. From the window, he waved at Beau, who stretched as tall as he could, trying to look old enough to enlist. Pearl threw Jesse a kiss, and Jesse launched one to her and Aunt Annie.

Something about this scene sent a longing through him. No use entertaining the desire to see Mama—hadn't the past eight years taught him that? How many times had he wished she could be here to watch him…his debate contests, his last basketball and football games…

The memory of her facial features grew weaker by the year—would he even recognize her now? Now and then, he'd meet some stranger on the street and do a double-take because of the imagined resemblance—freckles, clear-cut cheekbones, friendly jade eyes.

But when it came down to it, he had to admit his mind had grown blank about details. When you're eight, your mom seems tall, of course, and she'd always been on the skinny side. She would be crying today, Aunt Annie said, but he couldn't remember her expressing much emotion.

As always, he tucked these thoughts as far down as he could and turned to Willie. "Well, we made it, and so far, they let us stay together."

"They'd better. You're a decent sharpshooter without me, but the two of us together—we're unstoppable."

As the depot shrank behind them, Willie turned talkative. "Got any idea where Fort Wolters is? Anywhere near where you lived when you were little?"

"Way north of there, I think. Up near Fort Worth and Dallas." Jesse might have continued, but honestly, he had no inkling where their ranch had been in the huge state of Texas. And since his father died, Mama had moved away from there.

Now, the war was shrinking the whole world—after graduation, two girls from his class would be making bombs in California. Another would move to Pennsylvania to create radio crystals in her uncle's factory. Otherwise, these girls might have married and never left the state.

Along with the rest of the world, the entire nation seemed to be shifting from here to there. He and Willie were most likely headed across the ocean, but what difference did location make, anyhow?

Chapter Five

Miss M runs the boarding house, no question about that, with no lack of challenges. But she's unflappable…always composed. I don't know how she manages, with Elwyn to care for and all her other daily duties.

I've been here long enough to grasp that her quietude comes from within. It's easy to see she has a whole other life inside that no one sees. Maybe the plaque on her bedroom wall, opposite from where Elwyn's wheelchair sits, gives a clue.

> *The first rule is to keep an untroubled spirit.*
> *The second is to look things in the face and know them*
> *for what they are.*
> *Marcus Aurelius*

I suppose some folks might classify her as *bossy,* but this would be imprecise. Her actions show she believes in what she's doing, and you get the idea that following suit would be wise. But Miss M never demands that you do.

On my first Sunday morning here, for example, she donned her white gloves and hat after we cleaned up the kitchen. Not a word, mind you, about her intent, but overhearing Judson ask, "Anythin' I can do in here while you're gone?" guided me.

"The chicken should be all right in the oven till eleven, and the table's set. If you can turn on the fire under the potatoes, we'll just need to mash them and bake the biscuits when we get home."

While answering, she glanced at me. When she said "we,"

I knew she expected me to accompany her. So I did, but with no white gloves, hat, or Sunday dress. Nobody seemed to mind, and with a subject like *Peace During Wartime,* how could I not lose myself in the service? On the way home, we discussed the power of words, and I allowed as how I used to write.

"Used to? What did you write?"

She accepted my simple reply. "Poetry." Of course, that had not been all I used to write, but the topic ran so deep, I had trouble making a coherent reply.

We walked half a block before she turned to me. "Poetry? Why, I don't believe I've ever met a poet. How wonderful! I should like to read something you've written, Kin. Would you let me?"

"Oh, it's all gone…I mean, left behind."

"Hmm. Well, if you create something new, please do let me know."

Not a command, but a desire, a willingness. I said nothing more at the time, but her eyes sometimes remind me of my forsaken belief that I was meant to write. Somehow, though, when something worthwhile comes to mind, I avoid picking up a pencil.

But other forms of art have attended me here. From the very first, Miss M allowed me to help with the cooking, and this brings a satisfaction I cannot explain. Three meals a day—eggs and bacon, pancakes, grits, biscuits and gravy in the morning.

At four o'clock, my internal clock tells me it's time. A minute later, the floor above me squeaks, and Miss M begins her day. For an hour and a half we work in silence.

How did she do all of this alone before I came? At the same time, I look back at miserable, empty ranch mornings—how could I have possibly accomplished so little? All I can say is, maybe I'm making up for lost time.

During these early hours, Judson watches out for Elwyn. I think he may dress him for the day. I haven't asked and won't. But when I take up Elwyn's meal, Judson has already eaten his breakfast and gone off to his own work, leaving the bedroom tidy and Elwyn facing the morning sun in his wheeled wooden chair.

Most of our boarders heft heavy loads all day long and need hearty fare. They look forward to meat and potatoes every evening. For others, the evening meal strengthens them for the night shift, and breakfast equals dinner.

Something about putting ingredients together to form meals for these workers makes me happy. And bringing out a dessert like apple pie or rich chocolate cake—the expressions on their faces say it all.

They've eaten plenty already, but this last blessing proves better than the first. Perhaps it's my German ancestry, although these days, any sane person would avoid touting that. Still, a bit of sweetness after the meal, however small, sits well.

Always gravy over the potatoes and meat, served with home-made rolls and butter, and most evenings, a side dish. Sometimes green beans, often carrots, peas, turnips or buttered corn in season. All of this bounty grows out back, in the half acre set aside for the garden.

Judson waters every other day, a toilsome task involving dipping a pail into a reservoir built by early German settlers. After work, he lances his hoe at the weeds, striking like a diamondback. Often, he spends the early evening hours in these rows, right after dinner, his thick overalls gathering more grit for the weekly wash.

He barely leans when he strikes—no strain on his back that way. Mustn't risk his vocation of caring for Elwyn.

This evening, out picking vegetables for tomorrow, heat still hovers, so I stick to the shade. From there, backed by the setting sun, Judson's profile defies the eye. He might be a muscular eighteen-year-old recruit.

"Judson's the same age as Elwyn. A December birthday, as I recollect." Miss M shared this confidence over the washing machine one day when I first came. "So many likenesses…each the eldest in their family, set on fighting in the last war, but equally determined to get home, come hell or high water."

She twisted a towel to release some of the rinse water, and the old machine pumped on, its gas motor humming. "Both of them so interested in what's going on in the world, you know? Always something in the newspaper to catch their interest.

"At first, I feared this would upset Elwyn too much and interfere with his healing. But Doctor Graham said not at all—his active mind needs something to ponder."

The pump squealed. "Just a belt. Judson will replace it—he keeps watch on everything around here." Miss M's eyes glinted. "Elwyn still wants to contribute, too, you know."

The image of her husband's fading person flashes before me. As it is, what does he contribute? Perhaps a reason…a reason for Miss M's steadfast resolve, a reason for Judson. When you have a reason, your very best emerges.

Now, the last of daylight slips further from us. In a few minutes, Judson will lean his hoe against the inner wall of the shed, carefully shut the door and wash up at the pump. He'll sing a soft tune the whole time, his voice a muffled rumble, but I can never make out the words.

Then he will cross toward the house and climb the back stairs to his and Elwyn's side of the house. As he strides down the hall, he calls out, his voice low and sonorous.

"Almost full dark, brother. Time to get you out of this place!" I imagine Elwyn's face lighting at the sound of Judson's rich bass.

In ten minutes, Judson will wheel him outside, carry him down the front stairs and push him to the corner and back in the outdoor chair that matches the wheeled one upstairs. Then, with most boarders already in bed or gone to night shifts, he will seat Elwyn in his favorite rocker on the front porch. Many evenings I note the rhythmic process, Judson carrying Elwyn in his arms step-by-step, murmuring low, as a mother to her child.

A scraping of the front door, and Elwyn is deposited out in the fresh air for a time—removed from the four walls where he lives out his days. Miss M might go and sit with the men when they return from their walk, for they are family. Sometimes I join them, too, or find a chair down the broad porchway.

How must it feel for Elwyn to get another view of this world, to see the rare automobile pass by? This porch, some place to go besides his solitary spot upstairs.

They start their commentary on just about anything to do with the war—which most days amounts to everything. How many new recruits have come to our area? How many patients fresh to the hospital? Which battles are being fought and exactly where, which theater proves the most significant at the moment…or the most exasperating?

Names from the Philippines course between them. When I delivered Elwyn's breakfast the other day, Judson had positioned a map on his bed, handmade of thick cardboard with clay formed into the major South Pacific islands. Pins occupied a box with exotic names printed on small pieces of paper.

Judson had explained the distances between islands and given Elwyn a job—cutting the paper pieces and writing the names. This occupied his hands during the day, and when he came home, Judson guided their placement on the map.

Their porch discussions resemble guessing games about which power will strike first, the Japanese or our troops, and where. On the European front, they scathe the French for failing to realize the Nazi military build-up on their Eastern border, and both the British and French for declaring war after Germany invaded Poland, but then doing nothing for a full year.

Next they move on to the fall of France.

"Wounabeen no dunky if them Rencha'd…"

"Would have been no Dunkirk if the French had fought. Yes. The retreat might have destroyed the entire B E F—but the French could've pushed the Huns back. Can't understand, either. Men with no heart to protect their own country."

I'd grown in my ability to follow what Elwyn was saying. His utterances were in no way parrot-like—he had ideas of his own and steam to let off, too. Most often he did this when some confounded Colonel or General proved unworthy of command.

And Judson…he must have saved his vocabulary for these times with Elwyn. Hardly spoke a word otherwise, but in their conversations, his understanding bloomed.

When the German Bismarck sank the HMS Hood on May 24, Judson and Elwyn spent an hour on this disaster that killed fourteen hundred sailors. This would do the trick, Elwyn declared. Simply blast all enemy troops out of the Atlantic before they reached their destinations.

They discussed the history all the way back to Great Britain's loss of the HMS *Glorious*, *Acasta*, and *Ardent* in June of '40. Fifteen hundred British sailors vanished off the coast of Norway. Judson and Elwyn still recalled all of the details.

Such foreign names…I would never have heard any of them without these local scholars identifying places and dates and losses. After speculating about the Navies, they turned to another theater entirely.

In North Africa, a new German commander named Rommel is headed towards Tobruk, Libya, but thus far, the city has held against his attack. Americans—our GIs—living in tents in the vast African desert. Hard to imagine.

In Europe, Yugoslavia has surrendered, the British evacuated Greece as Greek Prime Minister Koryzis committed suicide, and Greece has surrendered over 200,000 troops to the Reich. South of Sicily, the Germans have bombed Malta.

In Great Britain, the Luftwaffe has carried out devastating air raids on London and Liverpool. Tens of thousands of British citizens have perished.

Judson and Elwyn have no compunction about calling out ineffective commanders. This one was "too cowardly to attack," or as Elwyn phrased it, *sho n bens* (short on brains.) The night they learned that the great German ship Bismarck had been sunk, their voices rose far above normal.

"Sabouti!"

"Right you are—*it's about time*. Everything takes longer than we think."

It probably helped that Judson had his own network—officers who had hired him to roof their houses or build garages, and enlisted men whose wives trusted him with what they'd learned on the "inside." Easy to imagine them confiding in him as he put in a new doorframe, painted a house, or fixed a washing machine.

Have I mentioned Judson's face, as fixed as granite? This man would never break a confidence, and looms inscrutable, self-contained. He has become a rock for Elwyn and Miss M, a shelter in their private storm.

Though I have gained weight since coming here, Judson seems larger than any human I have ever met. His massive high forehead and arched nose appear in my dreams at times, sometimes in scenes with Clyde.

Such opposites—Judson so powerful but keeping his might under control. Clyde, always longing to be seen as mighty.

The newspapers carry stories enough to ignite passions on the porch. Some of this involves incompetence at high levels. That's when Elwyn bursts forth.

"Tupa ijuts!"

"*Stupid idiots* is right!"

Hearing about our losses in North Africa, Elwyn shakes his head. "Dopoboys…oh, dopoboys."

"Those poor boys, for sure. Who sends men into a valley with an enemy dug in on the high places?"

Elwyn rocks back and forth, faster and faster.

"But we had some lunkheads in the last war, too. Remember? That's the way of war."

Judson always finds a way to settle Elwyn. By the time the temperature cools, they have held a magnifying glass to the war's progress, reacted together, and agreed to subside until tomorrow.

By then, the first evening star often sparkles above Kendrick

Lane, close to the city, yet with a rural air. Besides the garden plot, this large house and the garden shed, there's another building, the carriage house. Judson has begun to repair this to house the overflow of workers.

When he stays home for a day of pounding and sawing out there, he takes Elwyn for some sunshine, and after an hour or so, returns him upstairs. Doctor Graham has positioned his chair to receive the best light from his single window.

In those hours outdoors Judson works, and Elwyn grasps as much with his ears and skin as with his eyes. Such tight-wrought skin…Doctor Graham has mentioned new grafts, Miss M says, to ease his pain from adhesions.

But she holds reservations. Would the promised relief be worth the suffering the surgery would cause? Considering what I see in the wards, I wonder.

The carriage house still stores Judson's ancient rattletrap truck, waiting to tote whatever's needed from town. And the big front yard makes us seem even farther away from the hospital and the base with its pilot training and…well, a whole world springing up overnight like a wild mushroom patch.

On evenings like this one, when I have heard most of the men's exchange about the war, I draw a deep breath, thankful that Miss M absented herself from their rendezvous, glad she hasn't heard these specific woeful statistics. Nothing here to encourage or bring cheer.

If she had, would she have reacted? Listening to Judson gather Elwyn in his arms for the climb to his room, I think not. Even as they cross the porch, Judson breathes soothing phrases into his friend's ear.

"Terrible thing, war. We learned that young, didn't we? At least ours is over."

Through the parlor and up the first flight of stairs, fewer words come through. "…thought…never again, but…help them however we can…"

Horrific beyond measure, the wounds Elwyn still bears from

his war, and those unseen in Judson, unite them in an endless bond. Tonight, under this vast inky sky, all across the world, other *doughboys* like them must be recalling the Great War that turned their lives upside down.

Of course, this leads to pondering Judson's undying devotion to his friend. He might have sought various opportunities after they returned. Clearly, he had gleaned a good knowledge of the world. How had that come about in the Deep South? Another question to add to my list.

Miss M said Judson has never married. Even though he's over forty now, he could be called up for active duty if Congress so chooses. What a conundrum that would provoke!

How would Elwyn respond? I cannot imagine…and who could possibly take Judson's place? Miss M would manage somehow, I suppose.

A sudden wave washes over me. So many bombings, sunken ships, surrenders, prison camps, and lost civilian lives all over the world. How might anyone keep track of it all? Our front-porch warriors attempt to. They pay homage to the lost and shout *Bravo!* to those still in the fight.

Does their absorption with the war make a difference? Can some sailor taken captive in the South Pacific sense that way back here, someone cares? I wipe my wet cheeks and think of Jesse. Has he gone to one of these horrible battles?

Nothing to do but pace the length of the porch and empty my heart. "One thing we know without a doubt, our prayers are heard by the Creator Who made us all," Sunday's sermon declared. "When we pray, we give our very best."

So, casting aside my doubtful nature, I do my part.

"Oh, please take care of him, and do let this war end. Keep them all safe. Bring them all home." Almost adding *soon*, I recall a lesson learned on the ranch. For many a prayer, this word is unfitting. As Judson and Elwyn often note, not much happens *soon* in wartime.

Annie's careful handwriting, postmarked July of '42. I grabbed the envelope and sank onto a porch chair. *I will remember this moment,* I thought. *I just know this is about Jesse.* The envelope opened easily with my fingernail.

Holding two pages written on pale blue military stationery, I sat there thinking of the wounded boys I'd just left at the hospital. The late afternoon sky carried a hint of coolness. A mockingbird sang from the crepe myrtle, kitchen sounds and smells wafted my way.

Still not reading, I thought of anything except what faced me. This is my way, I've learned. It's what I did with Clyde, with our miserable life on the ranch. Every single day, I set it aside. Maybe it would go away.

True, it had, but at what cost? And even then, I had not made a choice to end that existence. No, not really.

The gun went off, Clyde crumpled to the earth, and I could scarce believe my eyes. At last, I knew I must leave. Not exactly a well-thought out plan.

Between my fingers, the inked blue paper called. Breathless, I unfolded the pages.

> *Dear Aunt Annie and y'all,*
> *It's October already, but no leaves are falling here in the middle of the ocean. They told us to avoid specific references, so I'll leave it to you to figure out which ocean.*
> *We're sunbathing on the deck while headed for some*

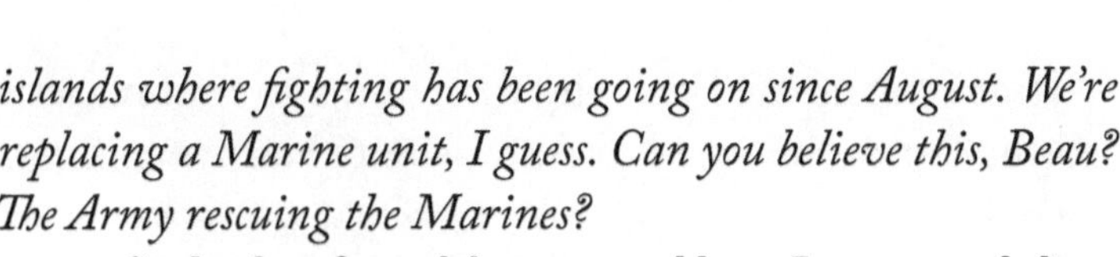

*islands where fighting has been going on since August. We're replacing a Marine unit, I guess. Can you believe this, Beau? The Army rescuing the Marines?*

*Such a lot of scuttlebutt around here, I try not to believe any of it, but it's impossible not to listen. One of our buddies named Joe revels in the gossip—he's a real storyteller.*

*That's fine, as long as he watches our backs like I plan to watch his. And he will. He's a sure-fire Presbyterian, so I know you'll approve of him, Auntie.*

*The food's better aboard ship than in training, and there's enough rain showers to keep us all smelling decent. Not sure how I ended up in this unit, except to say Uncle Winn had a lot to do with it.*

*Of all the things he taught me, who would have guessed I'd use his squirrel-hunting tricks the most? Beau and I learned from the very best and were sworn to secrecy. Of course now, every other private who watches us shoot can see it all.*

*Take care, Pearly, and be good to your brother. Beau, don't you be thinking about signing up any sooner than you have to. Do what I say, not what I did, all right?*

*This trip reminds me of the time you and I ran under Pap Murphy's porch when it started to rain hard. Remember how the dry leaves jumped like little mice when the rain hit them? It was like a whole living world under our feet. Feels like that now—nothing seems normal, but still, I'm all right.*

*If you could pass this on to Mama, I'd appreciate it.*
*Love always,*
*Jesse*


*P.S. Everyone has a nickname here. They call me Sharp and Willie Shooter. Probably will forget how to answer to my real name by the time I get back.*

"Oh, thank you. Thank you." I held the letter close.

Jesse remembered me—he wanted me to read his letters! I turned the last paper over and Annie's note had me smiling.

*Jesse can bag a squirrel from such a long distance. I'm not so sure I'm glad Winn taught him how to hunt, but it may save his life. The high school math teacher feels sure the unit is going to the South Pacific. Mr. Somerset, who teaches typing, has the same idea.*

*By the way, Jesse seems to have your talent for words, don't you think? Here's the address to write him, at least for now.*

*Love you, sis.*

*Annie*

How long I sat there in the sunny west window seat, I don't know, but Miss M's entrance with platters of food brought me back.

"Oh my! Sorry!" I leaped up to help.

"Some news about Jesse?"

"Yes. He's aboard a ship in the Pacific. And he asked Annie to send his letter on to me."

"Wonderful, Kin. Now you can be a bit more at ease."

I hurried to the kitchen. At ease? I wasn't so sure about that.

On November eleventh, the radio blared mixed news.

*Today at sunrise, without warning, the United States attacked Casablanca's French fleet, controlled by the Vichy government. Admiral Hewitt's fleet, superior in number and technology, ended the fight early in the afternoon.*

*Heavy French casualties reported—multiple submarines, cruise ships, and destroyers. The day of the ninth was relatively peaceful but drenched in confusion and apprehension.*

*In Algeria, Operation Torch had succeeded, so pressure was put on commander Patton. On the tenth, the French marine force, protecting Morocco's neutrality and supported by Senegalese riflemen, fought the American soldiers. You heard correctly. French against Americans!*

*Two French medium-sized warships escaped a fatal destiny against the Augusta heavy cruiser. Around four pm, while the surrender agreement had been signed but not yet communicated, the American forces kept attacking.*

*We can only assume miscommunication occurred between ships. After three days of furious fighting, Casablanca finally capitulated, although a great part of the French forces in the zone reportedly had been ready to join the Allies.*

*Not only that, but our Navy lost nearly five hundred men on four sunken troop ships, 150 landing craft, and suffered damage to several other ships. French losses include four battleships, twenty other ships, and five submarines. How many sailors perished remains to be calculated.*

*Ours is not to cast judgment, but we do entertain questions. Even with the possibility that French resources would fall into Nazi hands, why did our commanders feel forced to take this action against our allies? Could this great loss have been avoided had the leaders and operations been better prepared?*

The newscaster went on, and I began to detest the radio, bringing stories of such confusion and needless loss of life. Five-hundred American GIs! Everyone was talking about the situation. Now, we had destroyed French ships and lost some of our own, besides killing French sailors. Why couldn't military commanders simply talk with each other before acting—why must they be in such a dreadful hurry?

You can imagine how Judson and Elwyn tore into this battle. For days afterwards…weeks, they outlined the changes they would have made had they been in charge. On these evenings, Elwyn's favorite phrase for ignorant or egomaniacal military leaders, "tupa ijuts," ran rampant.

In North Africa, our young men were being lost in great numbers. It was one thing to imagine our troops slugging it out on the shores of Africa or out in the desert, but when Judson and Elwyn started in on news from an island in the Pacific, I took my leave.

My imagination already ran wild. Better not to know the actual details.

Scarcely had I washed my hands and changed into my uniform that late November day when Doctor Graham hailed me. He pulled me to a corner and spoke in a low voice.

"We're starting a new nursing program. You've had so much experience already and have risen to every challenge. What would you think if I recommended you?"

"I…well…" Until now, I had seen my duties here as temporary, my contribution to the war effort, but not something to continue afterwards. My long-held desire to complete my degree in English literature and writing passed before me.

I hadn't even thought of this lately. How long ago had that been? Let's see. Mama died in '20, so over twenty years.

Why not keep on nursing? Once I got used to each new process, the work became routine. And the doctors seemed to think I fit well here. Not that they had time to commend anyone, yet their appreciation popped out in small but significant ways.

Early mornings and evenings, I could still help Miss M as much as possible, couldn't I? And where else could I possibly offer more than within these walls, with growing numbers of patients in dire need?

"Take a couple of days to think it over. Oh, and did I say the training you've already completed will be credited to you? That would take some months off the total time required to earn your degree."

He pulled his pencil from its nesting place above his right ear, revealing white hairs I hadn't noticed before. Somehow, Dr. Graham seemed immutable to the ravages of time, but he was aging.

"For the record, I wouldn't be asking if I thought you'd have any trouble at all. You'd been through a lot before you came here, and whatever that may have involved, your past has given you a natural way with our patients."

He had not forgotten my origins, what little he knew of them. Out of the blue, I entered his life destitute. But his offhand assessment, that the past had increased my capabilities, struck me like sunshine on a chilly day.

If I poured out the whole story, I had a feeling he would understand, even the part about sending Jesse away. About the gun going off and Clyde breathing his last, the way Old Drake and I managed to hide everything…even that inviting bottle waiting for me under the trees.

Hadn't Dr. Graham taken me in from a summer storm, helpless and covered with dust turning to mud? Hadn't he brought me to Miss M and a new beginning?

In all this time, he had never asked one question, but reached out for me as for a drowning woman. Gratitude welled now as I considered his kindness for the millionth time. He'd accepted me *as-is* and pulled me up from an unspeakable abyss.

Because of him, I now faced this choice. I must focus on my decision. The first step occurred right away—Miss M would have a good perspective. I'd discuss this with her tonight while Elwyn and Judson bewailed the fall of Singapore, the Allied victory at the Battle of Midway, and the disastrous situation on Bataan in the Philippines.

Aghast that nearly eighty thousand American and Filipino troops had surrendered to the Japanese, Judson and Elwyn went over and over the scenario. Why hadn't the military sent enough supplies before the siege began? What had gone wrong with the Allied commanders?

"'You men remember this. You did not surrender—you had no alternative but to obey my order.'" Judson enunciated every word. "That's what General Edward King Jr., the commander on Bataan, told his men."

The best I could translate Elwyn's reply: "Why couldn't the big brass quit arguing long enough to wipe out the Japs? Our boys signed up to do just that, but in the POW camp, the enemy will be merciless."

Jesse could not be among those who surrendered, I told myself. He might not even have reached his destination yet—surely he was headed to some other islands. I must believe this and keep myself busy.

Maybe I would ask Miss M to take a short walk when we finished in the kitchen. With so much bad news on the Pacific front, listening to Elwyn and Judson's analysis might become overwhelming this evening.

They lost no time pondering which General ranked worst of all. Was it French General Robert Nivelle, who caused such damage to his own forces during *their war*, or Field-Marshall Sir Douglas Heid of Great Britain?

What about the Austro-Hungarian leader General Franz Conrad Von Hotzendorf, Bavaria's Crown Prince Rupprecht, or General Luigi Cadorna, Chief of Staff of Italy's Army? Oh, the evidence that mounted, all on our peaceful front porch!

I wanted to ask, "Do you think there were any *good* commanders?" Better to hold my tongue, for they had not yet started in on the Americans.

Now I understood why Miss M sometimes retired to the second floor. Tonight, my questions would give her a diversion.

"Why Kindred—what an honor! Doctor Graham asked you? He's the best of the lot over at the hospital, you know."
I agreed—his deep concern for patients had impressed me over and over. And without doubt, his foresight had been instrumental in establishing this nursing course.

"But if the classes go all day, how will I help you with Elwyn? How can I possibly earn my keep?"

"Pshaw! You long ago earned *your keep* for many a year. Having you share the load helps a lot, especially in the mornings with Elwyn, but we'll get along. For one thing, Judson has four holes to repair in this roof, so he'll be working right here for some time, plus his work in the carriage house.

"Maybe he can spend the early mornings here for a while and work out in the afternoons. I have no desire to decrease his paying labor, but when he brought Elwyn home, I wore myself ragged after a few weeks. Judson had taken a room elsewhere but came over every evening.

"One night after Elwyn went to bed, he made a proposal. 'What if I board here so I can help more?'

"I'll never understand his dedication, though I've thought about it from every possible angle. But at that point, I knew this young man, strong and brave and intelligent, was intent on doing all he could for Elwyn.

"One day after Judson moved in, I finally asked him why." The skin on her prominent cheekbones radiated light from a parlor lamp. "Never again, mind you, for he could barely get out the words.

"He said, 'Elwyn took my place. That terrible day, I was supposed to go over the trenches but got a killing fever. So he went in my stead. I'm the one who should've been gassed.'"

With a faraway look in her eyes, Miss M paused. "How could I possibly argue with him? And he's been like an angel all these years. He might have left after bringing Elwyn home. He would already have done such a great service.

"At any time since, he might have taken his leave, believing his duty complete, but…"

We returned from our walk to find the men still war-bound.

In the parlor, the clock's ticking and the reliable swing of the pendulum reminded me how long I had been here now. You get into a routine, and surrounded by kind folks, time passes without your notice.

Outside on the porch, the men stirred. Soon they would pass through this room, and all of us faced an early rising.

Miss M cleared her throat. "You asked my opinion, but

perhaps the most important decisions in life find their answer inside us. That has proven true for Judson, I believe. And for Doctor Graham as well. For so many years, he lived alone and worked between two hospitals, ours and the one in Temple.

"Nearly met himself coming and going, he did. I expect he stayed so tired, his life seemed full.

"But then one day he saw Rosita with new eyes. They'd worked together and were used to each other. But suddenly he realized what lay in his heart. He had loved her all along."

Miss M slowly shook her head. "Who among us can truly understand these things? Just like that, in a split second, we know what we're about. I wonder if your decision might be something like that?"

The front door scraped, and Judson elbowed in with Elwyn couched in his arms, looking more shrunken than even earlier today. Without glancing our way, Judson set his foot on the first stairstep.

Miss M and I lingered a while, with that image and Judson's footfalls to instruct us. From the second story, the floorboard melody brought an unspoken comfort.

The next morning, I signed up for the nursing program. Every time I thought about this move, energy filled me. The desire to help, to do my bit for the war effort kept increasing until it filled me, and my intended life of studying and writing faded even more.

That night, Miss M and I worked out a plan. After dinner dishes, I would mix up what I could—pancakes, biscuits, gravy—and put them in the fridge for the next morning. I'd get up half an hour earlier to do whatever I could before leaving for the hospital.

Miss M said I should concentrate on what lay before me, not on the work here, but making these plans helped. No matter what she said, the sense that I was abandoning her lingered.

Chapter Seven

Pearl Harbor would be with us forever. How could we in Waco forget, when one of our own became a hero that day? In May of '42, we all had listened to the radio report about Admiral Nimitz, also a Texan, pinning the Navy Cross on Doris Miller, a mess attendant on the USS West Virginia.

We memorized the story of Miller's bravery. Elwyn seemed touched the most, and his thin face contorted as the news anchor reported the sailor being honored for moving his wounded captain to safety on the beleaguered island.

As a Negro, Miller had received no previous training, but still grabbed the controls of an anti-aircraft gun and began shooting at the Japs. The image of him plying that feeble defense—the only one possible at the time—against the enemy made our hearts burn with pride.

Obviously devoted to his comrades and a patriot, he took up arms with no hesitation, even though greatly outnumbered. The image of him shooting at deadly enemy bombers struck awe in our hearts.

Judson and Elwyn discussed the sorry American laws that kept colored sailors and soldiers from being trained to fight. If Miller had been white, he wouldn't have been working in the mess, they declared.

A recruit with his physique would already have gone through gunnery school. Such a strong young man—how could Jim Crow still govern his service? Hadn't we learned anything from the Great War? What was wrong with our nation, anyhow?

This evening, I strained to hear, hoping to learn more about how Judson had managed to get into the Great War. Right into the trenches.

This did not happen, though Elwyn became even more animated than normal, jerking in his wheeled chair and crying out. This time, a few of his words fell beyond my grasp.

So here it was, nearly Christmas of '42—the Christmas we'd all believed would mark the end of the war. Instead, the fighting had not stopped in even one theater, and that prospect looked unlikely.

Another sad holiday. Another year of casualty lists and more battles ahead. Surely by *next* Christmas—that's what we all decided, as if we possessed inside wisdom about how long winning this war would take. As if we hadn't guessed wrong already.

Annie's latest letter came to mind. She filled in some details of Jesse's time in boot camp, two months before he wrote from aboard ship. Something in me bristled when she wrote that he'd been at Fort Wolters, up near Dallas.

Not so far away. *If I had known, I might have…* I envisioned taking the train up there, trying to find this grown son who might not even want to see me.

No, I decided. How could I have approached him? What could I have said? Annie had been wise not to tell me before, or perhaps she hadn't known his exact whereabouts either.

It was better that I hadn't known—better for us both. Reading a letter in Jesse's own hand, the one he asked Annie to forward, had given me something sturdy to cling to.

After the war, we would see each other. But the wounded boys who passed from this life in our wards day-by-day belied my hopes, for Jesse might soon be one of them. I knew this in my head but would not allow the truth to enter my heart.

*Oh, Jesse!* When I allowed myself to focus on him, I could do little else. *My dear son*—such a mix of pride and terror in these meager words. My task now, as Miss M so succinctly stated, is to set my mind to wait, write letters often and pray like crazy.

One…two…three. Sounds so simple.

"Fold each end of the fabric over a quarter-inch, if not already seamed. This will prevent the bandage from picking up undue dust and debris. Now, this simple triangle has become a cravat bandage, useful for shoulder and arm injuries."

Our instructor clearly had created this bandage often, and believed it worked. "Sometimes you'll need a safety pin or two, but tied at the top, this sling has been used successfully by the military since before the Civil War.

"Now, touch the right-angle point of your triangle to the middle of the long edge, forming parallel sides. Fold the shorter of the two over into the long side, then again, and a third time. You have created a band with as many as eight layers.

"Two of these will make an adequate tourniquet, as you see our nurses demonstrating. Four tourniquets like this can anchor a splint in place. Observe: place two above and two below the fracture or injury. Any questions?"

Lieutenant Baker glanced around our circle. "Well, then, it's time to practice on each other. Hop to!"

Twenty minutes later, when we'd all passed inspection, she leaned against a bed. "Nothing takes more attention than dressings and bandages, and nothing requires more sanitation.

"For now, working here in the States, making-do comes easy, but you never know where this war may lead you. You may serve in a field hospital overseas some day, without clean water and electricity access.

"Let me share a little story from my experience in Belgium some years ago.

"Nurses were always looking for ways to innovate—you have to in a field hospital. Most of us are by nature creative, so we came up with some unique side-uses for certain items. For example, the Kimberley-Clark Company supplied the front with absorbent bandages for cases of heavy bleeding. These were made from wood pulp fiber, and we found them invaluable for severe wounds. But one day, my comrade gestured me to the supply tent.

"'It's my monthly,' she whispered, 'and I tried one of these. It works perfectly!'"

"Her suggestion made sense, so I tried it. My sentiments exactly—these bandages proved immensely helpful, far superior to the wads of cotton or fabric we'd been scavenging. As you can imagine, our order list for this particular item grew exponentially.

"Don't get me wrong, it's tough to find a positive side to war, but our experience did make such a difference over there and after we returned. When the war ended, manufacturers started promoting sanitary pads. This improvement has made women's lives so much easier, as I'm sure you'll agree."

Little asides like this made the repetitive nature of Lt. Baker's instructions more agreeable. She did her best to relate our lessons to everyday life, since we had to memorize everything for tests, sometimes written, sometimes hands-on.

No more evenings lounging on the front porch, no more war analysis for the taking. I might have lost track of the battles altogether, but Doctor Graham set a small radio tuned to the daily reports in the nurses' station.

The hospital had no lack of GI patients, although most from the early North Africa theater were sent to hospitals on the coasts. Our second floor held mostly young men from air training crashes, many of whom suffered severe burns.

We spent time practicing our newly-learned skills on men who would never leave this facility. They were, as some whispered, just waiting to die. Miss M could have brought Elwyn here as his abilities decreased, but she would never consider doing such a thing.

Another trainee named Helen had lived at the boarding house until she married about a year before I came. As we got to know each other, she gave me a few valuable firsthand insights.

"When I first moved in, Elwyn worked for the Waco and Northwestern, on the line north to the town of Ross. He started a few months after he returned from the war, once he regained his balance. Let me see—I lived there about three years.

"But one day after Walt and I were married, I saw Millicent at church, and she said he'd had to resign. "That was in '29, when the railroad closed the line to Ross. I don't think he could've kept on anyway—his coughing at night had worsened, and he couldn't lift much by then.

"I always thought his nightly spells must've confused the coyotes. He had bouts with pleurisy, bronchitis, and laryngitis, one after the other. Seemed like one hardly passed before another showed up. That was when Dr. Graham started coming to the house to treat him."

"Not working any more must've been a tough pill to swallow."

"Yeah. But that fellow Judson—he took Elwyn with him to his carpentry jobs—until the sawdust got to be too much for him. Guess it all depends on how much gas a fella breathed in France. At least we shouldn't have to work with that sort of victim this time around."

Another nurse heard part of our conversation and spouted, "Ha! Haven't you seen photos of school children with gas masks in London? Don't think a ruling by some international court in Geneva will hinder those Germans and Japs from doing whatever it takes to win."

"These nurses will show you exactly what to do, so you can make a difference for our boys over there." Miss Abrams, a tall teacher as slender as a wood slat, gathered some twenty high school girls around Helen and me in her home economics room.

Glad that Helen led the way, I followed along. Something about these girls, all energy and excitement with a little competitiveness mixed in, took me to a bad place.

At their age, my teachers had advocated me skipping a grade to graduate early. By the time I would have graduated, I had two semesters of college under my belt, as they say, and was on my way to a sterling teaching career.

But then everything changed. With no warning, word came of Mama's passing, and…

No! I had made a vow to stop the flow of negative thoughts controlling so many of my waking hours. As someone said, our real enemies are the *ifs* and *oughts* that direct us backward or forward, out of the present. Today, even if only for this time at the high school, I determined to conquer my inner enemy.

As Helen explained bandage-rolling procedures, I leaned back against one of the long tables along the wall. Such attentiveness these girls showed—the war had become far too real to them.

They looked so very young, and already there had been two deaths among the senior class guys who went off to make quick work of the enemy. How often had we heard that prediction, *Once the Americans get there, they'll turn their tails and run?*

An idle boast, it seemed.

These days, we heard such exclamations far less often as the Japanese forces dug in on far-away islands. Clearly, they would fight for every inch of territory they had taken from native islanders.

Our dinner conversations were peppered with strange locales we'd never heard of—Fiji, Midway, the Coral Sea. Actually, I had rarely heard of Hawaii before the Pearl Harbor attack. Last night around the table, one of the men mentioned a Walter Lipmann newspaper column about the need to evacuate all Japanese living on the California coast.

"What if the Japs attack us there? If they have sabotage help from the inside, they'll be far more likely to succeed."

Judson and Elwyn speculated on this later, agreeing that the argument seemed logical. Judson had questions, though.

"But they're American citizens. Joe Dimaggio's parents were born in America, but can the government just haul them away because they have Italian blood? Don't seem right."

Elwyn's reply got lost in a tangle of syllables.

And now, Helen called my wandering thoughts to attention.

"Work in twos, girls. Arrange yourselves around one of the tables. Miss Fresh and I will answer any questions you may have."

In the half hour we stayed to get the students started, I received no questions, but did glean a few insights into girls this age. They feel the war deeply and are all about doing their part.

"My uncle's in California, working in an airplane factory. My sis and I may go out there to work this summer, even though Mom's having fits. But she's working full-time over at the Bluebonnet plant. If she can give her all for the cause, why can't I?"

"Can you imagine the number of sailors and airmen you'll meet? Not a bad stint, in my opinion."

"But the work days are long, and you've gotta wear overalls all the time." Someone else added, "I've heard it's mighty hot in those big hangars, and dangerous."

"Jodie Willard's first cousin is leaving for Alabama next week—I think it'd be worse making bombs or packing parachutes like her. Can you imagine how awful you'd feel if you made one little mistake?"

"Plus you might lose an appendage, or half of your face if the chemicals blew up."

"That's what supervisors are for. I want to be one."

"Not me. I've heard that some women pilots will soon be shuttling airplanes clear across the country. That's what I'm going for—the WAACs. You don't even have to leave Texas to get trained."

"Really? Where do you go?"

"Over in East Texas. My older sister saw a film about it in San Antonio. Girls are doing all of the military office and motor pool work so the soldiers can deploy overseas, and they even get to do some of the flying! Mom says Mrs. Hobby's the director, so she'll run a first-class organization."

Helen chimed in. "The former Governor's wife?"

"I think so. She's already held government offices, so Mom says she'll do just fine."

"Sounds safer than going to a factory in California. They're talking about routing all of the Japanese off the Coast, but if they don't, I wouldn't want to be there."

What an array of possibilities lay open to these young women! On the walk home, Helen and I noted how things had changed since we were in high school. Then, you either married and started a family, became a secretary, or went into teaching or nursing.

Then she turned down her street and left me lost in thought. There was something so young and innocent in those girls, so vulnerable it made my heart flutter.

Wherever they went, however they served during this war, I wanted them to be whole. And what did I mean by *whole*? The opposite of what I'd been after Mama died. For one thing, although Mama and my teachers meant well, I'd been too young to leave home.

Somehow, Clyde knew just when to show up. Even though I went back to my studies after Mama's funeral, I'd felt so alone, so out-of-sorts with the world. The literary realm lost its luster, so I slogged through each day.

Starting my studies so early might have paved the way for disaster. You can be brain-smart but know little of the ways of the world. And I could never have predicted how crushing Mama's passing would be.

I stopped caring about anything, even my beloved literature classes. My mentor tried to cheer me, but the loss held me fast. Even breathing came hard during that time.

What a deception, thinking that the sadness would leave if I married Clyde. Surely, he said, I'd feel better making a move out to the country, where we would start anew.

Like a misled child, I believed. But despite my determination to make things work during the first year, I knew I had made an irrevocable mistake.

Annie was grieving Mama too, and still wrote without fail. She knew things weren't right—must've read between the lines when I answered. Strange that healing would take so long, involve

Jesse going to live with her and Winn, and begin with violence beyond repair.

These speculations circled my consciousness like Elwyn's eyes seeking a landing place. I clung to the knowledge that out of misery rose a second chance. Out of despair came hope.

Still, I had no clear idea why I stayed so long, especially after Jesse left. Was it those three graves? I'd heard of pioneer women who refused to leave the place where they buried their children.

Or was the reason more like a curse, something other-worldly that gripped my spirit? You make one error, and then one more, and find yourself in a downward spiral.

Breaking free of the cycle seems impossible, so you bury yourself with mistakes, one on top of the next. You haven't the energy, or as Miss M calls it, the "gumption" to make a change.

Then one day there's a stirring, and you know that what you thought was the end will be the beginning of something new. You realize you've held your own soul at bay—allowed someone else to control that sacred part of you.

Unfortunately for me, the transformation took such a long, long time. Strength developed in pieces. With my wealth of experience, at this point, I could become a psychology professor—the thought made me chuckle. But several questions still defied answering.

What had Clyde been doing in my hen house the night he died? What caused the gun to go off? And where did that bottle under the tree originate? Who had put it where I would find it?

Did life sequester some inquiries into a back corner marked *Unanswerable*? Would more of these arise as time went on? Hopefully not—I balanced enough of them already.

Evening traffic slowed as I turned onto Kendrick Lane. I cherished the sound of our address, the very essence of safety and *home* that it represented. For in this place, over time, my spirit had revived.

The past, however sordid and lamentable, no longer held total sway over me. Little-by-little, neither did these questions.

No, each day started anew. I sensed this every single morning, traversing this route, going to work I loved, helping those who could not help themselves.

My flight from the ranch seemed eons ago, like the beginning of a movie. I recalled walking and walking and walking. Finally, with a storm brewing, I squatted against a tumble-down corncrib.

The camera focused on this stopping place. And then—a miracle.

Oh, the sense of stepping into Doctor Graham's automobile—the warmth and shelter, the security and protection, laced with kindness. Over and over, I relived that suspension of time.

And he brought me to Kendrick Lane, to Miss M, Elwyn, and Judson. How could I have known where that introduction would lead? That's just the thing—we don't know. We simply take one more step forward and realize that instead of offering only rejection, the world embraces us.

And then the hospital, with so much pain, yet a wealth of courage and optimism. So much promise and potential there, along with the suffering.

All of these positives drown out whatever fear might attempt to threaten me, whatever shadows the past casts. So much caring and giving and delight—the house down the street, recently painted. The way the couple works together, the intangible closeness they exhibit even to a passerby—is this not a form of beauty?

Dr. Graham's clockwork visits to Elwyn all these years, and his clear love for Rosita. The boarders' alarms ringing at dawn each morning, their steady work for the war effort. The milkman lugging his wares into the hospital kitchen at five a.m. every day… Is not all of this beautiful?

Later than normal, I step into our yard. Weary boarders sprawl in chairs on the front porch, chatting or simply sitting in receding daylight. I stop and say hello—some would rather be left to their private thoughts, so I honor that desire.

As I cross the threshold into the parlor, Miss M raises her eyebrows, acknowledging whatever has kept me. It's my work. My *vocation*, what I am born to do.

I give her a smile and take a platter of roast beef from her hands. This, too, has become my calling. In this, too, lies beauty and joy. The yellow rose bush just outside the front door proclaims the same, along with the set of the walls against this room's ceiling, the symmetry of plates and forks and knives all together, yet each one distinct.

In this frazzled world, the light in Doctor Graham's eyes passes before me. In each of us, this sort of light has the power to straighten things, to set things right. Adding the finishing touches to Miss M's table, I know a truth beyond all doubt. At certain times, perceptions heighten, not that I understand how.

If I were to tell my story—the whole tale—to Miss M, she would understand. *We all carry secrets.* Her expression would attest to this. *We all wonder about some turns we took and are grateful to have landed where we are.*

I set the napkins on each plate, napkins I washed, ironed and folded on Saturday. Still mostly clean, they wait to snare drips of gravy or catch unbidden tears.

I look in upon myself, so careful, so accurate in my folding. Hasn't Miss M commented on this? "Never knew a better worker than you, Kin." A professor from that other life long ago said the same.

The dinner bell sounds. Scuffles fill the porch.

Here I am, so scrupulous in my chores, as when I studied and taught, and at the hospital. And so fixed on the goal, but now a new one has arisen. Me, a registered nurse? Why, I never…

The boarders gather. While Miss M prays for our boys over there, and for strength for us all to continue making our contributions, I peek in at my soul.

With no conscious effort, the judgment always strung inside me, taut and terse, has loosened. Yes, I did fail my husband, my son, myself…and Mama. Yes. But now I make room for grace, even for myself.

Glancing around at regular everyday people who harbor secrets, too, I meet my neighbor's eyes as I pass the potatoes and gravy. Imperfect, lacking, each of us, but here, doing our bit.

We may not always be meant to understand, but merely accept the insights that come our way. Observed by fading rose wallpaper, during a hearty meal for a dozen hungry folk, this reality pervades.

Somewhere over in the shadows on the hidden side of Miss M's mahogany buffet, hovers Clyde's image, but its severe, condemning lines fail to startle me. The perennial scrutiny of his sharp eyes can no longer unsettle me.

No, and the next time I lift my eyes, Doctor Graham's countenance has overtaken Clyde's. His dark eyebrows and Santa-like nose, his clipped mustache, vigorous gaze and ready grin cheer me.

He employs his talents on behalf of the world around him. And I, too, have gifts to offer. Even in war's ugly shadow—perhaps especially now—each of us can be that light for others.

But we must leave the questions behind, for they smell of the past. Those of us given to constant hypercritical analyzing must embrace the present and set aside our judgments, especially of ourselves, in order to take up a new way.

Chapter Eight

"Where are we, anyhow?"

Jesse glanced around, wiping his forehead in intense wet heat beyond anything in Kentucky or Texas. Palm trees stood tall, except for those shattered by enemy fire, and a rickety runway had been slapped together by weary engineers. Still, he had no visible clue.

"Someplace mighty hot."

"You said it." With his sleeve, Willie wiped his dirty face. Sand crawled up his arm, itchy, ant-infested sand. So much for the sunny beaches the guys foresaw on the way here.

Their long ride on ocean waves had transformed the word *island* into a paradise. After passing through the Panama Canal, they'd stopped in Samoa and heard plenty of terrible reports from farther south. Ships that stopped by on their way back to the states, filled with merchant marine workers, carried more than cargoes. They brought men's perspectives on what they'd seen in the islands, and most of them seemed ready to share.

Now, not far from Jesse's boot, a snake slithered through the rocky terrain. Poisonous? Who knew, but no use taking chances.

"Attention!"

Willie and Jesse formed a reasonably straight line with their comrades and waited. The Army might've been called WAIT, to be more accurate. Or *hurry up and wait*. How many lines had they stood in at Fort Wolters, only to near the front and be moved to a new one? Lines for foot inspections, inoculations, hair-cutting, dental exams. Lines for everything.

But today, things seemed different. Besides the heat, a certain sharpness laced the Captain's tone. They'd gotten here, even if they had no clue where they were.

"I'm sure you're all wondering one thing—where are we? We've kept that quiet for good reason. We use this small island as a training area, and don't want to tip off the enemy." He ran the back of his hand across his wet upper lip.

"The jungles of these parts offer challenges we haven't faced as yet, and we can learn a lot from the Marines we're relieving. More than 7,000 of them lost their lives here, with 8,000 more wounded."

His pause had the desired effect. *Seven thousand dead…* "So get used to the heat as fast as you can 'cause we've got mighty important work to do. Get used to the mosquitoes, too, and don't think you can go without your netting—malaria's no fun. Every mosquito you slap, think *vengeance!*"

After a grueling uphill run in full battle dress, the men, too exhausted to complain, set up camp. Hammocks swung from trees with mosquito nets all around, and a few elevated supply bags kept the food and medicine from wild animals.

Nobody knew exactly what creatures roamed this place, if previous bombings and fighting had not driven all forms of life into the sea. But everyone had ideas, and the craggy landscape ignited Willie's imagination.

Every bombed-out crater kindled questions, even though a crew had already come through to remove bodies. But the stench remained. Far too many corpses had rotted in this heat before they could be processed.

Huge flies hovered over certain areas—it didn't take much to conjure up what might have occurred there. The officers seemed ready with explicit descriptions of hand-to-hand battle.

At times, bombing and machine gun fire, rifle blasts and mortars still made their impact in the distance. They'd been exposed to these in training, but here on this island, with mutilated palms in easy sight, the struggle became more vivid.

The men had heard about the Seventh Marines and their

stand to defend Henderson Field on Guadalcanal. Bloody Ridge, or as later re-named, Edson's Ridge, for Edson's Raiders, became the line to hold, and through heavy losses, the Marines did just that.

"Some day, they'll name a ridge after you," one guy joked to another.

"Yeah, just what I always wanted. To get something named after you, you gotta die."

Some in the unit seemed intent on bragging before they'd even been in battle, but after viewing this island's bomb craters and other battle remains, Jesse retreated into his own thoughts. Being here seemed impossible. Sometimes he still woke up in the morning expecting to hear Aunt Annie downstairs cooking breakfast.

Often, he stared at his trigger finger, the main reason he'd made it into this rifleman unit. He'd seen the results of gunshot up close. The worst, Uncle Winn's after the accident, proved impossible to forget. He had done all he could to stop the last of the bleeding, but his efforts had come too late.

No need to allow that scene to inundate him now. He tamped down the image into the deepest recesses of his being. It was one thing to dress a deer, another to witness a ravaged human body.

So far, he'd never shot at a man, except in training, when using blanks. The maneuvers amounted to good experience, but they still weren't the real thing.

During a true fight, with bullets whizzing around him, would he remember what Uncle Winn had taught him? Would he be able to block out everything but the enemy, recall that these squinty-eyed devils were the scourge of the earth and hit his target with cool objectivity?

He sure hoped so, but definitely had no urge to claim success before his time. The guys who blabbered most were nervous, he suspected. They just needed to let off steam through their big mouths.

Willie hung back, too. Reassuring, because the two of them would fight together—hopefully the whole way, no matter what happened around them. When this was all over and the world returned to something akin to *normal*, Kentucky would welcome them back.

With Willie just down the way, another punishing day became bearable. Those bruises they'd gotten on Senior Skip day to the Red River Gorge had been replaced by far deeper ones.

The commanders knew what they were doing—this unit needed hardening up. Like they said, no amount of training could ever be too much.

Keeping track of the war news on the way had helped some. Details about the hard-fought Task Force 53 battle at Tarawa Atoll heartened the privates. For the first time, the Marines faced fierce opposition in their landing, which increased casualties.

But their captain said, "We learned a lot through that landing. Now we know the Navy bombardment has to continue throughout the whole time."

"By the time we land, they'll have it all figured out, don't you think?" Each of them might have asked Willie's question.

"Yep. We won't be in any danger at all."

So here they were, not yet in the fight, but all right. A guy or two had cut up their legs on merciless slippery rocks, a few had caught malaria or some other disease or suffered bug bites, but that was about it.

As one fellow put it, "By the time we get to the Marines we're replacing, we'll have wised up about this crazy terrain. Oughta be grateful for this extra time to work out the kinks."

On this train of thought, Jesse allowed his shoulders to relax into the forgiving hammock. Forgiving, but not exactly comfortable, yet far better than this rocky earth crawling with vermin.

He had been plenty tired before, but never like this. More than exhausted, it was as if his very cells cried out for relief.

Eventually, the mouthy guys fell asleep. Wild bird calls still filled the night air, and intermittent snarls, a lot like Kentucky polecats that ruled the night. He'd brought down a few himself when out coon hunting.

Finally, sometime before dawn and reveille, he managed to doze off. The next thing he knew, he lurched awake, sending his hammock into a wild sway and alerting some fidgety native bird that danger must be near.

Amid the wild squawks, he lay back sweating. The nightmare had been far too real—had he screamed out loud?

In his dream, a wild-eyed Japanese about ten feet tall had crouched right below him and suddenly attacked, wrenching him from the hammock and drawing a silver sheath to his jugular. He'd been helpless and for long moments before waking, looked death in the eye.

Somewhere, a shriek split the night, followed by a muffled whine that sounded almost human. The long sigh Jesse let out led to a whisper from Willie's direction.

"Hey, man. You doin' all right over there?"

"Yeah." Jesse rolled over the best he could. "Just a bad dream is all."

Chapter Nine

What a day—at times, I thought my shift would never end. Yet when it did, I felt somehow disheartened. What it took to learn my lessons nearly crushed me. Helen felt the same, if her blanched expression meant anything at all.

My third-floor room, as I mentioned, sits right above Elwyn's. Tonight, I was asleep, for all practical purposes, before lying down, asleep on my feet. Yet when I took to my bed, blessed slumber turned into a stranger with so many thoughts churning in my head.

Doctor Graham sent us to visit another hospital for special instruction in dealing with burns. That facility recently received several victims from airplane crashes.

I thought that being so familiar with Elwyn's visible scars—I could trace them in my dreams—would have prepared me. Besides, I had already dealt with burn cases in the wards.

How wrong we can be!

Charred areas of these new patients' bodies had to be kept moist, so the nurses taught us how to wrap wet saline bandages 'round and 'round the affected regions. With no anesthesia, this process caused awful pain. The process resembled surgery, since with every move we disturbed fragile skin.

Helen and I walked up and down the ward to wrap those confined to bed. The whole day, we changed dressings, up-and-down each aisle, up-and-down.

In one corner, gauze covered a would-be pilot's face except for a breathing hole. At the next bed, the doctors had decided to leave a soldier's devastated cheek open to the air.

A young wife visited her wounded hero. Her obvious distress made my heart ache. He kept pointing to a photograph on his side table, as if to give her hope—these docs could fix him up good-as-new. Her efforts to look convinced fell short.

Outside the unit, one of the nurses explained, "He believes the surgeons will make him look exactly like he once did. I think he needs to see some of the post-surgery fellows to bring him back to reality."

Another added, "But at least his wife is *here.* Can't imagine how much that means to him."

During our midday break, even more patients had been added to the ward, so we wrapped them right after their surgeries. This time, Helen had to excuse herself—the still-present ether smell mixed with that of torn flesh nearly did me in, too.

But I thought of Elwyn—during the Great War, some nurse in an evacuation tent most likely tried to help him. Those lines of soldiers who'd been gassed, hanging onto a buddy's shoulder to make it back to safety from No Man's Land—he had been one of them, and each of these young men deserved my best.

Hours later, I lie here, as wide awake as a rock badger protecting its burrow. As I stand watch, a coyote's call fills the distance. Leaves rustle somewhere outside my window. The rock badger and I become one, keeping vigil when no one sees.

When a mockingbird breaks into song, the badger rolls his neck around, searching for danger.

Dr. Graham says Texas adopted the talented mockingbird as the state bird in 1927. So agile they can sing up to two-hundred songs, including the tunes of other birds plus sounds from insects and amphibians, mockingbirds also excel at protecting their homes.

Often, we see one of these feathered warriors swooping down at a vagrant bird or squirrel too close to its nest. I discovered only recently that the Texas State legislature proclaimed the mockingbird "the most appropriate species for the state bird of Texas, as it is found in all parts of the state, in winter and in summer, in the city and in the country, on the prairie and in the woods and hills, and is a singer of distinctive type, a fighter for the protection of his home, falling, if need be, in its defense, like any true Texan."

This last, Judson inadvertently taught me as he took to reading an ornithology text to Elwyn. The book details the night songs of this species, noting that unmated males fill the ranks of nocturnal singers.

Despite my desperation for sleep, one of them perches in a tree below my window now, warbling a compilation of six or seven different tunes. His song attends me as I fight for rest, for tomorrow Helen and I must make up for time that will soon be lost due to our training.

Next week, Doctor Graham says, we will visit a second hospital for another instruction day. The idea is to have at least two of us available for what may eventually be an urgent need here. Burns this week, and next week, childbirth.

That seems strange, but the hospital down in Temple, just a half-hour away, delivers more and more babies these days. Overnight marriages and deployed soldiers leaving expectant mothers behind has awakened McCloskey General to the need.

Activated just a few months ago, the hospital's newness is, as Helen says, "kinda nice." And what better news to send a young man fighting in faraway lands than the birth of a healthy child? Why not build a wing specifically to assist these wives?

Still, in the midst of war, learning about birthing babies seems odd. I have never even assisted in a delivery—I tried with Sophie's, but hers always came too fast for me. I have to say, the deceptive specter of jealousy visited me then. Why had my deliveries been so fraught with disaster when she gave birth with such ease?

My memories of childbirth do not serve me well. Turning over in bed, I know my thinking must change course.

Instead, I consider whether—or how—one can make up for time lost, or for time one knows will be lost in the future? Helen and I will be behind when we come back from this next short trip—knowing we'll have to work extra hard before and after spurs this question.

We send off our boys, knowing time will be lost. Such precious time, and we have no idea how much. Doctor Graham sees things the long way and seems quite capable of holding past, present and future losses in tension.

He says the new sections of the Temple hospital now under construction will offer three-thousand rooms. This huge complex will be named after the first medical officer to die in this war. McCloskey General Hospital. "A forward-looking institution," says Doctor Graham. "The planners are wise to consider the obvious yet often-overlooked ramifications of a conflict this enormous, such as vastly increasing numbers of births."

In other words, focus on what you can do *during this time*, not on the time that will be lost.

The mockingbird sings on and on into the night. Knowing he seeks a mate increases my tolerance—he's only doing what he can to win someone's heart. That being said, his array of melodies reveals laudable ingenuity.

Just the sort of determination the burn victims we worked with today require as they face more surgeries and wrappings, re-dressings and constant pain. Time stops during these procedures—time lost in all dimensions.

One nurse said she makes a point of going on a "date" with each of the men as they make their entrance back into the world, a world that will stare and point at them. She wastes no energy wishing people would *stop* staring. Instead, she plunges into her patient's life and experiences the stares with him.

"I act *as if*," she smiled. "As if nothing's out of the ordinary. As if I go to a restaurant with a barely recognizable fella every day. People might as well accept him. He may have a patchwork quilt for a face, but we have to learn to *look* at him anyway, because he made this sacrifice for us, and he's not going away."

A sudden scream shatters the night. Down below, Judson's

door screeches open and he hurries down the hall. The resonance of his deep voice rises through the ceiling—not loud, but strong. Another example of embracing loss as it comes.

Miss M and Judson perform their ongoing ritual in silence. Past, present, future—they balance their loads as one, yet individually as well. I am a mouse sequestered in a corner, far removed but yet a part of whatever occurs.

In the daytime, they and Dr. Graham act *as if* Elwyn is not passing from this life. *As if* he isn't becoming more vexed by his daily existence, more muddied in his thinking.

Not a bad tactic, all things considered.

*Christmas Eve, 1942*

As usual, this idea originated with Doctor Graham, but he waited until the end of a long day in the wards to pose the possibility. Though December twenty-fourth had arrived, Christmas probably sat last in most of our minds.

"Tonight, would any of you like to help Rosita and me serve the traditional meal—*los pambazos, los tamales, y los churros para los niños?* Their parents and grandparents are working so hard for the war effort, they have no time to make all of the preparations."

"Where exactly, and what time?" Looking wearier than normal, Helen had been headed for the cloakroom.

"We've already cooked most of the food and will heat it right here in the kitchen after work. We'll carry the platters across the way to Beverly Hills, you know the new housing area.

"Many parents are working southeast of town, taking double shifts at the Bluebonnet Ordnance Plant. A few might be able to attend, too, but still would have no time to cook.

"Last year, Rosita and I started preparing *la Navidad* meal, and the children's gratitude made the work worthwhile.

"The war has taken many of their fathers away—some forever, and most of their mothers work seven-day shifts. Seems sad for such bright-eyed little ones to miss celebrating Christmas, on top of everything else."

"Ah." Helen's sigh issued extra heavy as she pulled on her sweater. "I don't know what time Walt will get home, but if it's reasonable, we might come."

My feet ached. I wanted nothing more than a steamy bath, if the hot water didn't run out tonight. But I heard myself say, "Some of the boarders have gone to see their families overnight, so dinner shouldn't take as long as usual. I think I can make it."

"All right. We'll be here, cooking away."

"Should I bring anything?"

"Nope. Just willing hands and a willing heart."

A long time ago, I learned that *small* can be satisfying when it comes to Christmas. Back in Kentucky, the simplest hand-cut pine with our homemade popcorn and wild berry strings brought out the lights in Mama's eyes.

Way back then, when we had to root for tubers to eat at times, a gift lay in those lights, and I'm certain Mama saw them in mine, too. That's the thing about children, their eyes.

It's Jesse's eyes that haunt me most. By now, he might have developed a stone face like his father at times, but his eyes always tell the real story.

Those lights—in the eyes of Rosita's community of children— were why I hurried over to the hospital kitchen after doing dishes with Miss M. When all of the helpers arrived Rosita explained, *Los Posados* normally includes singing processions, traditional food and drinks and ends with breaking piñatas.

"Even though our procession might be shorter than normal this year, our two small piñatas quickly broken and the sweets eaten, the children will understand the meaning of this festival. *Gracias* for taking the time to come."

An hour later, the children's expressions testified to her

prophecy. Dr. Graham explained that *Posada* means *inn* or *lodging*, exactly what Joseph and Mary sought on their long journey from Nazareth to Bethlehem the night of the Savior's birth.

Heavy with her first child, Mary desperately needed a safe place to give birth. A haven.

*Las posadas*, normally celebrated several times from December sixteenth until Christmas Eve, would be reduced to one procession this year. Though some of us recognized a few Spanish words, we hummed along as the carolers sang, following a young child dressed as an angel.

Once we set up the food table, Rosita hailed us, "Come along!" So we did. The angel child led us to Bethlehem, staged to the right of the church. There, lighted by luminaries in sand bags, a young woman with a baby in a manger magnetized the youngsters.

Their eyes shone with curiosity and delight. The scene drew me in, as well. My journey from the wilderness of our ranch came rushing back, and those buried infant faces—my babies, all three—appeared.

For a few moments, I returned to my stone seat along the dusty path. Above me, leaves brushed, creating the shade that guarded the bottle I found. What had this all meant? I still couldn't put words to the experience, but realized it had to do with light finding us when we need it most.

Here, even though recent days had been so filled with adults in pain, the serene image of this young robe-clad girl revolved around the same concept. She played the part of a new mother. I knew what occurred in Bethlehem so long ago, but until this moment, my thoughts of birthing all centered on next week's training.

This evening, however, belonged to a humble peasant girl of ancient times, black haired with luminary flames reflecting from her face, shadows around her, a fledgling Joseph beside her. A few feet away paused some scraggly shepherds and wise men.

The placid scene drew me. Two sheep and a few goats, a cow

and even a donkey gathered around the couple. Something about this simplicity arrested me.

Lately, time had moved like a fast train with no stops, but now a halt occurred, as though Doctor Graham had held up his hand and demanded we take a moment. All the flurry of days run together with bandage wrapping, racing home to do what I could for Miss M, and falling into restless sleep fled.

Here I stood in the midst of that old, old story Mama always read to us. I kept up the tradition when Jesse was young, and tried to produce a meager Christmas for him, even though Clyde wanted no part of it.

But a vast chunk of my heart boarded that train to Kentucky the same morning Jesse did, so after that I gave up all attempts. Christmastide became a forgetting season—neglecting the significance of the long-ago Bethlehem birth.

As if a crust formed over my heart—and no fragile pastry crust at that—my spirit closed. But this twilight revelation produced a crack in that crust.

Standing here and staring was all I could do. As I did, the intense sorrows of my babies lost, Jesse gone, and the future stalled in nothingness on my trek through parched Texas fields. Salty tears washed away such powerful scenes from the past.

People walked by, but I remained, transfixed. Families hurried to the food table, greeting their neighbors and friends. There, Helen and Walt manned giant metal spoons to dish up hearty fare.

As they filled children's plates, Doctor Graham and Rosita, like kindly grandparents, supervised the plate-carrying. With radiant smiles, they spread good cheer.

Each child received a touch on the shoulder or head and a personal wish. The adults ate then, and afterward someone announced the *piñatas.*

All of this I observed from the side but felt no compunction to join. No, I belonged here, gazing at this miracle birth, this child in a hasty manger. Suddenly, in a pool of light from a candle, Jesse stood with me—wherever he had gotten to in this ugly war, his image hovered near.

The photo Annie sent of him in his uniform, taken before he left for his training, came to me. The picture on my bedside table, that I prayed over each night.

In the evening chill, my whisper quavered. "Forgive me for the way things were, Jesse—I'm so sorry. Please stay well. Please stay alive…"

In that crucial moment, the glint in my son's eyes became as evident as the children's voices around us. Something passed from him to me—how can I even begin to describe what occurred?

I only know that what I needed entered me. The forgiveness I pleaded for, or was it love? Perhaps I shall never know.

And then he faded. I reached out to touch the coarse wool of his uniform, but too late. Still, a new richness existed—he had left, but I felt not quite so empty.

How long I stayed there, I have no idea. After some time, a hand touched my shoulder.

"Kin? Did you get something to eat?" Doctor Graham, his voice low and sheltered, as though he knew.

"I…yes. This is just so…" My tongue failed me as it had when we first met, but he seemed to understand.

"*Los Posados* has changed me, too. Beautiful, isn't it?"

"Yes, and I…"

He waited.

"Some day I need to talk to you about…" My voice shrank to a whisper. "About my past."

"We'll find a time." No note of prying. No hurry… Simply acceptance, as if human mysteries and miseries presented no enigma.

He guided me toward the crowd, a gaggle of folks from the Beverly Hills area, others from nearby sections of town. Walt, a tall muscular fellow, chatted with Rosita's uncle, people helped clean up the remains of the celebration, and Helen grasped my hand.

"Working all day tomorrow won't be quite so bad after this, will it? Can't believe I almost didn't come. Walt said no at first, but I'm so glad he changed his mind.

"I really miss my family right now, and it would've been so easy to stay home." Her sigh reached all the way down to her sore toes. "But I'm glad we came."

Walt joined her, saying good night to Doctor Graham and the rest of us with, "I almost felt like I was home again tonight, and that's a good thing. We'll have to do this again next year."

Walking home, blue stars that had been exchanged for gold ones in several windows caught my attention. Gold meant a son had perished. Rosita, having lost her only son very early in the war, surely had one in their window.

This would be the first Christmas with the effects of war displayed in front porches across the land, the first Christmas with places set at the dining table for departed loved ones. And empty chairs.

From one million young men deployed last year at this time, the number had grown five-fold. And every day, more recruits arrived for training at bases across the nation.

In the side yard, near the door where Dr. Graham knocked when I first arrived, I lingered. The yellow rose bush, barren now, would produce its bounty in a few months.

So much behind me, but so much lay ahead. Elwyn and Judson's voices drifted from the front porch—mostly Judson's, for Elwyn's grew weaker by the day.

A few stars shone above as I replayed how Jesse had come to me tonight. A shiver took my shoulders, for there was no doubt— just as when I had sipped from that small green bottle.

Where had the Army taken him? Annie's last letter, with the one from Jesse, contained few details—only that he had qualified as a sharpshooter, and his unit had boarded a ship out of Virginia with a secret destination.

Annie longed for information, too. Surely there must be

something we could discover. Perhaps Doctor Graham would have some suggestions, but that might mean disclosing the truth… the way I had treated my only son—how I sent him away.

And when I told him that, of course I would have to explain about Clyde. What would Doctor Graham say? He might advise me to return to our little ranch town and tell the sheriff the entire tale.

So many questions rose, questions whose answers depended on others, like pieces of firewood piled carefully for winter. Judson's array out here could hardly be called a wood pile, he had developed such an intricate pattern.

Always my thoughts had fought like this, stalling my progress, keeping me from moving one direction or the other. And here I stood, wavering once more.

But tonight, a mysterious age-old scene, the image of heaven come to earth, had gladdened me anew. The image of justice kissing righteousness, a message of hope for this hurting world. In spite of my eddying thoughts, contentment had sneaked in. Like the shepherds and wise men, in spite of everything, I had come to a good place.

The future remained obscure, but guidance had attended me in the past. Surely more would arrive for the rest of the way.

Yes, despite my failings and a ruthless world war.

The evening breeze, such a boon on a Texas evening, cheered my heart. Like a child caught up in wonder and awe, I skipped a step or two, ready to go in and wish Miss M a Merry Christmas.

*Guadalcanal, December 25, 1942*

In late morning's oppressive heat, Santa Claus, complete with a fake white beard, shorts and hairy legs, made his way through sick bay handing out hard candies and peppermint sticks. The candies would not slide into Jesse's mouth.

No matter how hard he tried, the slippery devils wouldn't fit through the tight wires holding his jaws together. No choice but to let the sugary red and green treasures slip from his fingers.

Seeing his struggle, Willie volunteered. "Want me to try?"

"Nah. I guess I remember well enough how they taste." Jesse worked his little finger through a gap in the wire to loosen something that clung to it. Amazing how much stuff got caught in there in the course of a day.

"How long have we been here? Three years?"

"Nope, not quite a month. No use making it any worse than it is." Willie always found a way, as he did right now, cracking one of the sugary treats into bits with his knife and pushing them one-by-one between Jesse's lips.

"Make this worse? How could I possibly do that?" Jesse flicked a mosquito from his forehead.

"We're stuck here, but we gotta keep *home* in mind. That's what we're fightin' for. Think of your favorite food and how good it'll taste when we get back. Can't eat it right now, but…"

"Yeah. Mashed potatoes."

"But are you really listening?"

Jesse pulled his cap over his eyes. Answer enough. Willie meant well, but it sure was hard to keep memories of home front and center when every inch of your head throbbed and your knee had swelled double its normal size.

Besides, it was Christmas. Christmas in a godforsaken spot of the globe teeming with bugs and serpents, not to mention constant artillery shells from the American and Second Marine Divisions. Word had it that more support would soon begin from Navy destroyers offshore and the Second Marine Air Wing.

"Oughta be thankful for that, and for the turkey dinner the mess hall somehow cooked today." Jesse reminded himself of the wonderful smell. Thankfully, the mashed potatoes and gravy had gone down well, little-by-little.

But all of the noise in sick bay spelled not a moment of

peace for a guy held up here. Rolling over on his stretcher-like bed, he tried for some shut-eye. Instead, recollections flooded in.

Aunt Annie at the kitchen table, forming perfect sugar cookies with her cutters. His little cousin Pearl adding frosting and smearing the sticky stuff everywhere. Beau taking him to the back forty to find a tree fitting for the occasion.

There'd be a giant pork roast or ham later, complete with succulent sweet potatoes and homemade biscuits so rich they melted in your mouth. His groan signaled Willie to start up again.

"I was just remembering Granny's pecan pie. You?"

"Knock it off, wouldja? Can't a fella even dream about Christmas dinner back home without you chirping in?"

"Uhhh…sorry." Trying to think of something to say, Willie turned his cap in his hands with a woebegone glimmer in his eyes.

Jesse turned his head away. No way to treat the guy you counted on to have your back. But too much was too much. Finally, Willie shuffled from the medical tent.

The last thing Jesse wanted was to hurt his best buddy. Earlier today, Willie had cut his turkey into tiny pieces so he could swallow a taste with the gravy. They'd been through hell and high water together here on Guadalcanal, but being cooped up seemed worse than battle.

If the doc was right, in two weeks he'd be healed enough to get back into the fight. Since basic training, he and Willie had handled everything together, until three days ago. An enemy bullet found his chin, and when he fell, his knee crashed into a merciless rock.

Willie bemoaned that hit. For a few seconds, he'd turned to meet fire from another direction. But how could he have known that just the right incoming bullet would find Jesse's face?

For some reason, this circumstance—being holed up in a miserable, moldy tent—nearly sent Jesse over the edge. Ah well, he'd have to figure out a way to make up for his testy attitude later.

Chapter Ten

*Early January 1943, Guadalcanal*

Torrential rains beat down on the canvas forming a so-called roof over three rows of wounded soldiers with bodies in various stages of disrepair. Giant drips cascaded like fountains along thick tent poles to bore miniature waterfalls in the sand.

Just like those dirty Japs to pick such a miserable day to launch their fiercest attack yet. And though he'd begged the doc to be reinstated from sick bay, Jesse could only watch and wait as the casualties mounted.

At least on the day he'd had to wait in line to be sewed up, rain had not soaked him to the skin. "You can always find something to be thankful for, and someone who's got it worse than you."

Aunt Annie had said that, he supposed. Or had Mama uttered the sentiment back in Texas, even longer ago?

Although he'd put those distant days far from his mind, he decided it must've been Mama. She touted sayings when things looked darkest, when the goodness seemed to drain out of life and the present painful moment clutched your heart with agony or fear.

Thanks to his father, a consistent stream of those frightening days had filled his childhood, but his move to Kentucky almost shoved memories of them into oblivion. Strange, really, how when Aunt Annie said his dad had passed from this world, he'd experienced no emotion. Not even curiosity.

When Mama wrote her, Aunt Annie gave him only the bare details. Mama had already moved on somewhere else, Annie said.

"I wrote back to her and asked where but haven't heard yet—she used a post office box for the return address."

Like always, no mention of her coming to Kentucky. So Jesse cherished his last image of her... close to his heart, but hemmed by a million questions.

That final picture stuck with him, Mama settling him into a train seat and hugging him so tight he couldn't breathe. He'd never forget that morning. The smell of perspiration on her face and the leather of the train seats still returned to him from time to time.

Her glistening eyes seemed painfully vivid as she released her hold. With the conductor's reassurances, she'd backed away, out of the train car. Out of his life.

Later, in Kentucky, in what he considered his first real school, he'd learned the word *ambivalence*. Two things could be true at the same time. You could want to stay with Mama, whose breaking heart had flooded her eyes, but also long to get away and start a new life.

He remembered fingering the word *ambivalence* in the massive Webster's Dictionary Miss Stewart, his English teacher, kept on a special tall table in her classroom. This was his feeling exactly—the word described the trip to Aunt Annie's, too.

The conductors watched out for him, and strangers were nothing but kind. But he'd been leery of everything and everyone, especially at the stations when he pulled a quarter from his pocket to buy food. He'd never handled so much money before and let his stomach get growling hungry before parting with a cent.

As the land turned from crusty dry ecru to every shade of green and hills started to appear, hills with healthy-looking cattle grazing rather than Texas longhorns with their ravenous eyes, his fears lessened some. Kentucky hills offered brown-and-white Herefords or Guernseys with meat on their bones, a promising lot.

And the rivers flowed so big they needed big bridges for automobiles and trains. In cities, vehicles passed the depots on paved roads, and people milled about everywhere. So different from the scant hole-in-the-wall town he'd gone to a few times, with a mercantile, a sheriff's office, and a bar.

In the dark that night, a conductor sat down beside him for a little nap. When he woke, he whispered something, so Jesse asked what he was saying.

"Why, my mornin' prayers, boy. Gotta put my fam'ly n' ever'thin' else in the hands of the good Lawd. He's the only one kin' take care of it all."

Something about that quieted Jesse's fears. But it took days to truly relax, although he instantly recognized Aunt Annie. She looked a lot like Mama—not many folks had eyes that shade of emerald.

Meeting Willie had surely helped. As they fished or swam in the creek or hunted together, the quietude inside Jesse grew. He'd come to people he could call family, to a place he could call home. Mama sent him to the right place. True, she wasn't here, but at least Papa could never reach him.

Time and the war only added examples that he had landed where he was meant to be. Seemed like Mama could never come to visit—she had things to take care of, Aunt Annie said. So Jesse tucked way deep down the lingering pain of missing her and let life gradually fill in the holes.

Mama had read to him, taught him his ABCs, sat by him at the kitchen table as he learned to write his name and cipher. She never seemed to tire of teaching him or of learning herself. She communicated the importance of reading books of all kinds.

And she had saved his life, even if he lost her in the process.

But was what she said true—could things always get worse? Especially now, he wondered, as cussing GIs carried even more loaded stretchers into this tent. With their precious cargos hanging between life and death and the deafening clash of bombardment mixed with an endless lashing downpour, could things really be worse?

Well, he supposed so. He could be dead, for one. The last two days the doc had been letting him sit for a while each day. This morning he walked a little, sat some more, walked again.

"You suffered a severe concussion, Kline. Can't have you out there shooting yet."

But awash with the odors of blood and ether, this tent seemed no place for the likes of him. He should've been moved to a recovery area by now, but nobody had time for protocol when the never-ending flow of casualties kept deluging the orderlies.

The Japs were like worms, Willie said. Like maggots, they streamed from every cave and potential hiding place on this island. They'd already killed thousands of Marines, but here they were, still crawling everywhere, still filling this tent with unspeakable horrors.

For a while longer, the chaotic scene immersed Jesse's senses. Then an idea occurred to him. Who would notice if he slipped out for a while? For sure not the docs, up to their ears in surgeries.

True, he had nowhere to go, but even the slipshod mess tent wooed him. Maybe he could find a hot cup of coffee, at least, and practice walking there.

Enveloped by yelling medics and outbursts of jostled wounded servicemen, he took his chance, hurtling through great swaths of rain and skirting mud akin to the hogwash back home. Across the boardwalk, skidding and sliding, he aimed for the meager swinging lightbulb that kept the mess tent from oblivion.

And he made it, though the makeshift railroad tie threshold threatened to throw him face first into a table. A hand reached out to grab his arm. When he glanced up, crystal blue eyes met his.

"Sergeant Adams?"

"Yeah. What're you doin' over here? I was 'bout to come 'n find ya." The burly sergeant guided Jesse into a camp chair. "Got some real bad news for ya."

"I don't want…"

"'Course not. I didn't want to hear it either, but facts is facts. And the fact is, Private Wilder…"

Jesse's breath caught in his throat. *Willie.* In a flash, all that they had shared crossed his mind's eye.

"The fighting got brutal today up near that blasted pocket

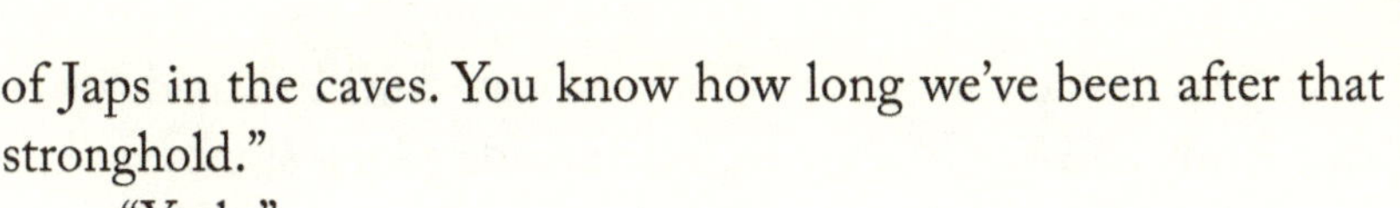

of Japs in the caves. You know how long we've been after that stronghold."

"Yeah."

"The medics got Private Wilder out, but he came back from the field with…"

Usually not one to dither, the sergeant pushed back his cap. A half-day's beard growth caught the light in hundreds of blond spikes on his jaw. He rolled in his lips and shook his head.

"Massive injuries. With that square of a hit in the chest, Willie never stood a fighting chance. At least he didn't suffer for long."

The tent revolved, poles swirling into poles as Jesse stared at the sergeant. He must be mistaken. Had to be.

"Jesse? Are you with me? I'd give my right arm to give you better news, son."

Heat filled Jesse's throat as those crystal eyes, so much like his father's, peered at him. But the Sergeant's gaze shone honest and fair.

*Gotta get out of here.* Jesse scrambled up the same way he'd come in, out into the deluge. Behind him, Sergeant Adams' heavy boots slithered right behind him.

*Two weeks later, somewhere on Guadalcanal*

Squinting through his scope, Jesse took aim at one Jap in particular. *Maybe this one had killed Willie.* Of course, he had no way of telling, but a thrill ran the length of his spine after pulling the trigger. His bullet blew the enemy soldier sky-high.

For a moment he forgot about the continuous twinge in his jaw and the insistent sting in his knee as he aimed and hit another mark. *For Willie.* From now on, every single shot would be for Willie.

After training in Texas, they'd suffered together through the worst heat and humidity Louisiana could offer. How they both ended up in the Composite Army-Marine Division made up of two Army and one Marine regiment made a long story.

They figured they'd laugh together about their fate in old age, rocking on somebody's front porch. But now, who cared about stories? Only one thing mattered: revenge. That, and winning this damnable war.

Aunt Annie had never allowed swearing under her roof, but out here in this hell-hole, cussing seemed to fit. Here, nothing made sense. It had been some time now, but how could Willie possibly be dead? And how else could a man release even a small measure of the seething inside?

A sudden shadow fell, along with a yell that sounded like it came from his new partner. Half-turning, Jesse released an inhuman cry as his new buddy, Joe, wiped out the side of a Jap's face with his gun butt.

An ocean of disgust swept him as Joe kept up his furious fight, oblivious to all else. That Jap had set his eyes on *him*. Without Joe's intervention, he'd be dead right now, or thrashing on this loathsome piece of earth.

He ought to say thanks. Maybe later. But even as he considered Joe's rescue, the outline of Willie's face masked Joe's. No one would ever take Willie's place. Half of the time, Jesse still expected to turn toward Joe and see Willie.

Oh, these hordes! Would the enemy never stop coming? True, they had bodies like American GIs, but apart from that, they might as well be termites.

Suddenly, Jesse was twelve years old again, deep in the Kentucky woods with Uncle Winn, who taught him everything he knew about using a gun. Instructed in patience, timing, and keeping a steady trigger finger, he had learned to meld with the weapon.

How many times had he waited for a good shot that would reap them a tasty supper—rabbit, squirrel, or deer? Uncle Winn showed him how to be certain of his shot before he made his move. The animal must not notice him—otherwise, what was the use?

This scenario required no such deception. The laws had changed. This amounted to a hunt, for sure, but everything came down to: *shoot or be shot.*

Strangely, Winn had died of an accidental rifle shot on his way home from helping a neighbor one day. His gun must have misfired when he crossed a fence, the neighbor said. Odd this should happen to a man who stressed strict care with firearms.

Normally, Jesse kept that memory at bay, but here on Guadalcanal in the stench and intense heat, the unthinkable scene returned. That awful muggy summer day, he'd been the one to go search for Winn when he failed to come home by chore time.

He'd been the one to touch the place on Uncle Winn's neck where a pulse ought to be and feel nothing at all. The one to race back to Aunt Annie so they could fetch the wagon. He'd kept silence as she held out hope.

"Maybe…maybe somehow, we'll find a pulse now." Later, disbelief and horror crossed his cousins' faces, and Jesse joined the family circle as they wept together.

During that time, Mama came to mind often, as if this new grief were not enough to bear. Another hole in his heart.

And now he'd lost Willie. A vast crevasse opened inside him when he heard that news. A part of him simply would not accept— could not accept—that Willie had fallen prey to the filthy Japs.

At this very moment, despite the noise of battle, Uncle Winn's voice sounded in his ear. "When you hunt, you gotta stay calm, Jesse. Cool as that lull before a big storm, you know what I mean? Still as the windless moments just before a tornado. That's the main thing—keep your mind on your business and your wits about you."

Joe felled another attacker. Another. The guy really was a good shot. For a few minutes, an eerie quietude reigned. Smoke from a thousand weapons hung like mist over warriors on both sides already swimming in island humidity.

Joe sank against a crumbling earthen wall to catch his breath.

Jesse maintained his surveillance as a sudden fresh draught of enemy troops appeared out of nowhere—three in a row for starters. One-by-one, he and Joe took them out.

In a slight lull, Joe scrambled up with a hiss. "Good aim!" A moment later, he glanced over again. "Hey, you doin' all right?"

"Yep." Serene as Annie and Winn's secluded back-forty pond with not a ripple in sight, Jesse re-loaded his weapon. "Just keepin' my wits 'bout me." He took a moment to look skyward and mutter, "Thank you, Uncle Winn."

Chapter Eleven

"Positive thinking. We want this ward to swim in positive thinking." The doctor gestured from the hallway just outside an amputee ward.

"These patients have been through Hell and back, leaving parts of their bodies behind. Some of them have accepted their situation already, some haven't. But either way, no good comes from rehearsing the details. What is, is. We need to keep our focus on their future outside these walls.

"Eventually they'll be fitted for artificial arms or legs. That's the goal, as much mobility as possible when they leave here. Their stumps are a fact of life—they have no choice but to accept them. And neither do we."

"Fortunately, the majority of them will adjust and be able to develop a normal life out in the world again." He stopped to survey us nurses-in-training. "Any questions before we begin?"

Four other recruits and I maintained silence. Listening to his introduction brought up only one valid question: would I be able to work with these fellows who had lost so much?

"You may be thinking 'what do I have to offer them?' That's the best possible perspective. I'll tell you what they need most. Listening ears, steady spirits, and a tranquil manner. What they do *not* need? Looks or gestures of shock, pity, or disgust.

"That's why the five of you will spend some time in a different ward right now, but with the same types of injuries and challenges. Listen and observe as I do my rounds—save your reactions for later. Watch how the nurses notice needs and meet them."

Glad for Helen's presence, I glanced her way precisely as she did the same. Her forehead wrinkles showed that she shared my trepidation. Silently we agreed we could hash this all out on our ride back to Waco. We took a deep breath in unison, and I relaxed a bit. We were in this together.

During those days we learned so much! How to apply dressings to infected stumps, how to rub the ends of healing limbs with various degrees of something like sandpaper to help convince the nerves that the rest of the leg or arm truly had disappeared.

The unfamiliar term "phantom pain" intrigued me. A patient might experience sharp stinging in his lower leg or foot, though that body part had been lost weeks or months ago in a battle.

Doctors *tricked* the nerve endings by using increasingly rough grades of rubbing material. Gradually these imaginary—but very real—pains and itches stopped troubling the patient.

"It's not so crazy," one young man quipped. Nearly through his recovery, he felt ready to serve again, but in an office this time. "Same thing we had to do when we trained—tell ourselves we were tough enough to defeat the Japs. We were just a bunch of kids, but we believed, anyhow."

The ride back to Waco gave Helen and me time to talk, even in a busy train car teeming with other passengers. I learned she was closer to my age than I thought. She had been married before she met Walt but lost her first husband to an accident.

She learned something of my history, too. Now she knew I'd moved from Kentucky, set out to become a literature teacher, married, and lost my babies.

After disclosing that much, I leaned into my seat for a while—had those words actually dispensed into open air? I'd never told anyone but Miss M, although Sophie had known. What had made me feel so free with the facts today?

But I hadn't mentioned the baby who lived. Not yet... I was not ready to risk breaking down. Helen offered such a sympathetic ear, but no. Maybe another time.

After today's lessons and practice followed by hours of bed-side experience with the wounded, neither of us minded slipping into silence for the remainder of the trip. The engines, with sounds of vast harnessed power—a little like Miss M's washing-machine motor magnified many times—slowed to an intermittent intrusion as the train approached the Waco depot.

My thoughts still roiled with the stories of those boys I'd met today. They had so many transitions to make. They longed for home, and families from all over the nation waited for them. One from New York had a wry sense of humor, and his accent forced me to concentrate.

"You come from around here?" I pondered how to answer his question.

"Sort of. Born in Kentucky, but I guess you'd say Texas-bred."

"How'd you end up here with us?" He gestured around the ward. "Must be kinda tough."

"That's a long story. And you're right. Sometimes it is tough." Just then one of his medicine bottles caught my eye. "But I'm just like the medicine in that bottle beside you—here to help you heal."

*Hiss…hiss…take your time…slow down…*the train sighed. *Even more change lies ahead.*

Deep inside, I welcomed whatever each day might bring. Now I knew I had something to offer. And surely, in all the tales this war would produce, my own challenges would one day fade into nothing at all.

Back at home, that message…more change to come…struck me in the face. I rushed into the kitchen to help Miss M, but all was quiet. Potatoes waited to be boiled, so I turned on the flame beneath the pot and peeked into the refrigerator.

Chicken in the ice chest, cut and ready for baking. I set to work breading the pieces in Miss M's secret recipe that set boarders raving. Nothing quite like the taste this side of the Mississippi, they insisted.

But the house stayed far too quiet, even for late afternoon.

This must have to do with Elwyn. The whole time, an ominous cloud enveloped me.

Someone headed down the back stairs, but not with Miss M's light footsteps. The door creaked open. Dr. Graham appeared, ghostly white.

He washed his hands. I'd never seen him like this.

"It's Elwyn." He wiped his forehead with his sleeve. "He went so…so fast in the end. Just like that, here and gone." This man who had witnessed many deaths shuddered. "It was as if he orchestrated his last moments, you know? I'm so glad Judson could be here… He and Elwyn had a bond like none I've ever witnessed."

Doc shook his head, and without pausing further or saying good-bye, let himself out the side door.

Change indeed.

Chapter Twelve

*February 1943*

The back-and-forth motion of the ship produced a moan from the depths of Jesse's being. Before he realized what was happening, he retched over the side of his bunk. The old gray-hulled vessel, once a merchant marine ship, yawned and squealed as he lay there covered with sweat.

The world performed a wild South Pacific dance around him, the smell and taste of vomit undeniable. This might be the first time he'd given in, but others around him couldn't seem to stop.

Finally, panting, he found his bearings again and rolled back into his swaying bunk. If only, for even one minute, everything would stop moving! But the ship's waltz continued—how on earth did Navy swabbies handle living on these things for years?

Amazing that the military somehow managed to supply pillows for everyone crammed into this hold. That's what Aunt Annie would say—she always saw the big picture and would notice something like this—a relatively clean pillow for every patient.

A seemingly insignificant object in the broad scheme of things, yet what a difference a pillow could make! Aunt Annie's eyes—bluish-green one day, pure green the next—against fair skin loaded with too many freckles to count, seemed quite close right now.

She'd been the one to clean up after her brood when they all got the flu and didn't seem to mind having one extra child in the mix.

At first, Jesse had been so embarrassed, having someone other than Mama dab a wet rag over his feverish head. But how many times had Aunt Annie told him, "Your Mama sent you to us for the very best reason—love. And you know what? I'm so very glad she did!" She explained little more than that, but Jesse's memories of the pain Papa had inflicted with his belt and his bare hands filled in the rest.

"She couldn't take seeing him treat you badly any more, Jesse. He was getting worse and worse, and she became so afraid for you."

This stream of recollections, though comforting, seemed too powerful right now. All Jesse could think was, *Hang on. This trip can't last forever.*

They were headed for California, that much he knew—California and hospitals prepared to deal with the likes of guys like him, wounded and re-wounded on Guadalcanal. And who-knows-where-else?

The Army, Navy, and Marines kept their members separated, mostly, but when it came to the Pacific Isles, things had gotten out of control. After the Marines' brave fight and the walloping they took, the powers-that-be chose to bring in a mixture of troops. At that point, officers paid far less attention to which branch of service you'd entered. The marines simply needed help, and fast.

Within minutes of Jesse emptying his stomach, someone set a metal bucket beside him and mopped the floor until a clean smell gradually overtook the putrid odor. Something soft bathed his burning skin as he tried to apologize.

"Shhh… No one can help it." Moisture bathed Jesse's forehead. Ah, nothing like a cool cloth for a fevered brow.

"Really, buddy. It's all right. Everybody's sick. Don't worry about it."

Like a pleasant stream, the woman's voice flowed from lips below gentle hazel eyes. The nurse leaned in a bit so he could hear her above all the other noise, and when she did, her necklace caught the light from a porthole. A small amber gem on a gold chain, a solitary jewel that settled in the hollow below her neck.

"They say if you keep your eyes on this bar…" She touched a metal rod above his head. "It'll help with the nausea. It has something to do with the connection between your eyes and your stomach."

She handed him a few crackers. "Might be best not to drink too much for a while, but it can't hurt to eat these."

A sudden stench wafted with the unmistakable gagging of another wounded man, and she looked for the source. "Oh, my. Just you rest now, all right? I'll be back."

Something about her expression, soft and caring, sent a wave of yearning through Jesse. She reminded him of… who was it? Someone in his past. Yes, even in the midst of all this, he recalled a day when he'd run outdoors to Mama, kneeling beside three small mounds southwest of the house.

He'd never seen her in tears before, or had forgotten, and when he drew near, she swept him up and kissed him. "Ah, Jesse. My sweet Jesse," she'd crooned, and rocked him back and forth.

With the memory came a scent, something like the lavender Aunt Annie wore. He must've been three or four—this might be his oldest memory.

Faster than she had appeared, the nurse slipped away, as did the recollection. But the sense of being cared for and of being worthy colored his dreams.


*Mid-March, 1943*


The small clapboard church bulged with well-wishers honoring Elwyn and supporting Miss M. They came from all over the city, and even further. The milkman, Doctor Graham and Rosita, former boarders who had married and stayed in Waco, workmen who labored with Elwyn years ago, Great War vets, and of course, members of this congregation gathered to say farewell.

They came for Judson, too. Planted solid as Texas pink

granite beside Miss M at the entrance, Judson wiped his forehead in midmorning heat as they shook his hand on the way in. These people for whom he had worked, neighbors and longtime friends, kindhearted folks, knew how close he and Elwyn had been.

The line they formed wound around the side of the church. Workmen in their denim overalls or khaki pants and checkered shirts, housewives in Sunday-go-to-meeting dresses and hats, clerks and professional men like Doctor Graham in tweed suits.

They filed in after greeting Miss M and Judson, and soon the service began. Elwyn's body rested in a simple wooden casket situated near the pulpit.

*Trust and obey, for there's no other way…*

An old piano in the front corner defied its humble appearance to produce remarkable chords.

The crowd sang louder, it seemed, than on any given Sunday. Most folks knew the words by heart and lifted their chins to bellow out the sentiments Miss M had chosen to send off her beloved.

*Trust and obey, for there's no other way*
*To be happy in Jesus, but to trust and obey.*

Over the past couple of days, Judson fashioned the wooden box that now held his friend's earthly remains. Yellow roses fresh from Miss M's bush adorned the lid, a tribute to Elwyn's doggedness. Miss M swore they bloomed early this year just for this occasion.

As Mama always said, "A rose that survives in Texas is worth a hundred anywhere else." Precisely what Miss M murmured to me when we cut the wiry stems this morning, and I had to agree. The difference between Kentucky and here, at least in my mind even after all these years, boiled down to fertility and color.

Bright and sun-bleached described Texas, vibrant and abundant, Kentucky, with so many flamboyant greens they hurt your eyes. Wildflowers galore sprouted in the back woods, aromatic pines and deciduous trees blasted their hues in autumn.

In contrast, Texas came washed-out. Her beauty, diminished

by the heat, lurked in corners. Tiny weedy flowers burst through rough-and-tumble red earth. Misshapen specimens sprang up where you least expected them. Running along the foundation of a dilapidated barn or peering at you from a ledge that looked like solid rock, they defied a gardener's eye.

And once each spring, such a violent outburst of purple massed in the meadows when the bluebonnets blossomed. Depending on the year, they simply overtook everything else, a one-time show to keep you through the rest of the year.

Early this morning, beside Miss M's rose bush in the hush of dawn, the image of bones appeared to me. Stark bones, beaten down by rays so strong they burned you smack dab through your shirt. Bones in a cornfield, dragged there by a horse and dumped.

This human skeleton made me shiver. When Miss M took me to visit Elywn that first night, he had been nothing but bones and tightened skin, yet he remained alive all these months.

These dark thoughts also led to Clyde, to nowhere, so I shook them off. This was Elwyn's day, Miss M's day. Not a moment to give to gloom, for as Miss M said, we would think on Elwyn's life today, celebrating what he offered to this hurting world.

Not much from the sermon stayed with me. It was all I could do to keep my nose blown. Why? I am not sure, but something touched me about this crowd's outpouring of goodness in his honor.

Towards the end, though, the preacher asked a question.

"Have you ever seen a better witness to the intrinsic value of human beings than Elwyn?"

Then he quoted from a book, a slender volume he balanced in one palm.

*Do not look forward*
*to what may happen tomorrow;*
*The same everlasting Father who*
*cares for you today will take care*
*of you tomorrow and every day.*
*Either He will shield you from*

*suffering, or He will give you*
*unfailing strength to bear it.*
*Be at peace, then, put aside all*
*anxious thoughts and imaginations,*
*and say continually: "The Lord is my*
*strength and my shield; my heart*
*has trusted in Him and I am helped.*
*He is not only with me…but in me…*
*and I in him.*

"These words from St. Francis de Sales, who lived centuries ago, describe the life we remember here. We honor a man who day after day, week after week, month after month, and year after year accepted unfailing strength and cheer to bear the suffering God allowed, a suffering he had no choice but to endure.

"We cannot imagine the particular cross the Great War left him to bear. No one disliked war and what it can do more than Elwyn, but he kept up with this present one. He embraced the suffering and hurt it is causing all around the world and supported our young fighting men.

"He pondered the battlegrounds in various theaters, followed along on his own map, recited the commanders and many of the units involved. No one knows how many prayers he lifted on high for our boys in harm's way.

"It remains for us to contemplate his example. How can we personally give our troops all of the attention they deserve?"

Two people Elwyn had affected rose to speak, and after the second one, I doubt any dry eyes remained. When Elwyn had still worked for the railroad, the middle-aged speaker said, he discovered her frightening situation.

Her husband, on-and-off a railroad employee, on when he was sober, off when he went on a binge, became violent after his benders. Almost always, he came home in the middle of the night filled with rage.

Every time, she would gather their two small children and

run to the train station—she had nowhere else to go. And coming to work in the wee hours of the morning, Elwyn noticed her. He opened one of the mostly-unused baggage rooms for her and her children, brought them blankets and something to eat.

"He never said, 'That's enough. This is the last time.'" She held back a sob as she continued. "Elwyn knew my husband, hated what he was doing to himself and us, yet did his best to help us all.

"After some time, he alerted someone at the hospital. I'm not at liberty to say who…

"Suddenly, word came that my husband would be admitted to a ward where he could find help overcoming his demons. He'd been in the Great War, too, and started drinking when he returned.

"I was flabbergasted at the effort Elwyn made to help us. I didn't know what to say. I tried to thank him, but he just shrugged and said, 'There but for the grace of God go I.'"

Walking home, I pondered—had my escape from the ranch, from suffering, been a good thing, a right thing? Elwyn lived with his troubles until he died.

The difference lay in perspective. What trapped me could have been changed. Elwyn, though, could not alter his condition. Still, once I realized the gunshot had killed Clyde, had my actions been the wisest?

On my worst nights when doubt refused to loosen its clasp on my soul, I debated. I could have gone to town the next morning and explained to the sheriff exactly what happened. Should have.

I might have seen respectfully to Clyde's body and given him a simple burial. Every one of God's children deserves that, don't they?

At the time, though, these alternatives never crossed my mind. But finally a way out seemed possible, so I made my escape. Once done, 'twas done, rash or not, but from this distance, I can't help marveling at the surge that empowered me on that fateful night.

For the first time in years, I felt in charge, and capable. In the matter of Clyde's bones being eaten by the pigs, Clyde himself had helped prepare me—I never would have thought of that. At times, though, I wonder how I accomplished what I did.

Where did such an infusion of strength originate? So many other times, I had failed to stand up for myself, so what spurred me in that instance?

But back to Elwyn. Each morning for more than twenty years, he awakened in the same body, hurting and miserable, needy and dependent. Yet he persevered without complaining.

Walking down the sidewalk, it seemed life spread before me like an ever-turning pathway. Whatever trials lay ahead, I determined he would stand as my example. I had entered his life toward its end, but maybe meeting him had been the main reason I came to Waco.

I'd never thought of my passage quite this way before, but how could I ever forget Elwyn's steady determination? His will-power as he tackled any small task, buttoning his shirt or bringing a biscuit to his mouth or placing a pin on the war map he and Judson pored over together?

Images of these movements, so difficult for him, would stay with me for all time. His life provided an example of perseverance to the utmost.

His slight grin, almost like a mischievous child's, often accompanied the most trying tasks. I would pause before placing his breakfast tray before him, and he would bite his upper lip, struggle up in the bed and reach for the napkin Miss M kept at his side.

"Let him tuck it in his shirt, no matter how much you'd like to do it for him. It's a small thing, maybe, but something he takes pride in," she instructed me.

This seemingly insignificant, sickly man had left me his life as a pattern. And not me alone, but so many others. Even in his death, his life kept speaking. "Take each day with a bit of humor. Endure to the end! Stick with it!"

For someone with such an inborn tendency to give up, this amounted to the best possible gift. I accepted the treasure as a souvenir to be cherished.

*November 1943, A California port*

Stretcher after stretcher lined up along the deck as medics and orderlies, privates pulled from other tasks, and in some cases, even dock workers carried the wounded down a long gangplank. *Like a parade,* Jesse thought. A very slow parade, akin to their journey from the Pacific in a merchant ship refitted for treating the wounded.

He'd been taken first to the New Caledonia islands, where an Army staff offered more up-to-date care than the field hospital on Guadalcanal. But after a week, the docs assigned him to return to the U.S. for further treatment.

Every stage of the long journey had offered its own sort of pause. His life seemed to be in a perpetual state of recess, as if he were crossing over from one world to another, but never quite getting there.

Once before, he had experienced a similar sensation—on the train from Texas to Kentucky, but only now identified the similarities. Too much time to think, that was the trouble. Way too much time.

And of course, he'd been just a kid back then, but the emotions fit perfectly. His mind had spun with questions. Would he ever really get to where he was going? Would he indeed meet Aunt Annie, Mama's sister, at the end of this journey, the aunt Mama had told him about so often?

Or at one of the depots along the way, would something happen to keep him from his long-awaited destination? He recalled feeling safe, finally, in the train car. But at every stop when he got out to buy food, this awareness—kind of like a premonition— struck him. He might be someone's prey, so he trekked with great care to the canteen, and each time, purchased something simple.

Grilled cheese sandwiches seemed safe. He paid the clerk and hurried back to his seat to eat. That seat attracted him like a magnet draws a nail.

In retrospect, a walk would have done him good, but he could manage no more than the quick trip to find food and the bathroom. Every time he returned to the car, the warm brown eyes of a conductor, all dark men, offered assurance, so he once again felt as though he would make it to Aunt Annie's.

He would forever be drawn to large men with dark skin and a kind manner. "Darkies," his papa used to call them, followed by a slew of uncomplimentary adjectives. But his father had been so wrong. These men watched out for him.

About ten years later, this recent voyage by ship had its own worries and fears. Torpedo boats weren't supposed to shoot at Red Cross ships, but this vessel had no such marking. From the outside it looked like any old gray-hulled craft on the vast Pacific Ocean.

The Navy had transformed its innards into a quite a hospital, serving 1,600 wounded at a time. But when torpedoes came screaming through the water and the alert sounded, general panic arose. Some fellows, if they could, flew out of their bunks and looked madly around them.

Others, like Jesse, remained quietly where they were, hoping for the best. After all, wasn't that what they had done in each scenario since basic training?

You did your duty and hoped for the best. Counting himself lucky to have arrived back in the States at all, Jesse took in this lovely California bay and the salty air.

A few weeks ago, after their first ship took torpedo fire from a Japanese submarine, the patients had been transferred to another vessel. How many had died during the shooting and the transfer, no one would say, but what a spectacle it had all been.

As someone announced over the intercom this morning, they were headed for a first-class hospital now. Thinking about that brought the hazel-eyed nurse to mind. He had only seen her a few times after she cleaned up after him, but he gave her high marks.

Once, she stopped beside his bunk long enough to explain that she'd been working on ships since Pearl Harbor. She'd said her name was Maggie, a good down-to-earth name. Every other time she came anywhere near him, she'd been busy helping some other guy.

She'd given him hope, just by being who she was. A few evenings after Jesse learned her name, after things settled down in the ship, she'd stopped by again. Without thinking, he told her how Mama had sent him away.

The story escaped like a rabbit from a snare. Wasn't supposed to happen, but it did. He felt like an onlooker, an eavesdropper as it broke free.

"My mother sent me away when I was eight." That was how he started out, but Maggie's response after hearing more details helped him rethink things.

"Sounds like she saved your life, maybe at great cost to herself. I bet you ten-to-one she prays for you every day and longs to see you."

Such certainy rode her tone, and the glow in her eyes underlined each word. Then she went on. "Private Kline…"

"Please call me Jesse."

"Jesse, then—that's my baby brother's name, too. He's ten years younger than me. Do you know what your name means?"

He shook his head, and she said, *"God's gift.* I bet your mother named you that for a special reason. My Mama prays every day for this war to end so our Jesse doesn't have to go."

For a moment, her eyes glinted. "Anyway, if your mother saw you off to safety like that, you can be sure it was the hardest thing she ever did. And you can count on her dying to see you face-to-face."

The memory of that conversation remained like the pleasant aftertaste of Uncle Winn's fresh-made apple cider, hot from a mug on a cool autumn day. After the nurse left, Jesse found himself asking for the first time, *I wonder what happened that day when Mama got home after taking me to the train?*

And this spurred other memories unknown as yet…Mama with large purple bruises on her face and arms. Sounds of a scuffle in the night after he'd gone up to the loft. What if, on the day she'd taken him to the train, Papa had laid into her because she dared to stand up to him?

Suddenly, his whole childhood paraded before him from an entirely new angle. Mama had been a fighter, his protector. He'd been all she had, her only living child.

This conjecture led to no solid answers, but the *what-ifs* wielded a power of their own. In the influence of this revelation, he felt less in limbo.

Long-held questions transformed into others that centered on Maggie, who listened so well and possessed such insight. If his leg healed and he became a whole man again, what if she didn't have a beau? What if she waited for a private just like him to come along?

Fingering the rough edge of the sheet that covered him, Jesse pondered the possibility. Nah—like a lot of nurses, she probably had lost the love of her lifetime at Pearl. Besides, a woman like her deserved a surgeon, a colonel at least.

But he did consider what it was about her that soothed him so. Maybe the composure that seemed so natural. She remained steady, confident and competent in the midst of the chaos aboard this huge ship filled with hurting GIs and some wounded docs and nurses, too. After all, some of them had been hit by the torpedo fire—nobody wore an *exempt* sign.

Something about her reminded him of a warm strength he once had known. Could it be Mama's? Awash with fear that night Papa attacked him, Mama had stood up to him. Unruffled, she came up with a plan lickety-split. The next morning, she carried it out.

After all of this time, he didn't even remember her face, couldn't conjure the outline of her profile. Although he suspected she looked like Aunt Annie, with dimples when she smiled, freckles and wavy reddish-blonde hair, he couldn't remember for sure.

How could he have let her features grow so dim? Would he even know her if they happened to meet?

As always, his brooding went further. How could someone as smart as Mama ever have married a man like Papa, with as much compassion as a cholla cactus? Aunt Annie told him very little about this, only that Mama had been in college when their mother died and Papa proposed.

Even as he pondered, tightness constricted Jesse's throat and he reached his fingers up to where Papa had held him against the cabin wall. A grip like iron. Eyes to make a cougar back down.

Some memories, like this one, never seemed to fade. He could still sense the pressure of those strong fingers. Even drunk, Papa somehow maintained his prowess. At that moment, only Mama could have saved him, and she certainly did.

If only he could recall her countenance like he did Papa's. That face always scowled, ferocious as a hungry mountain lion, furious about one thing or another.

During the battles he'd fought, and in all those days on the ship, he couldn't count the number of times some wounded GI called out for his mother. Something about that moniker, *Mama,* held almost a sacred meaning when you lay dying, or thought you might be.

Nodding off as he waited, Jesse wrestled with recent scenes from the war. But one searing inquiry cut through them all. Would he ever see Mama again?

An ocean wind swept in from the west, sending a shiver all the way to Jesse's feet, in spite of the scratchy olive wool army blanket covering him. What a weakling he'd become, shivering at the slightest breeze from the Pacific, the ocean that had altered his life so irrevocably.

All around, orderlies grunted under their loads as docs or nurses issued instructions. The tension threaded through Jesse, constricted his every breath. So many men, so much critical need.

All around, typical wharf echoes created background noise. *Smash! Thud! Screech*! A human *yowl* came in the midst of it all, probably some poor worker getting his finger caught in the wrong spot.

"C'mon! Bust a gut, fellas! We gotta get these guys t' the hospital 'fore it starts rainin!" Someone grabbed one end of Jesse's stretcher. None too gently, another orderly took hold of the other, shifting all weight onto his injured leg.

His own yelp startled him, but it was too late. No such thing as taking it back. Even his own voice seemed beyond his control.

An ache passed through his chest as he felt himself being lifted and carried, the sort of ache that finds no easy repair. Nothing in his life seemed manageable, least of all his own body.

His thoughts drifted off again. He didn't even know for sure where Mama was. The last he knew, after Papa passed on, she had moved somewhere in Texas. But he'd gotten busy in high school, busy with sports and debating.

Things that had meant so much to him before the war shrank

them into meaninglessness now. But how could a guy lose track of his own mother?

And now, fate had just landed him in California. This crazy war, with his back-and-forth travels, mystified him. Now he'd been to the Pacific and back again, this time by a different route than the first time. Where would he end up next? And if the docs weren't able to fix his leg, then what?

His thoughts were interrupted when his carrier leaped over something. Jesse bit his lip to hold back his reaction.

"Sorry about that, private. We're just about there."

*Just about there*, a comforting notion. Jesse flattened his chin to check out his chest, but his rank wasn't there. Oh yeah—they'd cut away his uniform in the evac tent.

After pondering a while, he did discover a vague memory of being promoted after the last battle, some mumbo-jumbo about leadership. But what mattered was remembering his name: Jesse Kline.

"All right! All right!" A puffy-eyed doctor who looked like he might've showered a week ago stopped at the bed next to Jesse's. "Private Tourney? Philip Tourney?" The doc flipped through some papers on a clipboard hanging from the foot of the bed.

"Yes sir."

"Here's the facts, son. Best case scenario, you never would have had more than five per-cent use of your right arm, but even worse, in the past seventy-two hours, the infection has spread. None of the therapies we've tried has made the slightest difference."

"But…"

"I'm sorry, son. We really have no choice but to schedule you for amputation."

"Ampu…?" Phil's voice broke. "But you saved that guy's hand…" He gestured to his left.

"Yes. The problem with your arm is the infection. We don't have a drug strong enough to fight it. Sounds like we may soon. In some places, military doctors are experimenting with penicillin. But there's such a demand, we can't count on a shipment.

"Looks as though we might be able to take only the lower part, just below the elbow, so that'll give you a little more control and usage. You're healthy otherwise, so you ought to get along just fine."

"But I…" Phil's voice quivered.

"I'm really sorry. We've tried everything we possibly can."

The doctor moved on to Jesse's side. "Wounded in the Pacific, eh? And not once, but twice. That's one way to rise in the ranks."

He uncovered Jesse's leg and poked around. "I hate to tell you this, but your leg looks like one more case where we're going to have to amputate."

A storm churned through Jesse's midsection. Not even a single question came to mind, and after the doc left, Phil lay there staring at him as if possessed. He blurted, "They're … they're givin' up! They're gonna take 'em both off!"

He glanced around furiously before fixing his eyes on Jesse again. "Listen, we gotta break outta here, man."

"Break out? But your infection will get worse, and you could die."

"I'd rather die than lose my arm. Besides, my folks live just over the border."

"Which border?"

"Nevada. Not that far." Phil lowered his voice to a whisper. "All we need is a ride to Las Vegas."

"Right. And all the world needs is Superman to end this war."

"No, listen! My Dad works for a magnesium company up there, and the government built a hospital for the workers. They've had some real bad accidents in the mines, and Dad says those docs can work wonders."

"Magnesium…?" Jesse's mind couldn't seem to take in what this GI was saying. What was he talking about, anyway?

"Yeah, it's mining, y'know. Dangerous work. They're used to dealing with mangled arms and legs up at the mine. And maybe they've got some of that peni…whatever it's called."

"How would you…?"

"Get a ride? Oh, that won't be hard. We'll find a diesel fuel station and wait for a truck headed that way. BMP, the Basic Magnesium Company sends a whole raft of 'em travelin' to the coast and back every week."

"You'd go AWOL?"

"To save my arm? You bet. But it's gotta be tonight…" Phil turned quiet.

Clearly, he was trying to form a plan. He hadn't spent a year working for a supply sergeant for nothing. Those guys knew how to get things done, and how to just plain *get* things.

As he muttered to himself, Jesse realized this was about all he knew about Phil. He'd been wounded serving with a logistics unit on one of the islands and was sent here.

A few days later, after transport from San Diego, Jesse arrived too. Phil's dark humor welcomed him to the ward.

"They're out to rid us of what's ailin' us, that's for sure. Looks like for you, that'd be a leg." From the beginning, Phil had used *we* and *us*. He hadn't lost his spirt, that was for sure.

During the evening hours, the ward quieted down for the day and an apologetic nurse finally got to them for baths. After that, Phil kept to himself.

Probably just as well. They were in Birmingham General in Van Nuys. Jesse had been relieved to finally land someplace and knew very little else about their geographic situation. Phil did, obviously, but going AWOL—that was a step too far.

An older nurse with thick dark eyebrows and greying hair came to check his leg and placed two large white pills in Jesse's palm. She brought him a glass of water and ordered, "Take these to help you sleep. Tomorrow's going to be a long day for you."

Swallowing them, Jesse entertained two last thoughts before falling asleep. Tomorrow he would lose his leg. He visualized himself with crutches or one of those new artificial legs, but the idea sent him into a tailspin, and he couldn't think straight.

One thing he did know. It would be no big surprise to awaken in the morning and find that Phil had vanished overnight.

"Git up!"

Something jabbed Jesse in the ribs, hard. Dazed by his last round of pain medication, he tried to rouse himself.

"Git up, I said!"

Slow as the heavy cider wheel he used to turn every fall at Aunt Annie's, Jesse obeyed. His body felt heavy, as if parts of it were attached to someone else, but a huge yank tore him from the bed and pulled him out of the ward.

Only a dim bulb lighted the hallway. Not a soul in sight.

"We're in luck, Jess. The nurses are changing shifts or somethin'."

The man—who was this, anyhow—shoved what felt like the barrel of a gun deeper into Jesse's side. Moving at all, especially dragging his left leg, created quite the challenge, but he managed a forward thrust down the hall.

Opening a door, his captor grunted, "Stop."

For a moment he removed the gun, and Jesse considered running for help. But his leg throbbed in protest as the door squeaked on its hinges. Surely someone would hear them. Surely someone would come.

Then the truth struck him. Phil had decided to escape and was taking him along.

"Git in, now!"

"I don't…" Jesse wavered, so Phil pushed him headlong onto some stinky towels piled in a deep wheeled object. A maintenance cart. Jesse's eyes watered at the odor. With a growl, Phil grabbed something from a shelf or hook and threw it over Jesse.

Careening the cart down the hallway, Phil veered left, then left again. They raced right and down some stairs, with Jesse's head bouncing like a basketball and thunder soaring from ear to ear.

Phil had turned into a madman!

Through more doors, along another passageway, down more stairs…would this ever end? A loud *thunk*, someone took a blow to the head, followed by a body collapsing on the floor.

"Got rid of the maintenance door guard. Whew!" Phil's heavy breathing still allowed him to sputter statements here and there. It was all Jesse could do to grasp at whatever thought occurred to him. Everything happened as though he were watching from a distance or still half asleep. Must be those pills he'd taken.

But then came the sweet smell of blossoms, an essence from Spring in Kentucky, sweetest scent in this wide world. Some kind of feathery white blossoms that took your breath away. Was it magnolia or a fruit tree? He couldn't recall which.

His nose functioned, but his mind still refused to work.

He tried to scrabble from the cart, but Phil gave his head a rude knock and snarled, "Don't know what's good for ya! One of these days, you'll thank me for this, buddy. The docs in Henderson'll save that leg of yours, and you'll thank me."

*If I don't die before we get there.* That was Jesse's last thought as Phil ground the cart to a halt and manhandled him, cart and all, into the back of a truck. At least, that was the general trajectory.

He landed in some sort of tarp or blanket as Phil leaped up beside him. Not a word about his wounded arm, but in the silence, he cradled it in his good one.

Within a few minutes, the truck motor shook awake and gas fumes encroached. Another minute and they were on a road. At that point, the meds mercifully took over. Despite his angst and the incredibly bumpy route, Jesse dozed off.

"But the Army'll say you've gone AWOL." A mature man's voice drove heavy sleep from Jesse's eyes. When he glanced around, he realized he was still inside a truck, surrounded by filthy hospital laundry.

"Nah, not when they hear my story. I'm just trying to get us both better so we can go back to our units. That'll never be possible if they amputate." Phil's voice, against a background of machines grinding and a nauseating sweet-sick gasoline smell, came from somewhere below.

Below what? Jesse felt around him but found nothing except stinky towels and a wooden floor. He touched all over his head. No swelling, no ache there, but his foot and lower leg cried out for attention, and his teeth filmed over with some sort of thick dust.

"You brought another guy with you? I can't believe this, son!"

"Well, it's true. When I saw the Basic Magnesium truck from our hospital window, I knew this was meant to be. You've always said God guides us in mysterious ways."

"Yeah, but this is different. You're breaking the law."

"Maybe so, but only temporarily. We need help, Dad, and quick. And just so you know, Jesse didn't want to come. I forced him."

"You what?" The man's voice rose as dawn streaked the East. Jesse lifted his head to see Phil's dad making a fist under the dim yard light. "That's kidnapping, Phil!"

"All right. Call it what you want, I won't argue. But do you have any water? We need some. And get us to Doc Adams quick, will you?"

Chapter Fourteen

*Late February 1944*

A normal Saturday morning at the boarding house as Judson's hammer and saw competed with bird chatter from the big cottonwood in the back yard. The garden called to me. Judson had been working day and night on the carriage house, so his weeding had fallen off.

With Judson busy elsewhere, I'd peeked into the carriage house a time or two. Soon, that space—two levels—would make some small family a lovely apartment. It could also become more rooms for Miss M to let out, but if she could rent it as an apartment, she'd have no extra cleaning to do. Such a wise tack.

On to the weeds. These intruders know no boundaries and possess no morals whatsoever. Unchallenged by storms, high winds or other natural events, they simply grow. No wonder Emerson described weeds as plants whose virtues have not yet been discovered.

That's for sure. I know Mama found medical help in what most people called weeds. Chamomile, for one, plus purslane, chickweed, plantain, and mullein. I wish I'd paid more attention to the concoctions she learned from Grammy, whose ancestors used them in the old country. Another regret.

As I took up the hoe Judson always left just inside the shed entrance, I surely agreed with Mr. Emerson, one of my favorite writers. He also wrote that most people simply don't know how to take a walk.

So true. These days, people walk everywhere because of gas rationing, but with furrowed brows. The walkers Emerson referred to knew how to saunter through a deep wood and lose themselves in its beauty. They had learned to allow nature to alter their moods and brighten their days.

But these weeds. How could they be so prolific? We struggled so to make sure our plantings prospered—protected them from rabbits with a sheltering fence and shored up the earth around their roots and applied manure to strengthen them. We did none of this to encourage the weeds, but they prospered anyway.

Weeding or not, I'd rather be out in the fresh air today. Actually, I enjoy pulling weeds. I could have worked another overtime shift at the hospital, but Doctor Graham said I needed a break.

With my first lunge into Texas soil, flimsy and rocky as it is, I knew he'd pointed me in the right direction. This labor would help my meandering mind and provide time by myself. I would be a much better woman for it tomorrow with even more to give.

I'd been at it for an hour or so when a shadow bade me look up. Then I noticed a sudden absence of sound. No more hammering and sawing. To my shock, there before me stood Judson, waiting at the end of the carrot row.

"Miz Kin." His rumble came from the depths, and with his back to the sun, I could tell nothing from his dark eyes or facial features.

"Yes?" Even as I responded, I realized that whatever Judson had in mind, I would say yes, for he so rarely spoke. If ever a man judged his words before they issued forth, it would be this one.

In over a year he had never before approached me. As he gestured me into the shade, I had no idea of the subject, of course, but knew his message would be well thought-through, most likely wrestled with for days in advance.

By the time he finished, a matter of a half-minute, I could only nod. "Why, of course, Judson. Of course I will."

Surprising that I could say even that much, considering the

import of his dispatch. He would soon be going West, he said, to work in one of the mines out there, since his body remained so strong and so many young workers were fighting overseas.

His strained expression testified that this short conversation took a toll. But the next part took my breath away.

Would I help him write a suitable farewell to Miss M? He would start out at night, leaving a note for her. When they were overseas together long years ago, Elwyn had taught him to read, but writing came harder.

One glimpse of Judson's gigantic calloused hands supported his words. Yes…virtually impossible to wrangle a pen or pencil with such fingers.

But he knew what he wanted to say—just needed me to write it down, a first draft of sorts. Then he'd copy the words line by line. In short bursts, he managed to communicate all of this, a thread of pain in his voice.

He turned a bit, and the tangled knot of wrinkles between his eyes deepened. Not an easy decision, and after such a long silence, speaking to me must have been such a difficult first step.

"I'll be sorry to see you go, Judson. You've been such a good friend for Elwyn and Miss M."

"Shhh…" He glanced around on both sides, put a massive forefinger to his lips and for an instant, resembled a small boy up to some minor mischief. Then his muscled two-hundred and fifty pounds disappeared into the darkness like a slender wraith.

After he went back to work, I imagined him slipping away some night. Under cover of darkness with a knapsack over his shoulder, his skin matching the darkness of the moonless evening, he would steal down the alley and work his way up to the railroad yard.

Whether he purchased a ticket to parts West or *rode the rails* like a hobo, he would proceed with a thoughtful plan, having researched his destination.

My own exodus had taken place in the light of day, willy-nilly, yet still led me to Doctor Graham and set me on my feet in safety.

Who could have pictured what purpose and meaning I would find here? Surely not me. My best vision had placed me subsisting in some wayside café taking orders and scrubbing floors.

But Judson, a modern-day saint, in my opinion—I foresaw passing steadily toward the kind of work only strong men could do, hard underground labor that would propel our troops to victory. Deep in a mine somewhere, he would support the troops in a powerful way.

His choice would honor all of those who signed up to fight… boy-men like Jesse. And as with his service to Elwyn and Miss M, Judson's reward would be known only to him.

One day, Miss M would catch my eye, and we'd sit down together as she told me about finding his note. Her voice would shake as she shared the news, but at the same time she'd be bursting with pride.

"It's a good thing you got here when you did." Doctor Adams pushed his glasses up on his nose. "And even better you could stay as long as needed. Thank God for the scientists who concoct new drugs, that's all I can say."

He perused Jesse's chart again. "You'll leave here with a limp, perhaps a permanent one, but you've kept your lower leg and foot."

Such a hodge-podge of emotions. How could Jesse accept the past weeks' events? Here he was in the Nevada desert, in a town that hadn't even existed before Pearl Harbor. The community grew around the magnesium plant the government had created to supply raw munitions material.

This hospital had been constructed specifically for the workers at that plant. Somehow, a magical infection-destroying drug had been available in this isolated location at just the right time. Penicillin, perhaps.

If that weren't enough, someone at the plant, a big-shot Uncle Winn would call him, with the right connections to pull strings in Washington, had managed to pave the way for Jesse to return to his unit, no questions asked. What a head-shaker!

At the same time, Phil would soon lose his arm. The doc had scheduled his surgery for this afternoon.

The irony gored Jesse. How could life be so unfair? From the time he'd met Phil in the Army hospital, he'd guarded his heart. Losing Willie and Joe had been more than enough for one war. No use getting close to another soldier. Clearly, he brought bad luck.

But then Phil had risked everything to get him to Doc Adams, who could help only one of them. What could he say to a guy like this when he came back from surgery? What could he possibly say?

"Some day you'll thank me for this," Phil had promised during the so-called kidnapping. Yeah. Thank-you would be all Jesse could muster, but that would be far from enough. What about Phil's arm?

Doc Adams tapped Jesse's left knee with his instrument and his foot jerked. "See? Your nerves are coming back just fine. Do you have any pain?"

"Not really. Not compared to before I came."

"To be honest, when they brought you in, I'd never have thought this would be the outcome. So much time had passed since you'd been wounded, I doubted we could do much to help you. But the next morning, the latest shipment of meds arrived, with exactly what we needed."

"But they didn't work for Phil..."

Doc Adams shook his head. "The government's built twelve other magnesium plants, but not all of them have their own hospital. We've been able to save some injured workers' limbs here, and word gets around. That's what Phil was counting on.

"I have to say his wild idea was worth the risk, but in his case, too much damage had been done. The nerves had been too badly damaged. I thought perhaps the specialist that flew in from New York might be able to work a miracle, but even he..."

"I can never thank Phil enough for bringing me here."

The doc gave a long sigh. "I know. He's a fine young man. Unselfish and so spirited. He'll find his place in this world again, I have no doubt."

"I hope so. I can hardly believe he's going into surgery and I'm going back to my unit, even though it's what I've wanted all along."

"In the Great War, I felt the same way. Mind you, though, keep walking like you've been doing and add a little distance each day. Walking's the best thing you can do to keep the healing going. Do your stretches morning and night and rub your leg down with this liniment like I showed you. It's a small bottle but should go a long way."

Doc Adams reached for the greenish-gold bottle that always occupied the table beside Jesse's bed. As he did, a nurse opened a curtain nearby, and the glass twinkled.

"Most of all, keep on taking these pills I'm sending along. One-a-day till they run out, you hear?"

"Yes, sir." As Doc Adams washed his hands, Jesse just had to ask. "Do you know who spoke to the Army for me? I keep wondering who made all of this possible."

"I do, but he asked me to keep his identity secret. His brother's a general with some pretty close connections to your unit commander. Interesting, isn't it? This war's full of amazing connections and coincidences, just like the last one. Throw together so many people from so many places and unbelievable things happen."

He extended his hand and they shook.

"As long as you appear at the ship for the trip back to the Pacific, no questions will be asked. They'll be glad to welcome a seasoned soldier rather than the raw recruits they're getting these days. And from the sounds of it, there's no lack of islands still waiting to be liberated from the Japs."

The doctor sure was taking his time. Phil had been moved to another bed. Would he visit him next?

"The ship leaves San Diego on Tuesday and has other Army

personnel aboard similar to you. Fortunately, we've got a convoy taking product down to a coastal factory tomorrow. Our driver has specific instructions about the ship, the time…it's all been arranged. He'll personally see you on board and report back to me."

He let out a long breath. "Still seems awfully wild how Phil got you here. He really used a gun?"

"Or something that sure felt like one, shoved in my ribs. It was the middle of the night, and I'd taken sleeping medicine. I remember only a little of what happened. He slipped up behind a guard at the back entrance of the hospital…"

"Used his training…"

"That's for sure, to get me to the truck. He threw me in, dirty towel container included, and with one arm."

"I've mulled this over and over. I'm pretty sure Phil gets his guts from his dad. It's not easy working here, especially supervising so many different workers, including women and some colored folks the company's brought in. Fights can break out, you know, and supervisors have to manage whatever happens.

"But Phil's dad never bats an eye. He treats everybody the same and keeps plunging ahead. Never seems to run short of ideas and stays pretty cheerful about the whole situation.

"All that to say, I expect Phil will do the same." He opened the door. "It's been good to work with you, son. Glad we could save your leg."

"And you, sir. How can I thank you?"

"Come home alive, okay? I do have one favor to ask. Don't go to see Phil before you leave, all right? When the war's over, look him up. I'll tell him you had no choice but to leave immediately."

"Yes, sir."

*February 1944*

Such a mix of impossible occurrences since the stretcher-bearers carried Jesse from the theater…being torpedoed, the weeks at the hospital in Van Nuys, the crazy getaway with Phil at the helm, and Doctor Adams' innovations delivering him from a lifetime of hobbling around.

Above all, the doc's expertise made it possible to get back into the fight. His unit had been transported to Australia for some rest, but which Japanese-infested island would they be invading by the time he arrived? No telling, but he'd be ready.

Every time Willie's face passed before him, which was often, Jesse fought the temptation to scream. Such a great guy Willie had been, and he died so young, so viciously. If only they'd been together that day, he might still be alive.

"Why did I have to get wounded, anyhow? I should've been there watching his back." Could he ever forgive himself for this lapse? This question gnawed at Jesse's soul like a ravenous rat in a ship's hold.

What could he possibly say to Willie's parents when he returned to Kentucky? How to rationalize standing before them alive when their son lay in a makeshift grave on some faraway island?

The bottle of liniment Doc sent rattled against the box of pills in his duffle bag as he walked toward the magnesium plant's truck lot. Interesting how something like this could help heal what ailed his leg right through the skin.

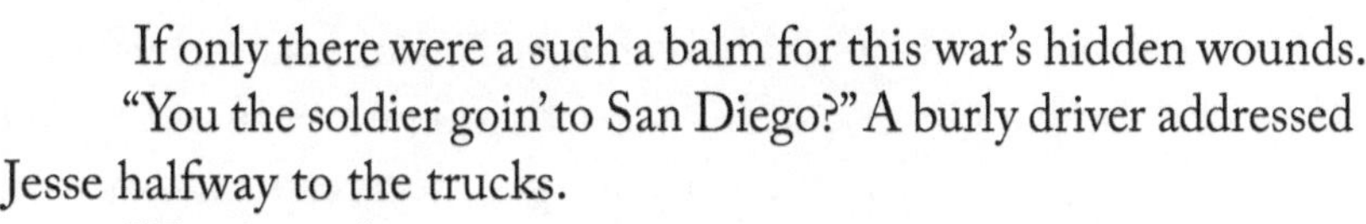

If only there were a such a balm for this war's hidden wounds.

"You the soldier goin' to San Diego?" A burly driver addressed Jesse halfway to the trucks.

"That's me."

"Name's Buck. It's a pretty rough road." He pitched his filthy cap back on his head. "We're in number 6. Time t' load up. Once we get goin', ain't no stoppin', just so's you know."

Jesse used the lack of facilities in some bushes at the edge of the lot, and ten minutes later, they barreled down a road as rutty as some island paths in the Pacific Theater. The roar of the engine took over, leaving Jesse to his thoughts.

After all he'd been through, he might as well relax and enjoy this final segment of his journey back to the U.S. Army. Strange how a guy could hate everyday Army life, yet long to return.

Buck, a master at the steering wheel, used his brakes and shift stick like a pilot. The treacherous trip transported Jesse to riding back roads with Uncle Winn in a rattletrap bubbletop pick-up that had seen better days.

*Ol' Suzie,* Winn called her, and like a faithful wife, the pick-up came through for him time and again.

Soon enough, Jesse would be in harm's way, but for now, he leaned back into the seat. More comfortable than an army truck, but that wasn't saying much. Still, he had nothing to worry about.

"Far be it from me to judge anybody's leave-taking. Especially Judson's."

I fell back on my bed. Something had wakened me and I'd pulled back the curtains to look out the east window. Below me, Judson toted a canvas bag past the carriage house down that soon-to-be sunlit alley that led nowhere but brought such joys.

Past the crepe myrtles he had nurtured, watching for powdery mildew, *Cercospora* leaf spot, sooty mold, and aphids, all enemies of the species. Past the carriage house where he had labored so long.

This must be the night he'd chosen. A warm wave enveloped me at catching a glimpse of his departing figure. A man I would never forget, he had earned my unqualified respect, however curiosity-filled.

In a couple of hours, Miss M would find his note in the kitchen when she got up to start the porridge. Aghast at the news, she would race to a window…

But then she'd drop at the table and hold her head in her hands. Judson, gone? How could this be? How would this place ever make it without him?

When the floorboards above me squeaked and Miss M. made her way down the stairs, I dressed in a hurry and entered the kitchen from the hallway. Sure enough, envelope in hand, there sat Miss M. But her countenance held little of the emotion I had expected. She seemed altogether composed. Serene, even.

"Good morning, Kin. Sit here with me for a minute, will you? I made us a pot of tea for starters."

The earthy blend stoked my senses, soothed my throat. No need for words yet. Miss M would choose when to speak and what to say. In the meantime, hot tea worked its particular magic, as Granny always said.

A spring breeze fluttered the curtains just a bit. Out in the back yard, a lone bird cheered for the sun to rise.

"I knew he was leaving." Miss M's voice tore at my heart. "Oh, not *when*, but I felt it in my bones."

"You…what do you mean?"

"Judson. He left during the night."

Embracing her meaning, I held my tongue. Should I have said something before? But no, that would have meant betraying Judson's trust.

"You knew, too, I reckon." A statement, not a question.

"Why, I…"

"Someone had to help him with this note." She peered at me, but without blame. "It was only a matter of time, and you sense things, just like I do. Of course, he did this the right way. Sometimes it's better not to say good-bye face-to-face."

Miss M studied the paper in her trembling hand, picking out phrases to read aloud. "Need to serve…mine out west…a buddy is going…take care of each other…."

With each assertion, some small alteration appeared in the lines of her forehead. All through Elwyn's last days, she rarely shed a tear, but now a sudden torrent engulfed her, and her utterances came in gasps. "Something about this…Even though I knew, this still…"

"Hurts." I wanted to say. But Miss M had kept her silence with me when I needed it, and now my turn had come. She showed me how to sit with someone in pain, hushed and respectful. After a while, I offered to make breakfast, but she crumpled her hankie and gave a big sniff.

"I'm fine now." She stood and started toward her big griddle. "It'll be pancakes this morning. Starting now, we have to—we must make some changes around here. Tighten our belt, so to speak, since Judson did so much. But he finished with the carriage house, and everything else will work out for us."

As she took a step, something from the envelope she held floated to the floor. Six papers, like spent cottonwood leaves in autumn.

We both stared at the bills—fifty-dollar bills. Miss M scooped them up and counted. Her gulp came in tandem with the clock's chime.

"Three hundred dollars. Why, Judson left us a fortune!"

She was using *us* again. I attempted to grasp the amount. "My goodness! How kind."

"More than kind." Miss M slipped the money into her apron pocket. "Sacrificial. He always looks ahead and knew I would have to hire things done from time to time, things he always took care of. He looked ahead and watched out for us."

It wasn't as if Jesse had never been thrown from a vehicle before. Back in Kentucky, he'd been about twelve or so when Willie's Grandpa took the two boys to the county fair. On the way home, they sat in the back of Grandpa Hoke's '31 Chevy truck holding a squealing pig, the wind in their faces.

He'd never felt so free! That is, until the low sideboard hit a deep rut and sent them all flying.

At least Gramps realized he'd lost something and took his foot off the gas. Probably was worried about the prize pig he'd purchased to fatten up for Christmas. Willie and Jesse, giggling so hard they could hardly breathe, shook off their scrapes and bruises and chased down the terrified animal. Then they traipsed back to the scene.

Today Buck wrangled the Magnesium Plant's truck around baby boulders growing up in the middle of the road. He really knew what he was doing, so Jesse fell asleep to the roar of the motor and the *r-i-i-p* of the clutch.

Despite his practiced hand, on a deep curve where the road had washed up to the edge in heavy rains last winter, Buck lost control of the wheel. The impact sent him sailing out the driver's door.

With no warning, Jesse's door flew open, too, as the truck smashed into the five-foot wash. The crushed right fender snapped in two and the chassis flew ahead several feet before it crumpled like a tin can where it landed.

*Hiss…hiss…*

Gasoline spewed from under the hopelessly tangled vehicle. Something was going to blow, for sure. But where had Buck gone? Twenty-five feet away from the chassis, Jesse lay stunned, smelling the fuel, hearing the sound, able to think but unable to react.

And then, *Whamo!* The blast transported him what seemed thousands of miles away from the flames. *Smack!* His torso collided with solid rock before the whole world went murky.

Closing his eyes against a stab of light, Jesse attempted to corral his rushing thoughts. Something skittered across his chest, so he tried to lift his head. Between his ears, a thousand drums beat without mercy.

Sweat, salt, and blood…these tastes vied for first place when he moved his tongue. Sand and dirt caked his lips. Another attempt to push himself up. Another scampering creature, a lizard, maybe, checking out this bizarre spectacle.

Dizziness swarmed Jesse, and nausea. But a flash of something out of place, scrunched against a rock caught his eye. What was that?

The desire to know made him groan to a sitting position. He gritted his teeth against the pounding in his head and remained still until the desert stopped spinning. A lizard stared at him from atop a refrigerator-sized rock. Yep, must've been the one that crossed his chest.

Finally, peering paid off. His eyes cleared, and he recognized an Army duffel bag down the way. His bag, with his medicine and liniment inside. Must've been clutching it in his sleep…

His shoulder seared as he made a quick move. He'd been riding in a truck. Oh man, what was the driver's name? To his left, perhaps two rods away, lay the mangled vehicle.

Crawling closer, he tore his pants on small jagged rocks and was barely able to support any weight with his right arm. But he must get a better look. In heavy dust, the remains of the burned, nearly unrecognizable truck clung to the edge of the road.

"Gotta see if…" Jesse struggled to his feet and stumbled ahead. "Gotta try to help…" The next thing he knew, he was falling, falling. Rolling against ruthless desert terrain, he tried to catch hold of a branch, but his arm refused to work.

Something stopped his fall, something hard and immovable. Once again, the world went dark and silent.

Chapter Sixteen

*P**op! Snap!*

A crackling campfire…was he back on an island? Other soldiers must be throwing snakes into the flames.

No. This crackling seemed more contained. Moving his head with great care, Jesse scanned around him. He was lying on a bunk in a room. A log cabin.

Across the room, perhaps twelve feet away, a stone pioneer hearth filled nearly a whole wall. Something—someone—rubbed his lower leg, the leg he'd almost lost. That, he recalled.

Finally, he connected those huge hands with the arms and torso of a giant sitting beside his lower body. Even stronger than the burning mesquite drifted a scent he could not place.

The figure's chiseled face, the color of burnt umber, reminded him of someone. Someone from the past. But who?

And where was he? Log walls, this bunk, and something bubbling in a pot on an iron stove in the far corner. He had no idea, but these homey objects eased his mind.

The door opened and another man almost as enormous as the one rubbing his leg, but tow-headed and sporting a bad sunburn, dropped a pile of kindling near the hearth. Sunshine from the open door illuminated the room like a searchlight, highlighting a glass object on the hearth. A vase?

The fellow with the kindling ambled closer, squinting at Jesse.

"Awright! Y' woke up! Thought y' never would!"

Jesse tried to reply, but his throat betrayed him. Meanwhile, the rubbing continued without a hitch. Such wonderful warmth spread through his leg, but his shoulder cried out for attention, too.

"That's Jud workin' on y'. You can call me L'il Wall. What's your name?"

"I…" Did that scratchy sound come from his own lips?

"Never saw nothin' quite like that melted Chevy truck. We buried the driver. What was he carryin', anyhow?"

L'il Wall came closer and peered over the darker man's shoulder. "Thought we'd have to bury you too, but you're a tough 'un, son."

"M…" Another gargantuan effort to speak resulted in coughing that ripped through Jesse's chest and shoulder. "My sh…"

The colossus sitting beside him stayed silent as L'il Wall responded. "Lemme getcha some water. You ain't the first soldier Jud ever tooken care of."

A tin cup held to his lips, Jesse took a first sip. Another bigger sip reached his throat and he nearly guzzled the rest.

"My…" He attempted to scan down his body.

"Musta' got throwed out on your shoulders, from the looks of it. But yer right lucky. That fall might could've teared open thet ol' wound in yer leg."

L'il Wall backed away and busied himself with something. Soon Jesse was devouring a brothy bowl of stew. Who knew what creature they'd shot to make it, but who cared? Full of the warm concoction, he fell asleep and woke with Jud tending his shoulder this time.

The stinging sensation, he'd felt often enough in his leg. Things sometimes had to get worse to get better.

Such a quiet fellow, this giant, but as he watched, Jesse could almost hear words from Jud's lips. Not hear, exactly, but sense, like when someone in his past used to say nothing, but he still could figure out what they were thinking.

Who had that been, and where? A woman, he thought. Yes. From the ramshackle table where L'il Wall was cutting something that looked like roots, came a question. "Been talkin' 'bout Kentucky 'n yer sleep. Born there?"

"I don't…"

"Where's yer folks live?"

*Folks…* what did he mean?

At last, Jud joined in, but with a mere, "Hmm." The resonance elicited a soothing sensation, as if he communicated, "No need to talk until it comes easier."

Now he rubbed Jesse's leg above and below the wound and began stretching the muscles. At the end, he paused. Then he proceeded back to Jesse's arm and shoulder, exercising it, too. He seemed to know how far the limb could bend without causing too much pain.

Did he want to ask something? That feeling prevailed, though Jesse could not have said why, but again it reminded him of the woman. She wanted to speak, but something kept her quiet. In any case, Jud maintained his reserve.

L'il Wall, on the other hand, kept offering information. "Reckon we was more'n halfway t' Californiyay when we come acrost ya. Come from down Texas way when we spied that ol' truck still a steamin'.

"Driver musta died right off." He shook his head. "Y' was pretty beat up, y' were, n' we was glad t' find this place. 'Jes' the ticket,' I says to Jud. 'This here boy's gonna git you well, mark my words.'"

Jesse lay back. Jud could speak. After all, he'd said '*Hmm,*' but seemed to have no desire. Yet questions clouded his immense onyx eyes.

What went on behind them? And why had these two men slowed their travels to shelter and care for a stranger? Jesse set himself to ponder, but within minutes, the weariness that plagued him encroached. He let go and in so doing, passed into a world of soft gossamer and gentle light, like when that vase had reflected the sun.

There, in a lush carpet of eighteen-inch needles spread across

a hillside by Longleaf Kentucky pines, or a curve in the creek kissed by the season's first snow, rest took Jesse in.

Sinking, sinking… He let go. No questions to answer, nothing to do but be who he was.

A chilly wind blew the curtains into my face. Startled awake, I shivered on this April night that felt more like late winter than spring. A cold slim moon offered little light, so I switched on the lamp beside my bed. Not that I wanted to stay up—this middle-of-the-night awakening had been occurring for several weeks. I'd learned the chances of stealing another hour of sleep before dawn were better if I got up and wandered downstairs.

In the kitchen, I warmed a cup of milk in a saucepan. "Like a child," I mused. "I'm a child needing some sort of comfort."

These nights seemed determined to haunt me. No use lying in bed to revisit all of my poor choices. Why, oh why had I married Clyde…allowed him to rule the roost on the ranch…sent Jesse away…? The list never stopped.

What good came from rethinking these actions? None whatsoever. Only a ceaseless Ferris wheel ride that led nowhere. Not that I would know anything about a Ferris wheel, but had at least seen one. I pulled my robe closer as a shiver took me.

Not a happy memory. Clyde had wanted me to take a ride with him, but I'd been in the early months of my first pregnancy. Even watching the seats progress round and round against the night sky made me ill.

He'd laughed at me—scoffed. Then he shrugged his thin shoulders and bought his own ticket.

I ought to have known by then, nearly a year into our marriage, that our vows would produce nothing but trouble, that he had no intention of *cherishing, loving, or honoring* anyone. He had made this so clear. Why couldn't I see? Why didn't I believe the truth?

Taking my warm cup out on the front porch, I rocked in

the wooden swing at the far end. Something so soothing about this motion…perhaps I could fall asleep here for a while. In the meantime, I could choose to pray—that's what the preacher had said on Sunday.

"Even when doubts assail and things look darkest, we still have immense power available." Clunks from iron hitting iron and a train whistle came from the depot. Day and night, those workers moved soldiers and ammunition across the nation.

You'd think by now, more than two years into the war, the branches of service would have received enough young men to finish the job. That brought Jesse to mind…such a long time since I'd heard word of him.

Faithful Annie kept writing, but her worry threaded through each line. Since she had signed for him, she felt responsible. I wrote back that any patriotic American mother would have written her signature in the aftermath of the attack on Pearl Harbor, including me.

But for months now, we had heard nothing. Surely the Army would let Annie know if he'd been hurt.

Wouldn't they? But they dealt with tens of thousands of young men just like him. If the worst happened, how long might it take to notify a family?

At the hospital, when I removed a deceased soldier's dog tag and put it with his watch and other effects, I always took great care, wishing this boy's mother could be here. I could never take her place, although in his last hours, the patient might have mistaken me for her.

How long until she would be informed of his death? No matter how far away she lived, I wondered. Did she clutch her heart at the moment of his passing, suddenly perceiving the loss of her son long before being notified?

The wind quickened as my uneasiness grew. Miss M had given me a warm chenille bathrobe just like her blue one, only mine, a deep rose color, still had all its fluff. She seemed bound to supply me with comforts, and gratitude swept in as the robe's soft folds surrounded me.

Another lonely train whistle…so many people far away from home during this horrendous war. So many mothers and aunts, sisters, brothers and cousins all across this nation wondering about their loved ones tonight. Loved ones like Jesse.

Before I realized it, a tear made its way down my chin onto my neck. I closed my eyes tight. Mustn't allow self-pity…my goodness! So many others, like the families of those boys who passed today, whom I pretended were my sons, bore heavier burdens.

*But oh, Jesse…how I miss you!*

At that cry from the depths, the flood I'd been holding back for so long broke through. At first, I fought its force, thinking a boarder upstairs would hear me and wake up.

A time comes, I know now, when fighting any longer simply won't do. Your emotions, however long you've kept them under control, rise up and rebel. You've no power over them. Not any longer.

And so I wept and sobbed, pounding the back of the swing. Then I jumped off and ran behind the house, where no one could possibly hear. Raced down our alley and wailed to the nearest tree. My fingers shook like those agonized older men in the hospital's very far reaches, sent there to withdraw from the drink.

The tree bark caught on my robe as I sank to the ground, this recalcitrant earth that Judson had toiled over so dutifully. This earth that, not far away in the nearby family cemetery, had received Elwyn's earthly remains. This earth, like a sponge, soaks up all in the end. Storms strike, rivers overflow, people perish, and the earth must deal with the results.

So it was this night. My storm seemed interminable, yet finally my crying subsided and I leaned into the tree, onto the earth, spent. I would like to say I composed myself and returned to my bed. I intended to, but someone neared.

Miss M, in her nightclothes, too, halted a couple of feet away, hovering like a specter. "Kin?"

"Yes, ma'am," I tried to say, but the stubborn words stuck in my throat.

"Kin? What is it? How can I…" She reached for me, pulled me into her arms. Mama was there, I swear, and all of the times I had sought her in vain piled into one. Unbelievably, I wept again, as though I would never stop.

"You have some deep sorrow…" Not a question, but the decision was mine. Should I let her in, when I had worked so hard to keep everyone out?

In that second a breeze stirred, and one of the crepe myrtle trees let forth a sudden draft. Odd, with the blossoming season nearly past, but there it was. Not blooms alone, but leaves, bear fragrance. Taking in the spicy sweet scent, I listed a bit, and Miss M steadied me.

Then, "Oh Miss M, I have a son. He's fighting somewhere in the Pacific. I haven't heard from him for…"

"Ah. A son. How wonderful." Her pronouncement startled me.

And then she asked about Jesse…anything I wanted to tell her. The whole story, the details I'd kept under lock and key, starting with the night Clyde had nearly killed Jesse, teemed out.

Like thousands of ants from an ant hill, tens of thousands of bats from a Texas cave at twilight, the truth unfolded. How I had delighted in this one living child, but eventually sent him away.

And back to Mama dying, how I had done the inconceivable. How I had consented to marry Clyde. Those three graves I'd left behind, my lost babies, the horror of living with this man. Shuttered inner windows opened, locked doors screeched wide.

All came pouring out. Behind Miss M, that old crepe myrtle rehearsed the time…its heavy, tired blossoms, radiant with sunshine earlier in the day, had dulled bit-by-bit as evening fell. Now, only pinpoints of moonlight showed through the branches, just enough to gild my dear friend's hair.

In the evening, walking out here in the slightest breeze, one could still trace the positions of these trees by their scent. A peculiar revelation in the midst of all this, but full of solace. Finally, the gush of words ceased. I waited. Would Miss M leave me in silence, loathing the foolishness of my youth, my rashness? Would she ask me to leave…

"Well, then." She grasped my hand, as firm a hold as I had ever known, and pulled me up.

Scarcely aware that we were walking, I let her lead me. "After all of that, things that might could've killed someone less strong, here you are. Here you are right beside me. Surely the Almighty led you here, and I am so grateful, Kin."

In a pause pregnant with feeling, she worked her lips. "No one can ever comprehend our private griefs, our great losses. I've been so lucky, with Elwyn to love me all these years."

She glanced off into the distance, to the echoing sounds of laborers working into the night. Always building, building. Then came her one lasting observation.

"You kept waiting for Clyde to change." Not a question at all. "Waiting for him to love you, but he hadn't the ability."

More blows, hammers and pick axes striking their mark, sledgehammers on stone. Then an owl who-hooed somewhere up in the trees.

"Always creating something new, aren't they? Just like Providence with us, don't you think? Something new rises from where something else used to be, or where we thought there could never be anything."

Her voice lowered. "Soon, it'll be sunrise, and the sunshine will warm us. All we must do is put ourselves in its way. Elwyn taught me this. Before we met, I knew so little about love, about what it meant to let someone care for me. Believe me, Kin, he gave me more, in his own way, than I ever gave him."

What to say? She so rarely mentioned their relationship.

"Do you understand?" The expression in her eyes held no pressure, still I wanted to answer.

"Maybe not…not fully. Not yet."

She halted, perhaps halfway to the house. "Ah, *yet*…what a lovely word! This one syllable portends the future, says that one day we *will understand*." She waited, giving me time. "You love words—we have that in common. Let's you and I hold onto the hope in little ones like *yet*, shall we?"

"Yes. You've been so good to me. You took me in, shared your home with me all this time."

"But this *is* your home. I knew that from the first, and so did Elwyn. You came here by design. Elwyn and I talked over these things, you know."

Not wanting to hurt her, I blurted, "I do feel at home, I do. But I guess I never feel quite…" I searched for a phrase, and finally, a word came. "Worthy, I think. I still have a lot to learn about letting the sun warm me."

The squeeze she gave my fingers ran right down my backbone. Her eyes glowed.

"Yes, my dear—as do we all. When Elwyn was healthier, but after he had to stop working, he used to walk our alley in the mornings. He could barely make it, but he called the path *Sunshine Alley* because the sun fell just right.

"Once he said, 'It's as if whoever designed our place planned around the light.'"

We had nearly reached the house when she turned to peer into my eyes. "Just you stay on the path and let the sunshine do its work. That's all any of us are asked to do."

Stepping after her through the doorway brought back the very first moment I entered this cheery kitchen, so bedraggled and lost. From that day to this, the welcome in her eyes had remained unchanged. Now she took both of my hands.

"I shall add your Jesse to my prayers without fail. I expect that boy will come back to you some day. I feel it in my bones."

My breath caught hard in my throat. She gave voice to more than I dared dream, and knowing she had faith made believing easier.

"When you came here, I had been longing for someone just

like you, someone kind and gracious, willing to lighten the load…a friend. But I never really expected Dr. Graham to knock at the door and deliver you directly to us."

I stood there, silent. How could I ever…

"Do you think you might be able to sleep a little more now?"

"Maybe."

"Off you go then. Today's an easy breakfast for me, biscuits and gravy. You have a long day ahead of you with all those dear boys to care for."

I floated to the upper hallway, light-held, transparent as air. Each creak of the floorboards under my feet reminded me, though, that this ascent was real. With each step, weight that had burdened me for so long released.

*…he hadn't the capacity….*

Clyde had been unable to love.

Of course, this rang true. He had no such ability. I'd expected something from him that he could never give.

Someone had taken in my story, filtered it, and sent it back. And that someone still cared for me, still accepted me *as is*. Only one portion I had held back. Only that night with the gun and my hens.

But as I lay down, I saw that the rest of the long-hidden past had brought me to this place. I might never know why Doctor Graham drove down that road just when he did, or what motivated him to take me in. But he had.

In dawn's cool ascent, merciful sleep descended. Some time later, for the first time ever, Miss M came to wake me for my day at the hospital.

Chapter Seventeen

The massive man nearly always sat nearby when Jesse awoke, as if to shield him from all but healing. And now, with a hand that could have wrenched his patient's neck in a flash, he wiped his hot brow with a cool cloth.

Never, not even aboard the hospital ship, had a touch felt quite so restorative. And never had eyes like this, impenetrable but wide with concern, intrigued Jesse so. Who was this man, so much like the fellow Uncle Winn had pointed out on their hunting treks in the Kentucky hills?

"See that slapdash cabin? Honor lives there. Honor Wilke, with a surname like other men but warrior blood running through his veins."

To Jesse's questions, Winn had replied, "Indian warrior, but from Africa, too. A half-breed, stronger'n anybody I've ever known, but somehow he got himself a tender heart."

Finally, this real memory flashed through Jesse's mind before he could grasp and hold it. Then it fled, and the concept of *Kentucky* became nondescript once more. The kind man named Honor, along with Uncle Winn, vanished into nothingness.

All Jesse knew for sure was these two fellows taking care of him, the stabs in his shoulder, and this small cabin. Fire, he knew, sunlight when the door opened, food, and care.

Still, a smidgeon of understanding remained. A tender heart—surely this giant leaning over him possessed the same. He seemed never to tire, like a superhero from the comics, where Captain America led a team called the *Invaders*.

For some reason, Captain America's kid sidekick Bucky Barnes, Jim Hammond, the original Human Torch, and his kid sidekick Toro came to mind, complete with names. And Namor the Sub-Mariner, of course.

Years ago, Jesse and someone…a friend back in…where was it? Anyway, they had pored over these comics for hours. Now, the made-up characters seemed more real than the actual folks he had known at the time.

So many questions, but gradually, his conscious times lengthened. Once, when the tow-headed man appeared in his nurse's stead, he repeated his comrade's name. *Jud.*

"Tol' y' b'fore, but y' don't recollect, do y'? Figger I better jest keep on tellin', so's some day, you will. They call me L'il Wall. Jud, he don't talk much, y' know. but he's always a-thinkin'. Got one a' them brains like a coal furnace, always churnin', churnin'.

"Lately, he's been figgerin'. All the time a'figgerin' how we's gonna get y' back t'where y' belong."

"Where I…"

"Most folks b'long someplace. At times, we don't nec'arily recall where."

"Right." Jesse let his head fall back onto some sort of pillow these men had fashioned for him.

"Took yourself a mighty blow to the head n' shoulders, son. Musta hit them hard desert rocks with a terr'ble *thud.* Jest let time remind y' who y' is and where y' come from. We be a'waitin'."

A few days later, Jud went outdoors for a while, and it occurred to Jesse to ask his companion where *they* came from.

The answer helped little, since the place name meant nothing.

"Waco. That's in Texas. But Jud, he hails from way back out east, where ever'thin' began, somewhere's in the swamplands. Sometimes, I think he's from 'nother world 'tirely."

During Jesse's next deep sleep, heavy moss hung from cypress trees, and alligators sneaked in and out of murky water. When the cabin door screeched open and he shook himself awake, a mighty scream lodged deep in his throat, for he had expected powerful jaws to collapse on him any minute.

But other images began to return one-by-one, like forest elves at play. Somebody with skin wrinkled up like an apple held over from winter had spoken often of such from the old country, as if they truly existed. One morning, a dilapidated ranch house took shape around Jesse, with nothing to distinguish itself, but on the table perched a glass jar with flowers in water.

A jar like the vase on the hearth that flashed when these men opened the door. Flowers in water, and a woman kneading nearby, a woman with red hair, humming a tune. And then she spat, "Oh, chicken fat! I forgot to add the salt! Whatever was I thinking, Jesse?"

*Chicken fat. Jesse…* Who had she been talking to? And why would she mention chickens?

All of a sudden, her laugh bounded through his memory. No girl's silly titter, but a solid chuckle allowed in the midst of a tawdry cabin, in the midst of a day's work, in the midst of… He grasped for more of the recollection, more of her sentient expression, but gleaned only a fleeting flicker of green eyes with a streak of sadness.

Green eyes against the aura of ginger hair in the sun. *Ginger Rogers…* No. *Maureen O'Hara…* No. No.

The image floated off, and he slept once more. The next time he danced between waking and sleeping, the big man called Jud was speaking in a low tone, like thunder rolling from a great distance. He stood near the door, a pack strapped on his back.

"Get him walkin' 'roun' here. In three days, start out for Fort Irwin if he's able. Follow that new highway over yonder. I'll meet you along the way."

*Fort Irwin.* And that other place, *Waco. Waco, Texas.* In a hasty moment as Jud left the shack, a map appeared in Jesse's mind. All of a sudden, East and West became clear. Fort Irwin. California? They were taking him to California?

Over the next day, other memories slid into place. Maybe

walking helped. A hospital…a doctor. One thing Jesse knew, it felt good to be back on his feet. His shoulder and neck were still sore, with L'il Wall applying some ointment there, too, when he dressed his leg.

"You still got a limp. 'Member where it come from? Where was you fightin' in the service?"

*The service…* Like hail pelting inside his head, a thought struck Jesse. One clear missive—The Pacific Theater. He must have said it aloud, for L'il Wall raised his eyebrows.

"Got wounded on one a' them islands, didja? Heard 'bout how bad them was. Sentcha back on one a them hospital ships, did they?"

*Hospital. Ship.*

"Say! Didja hear we kilt General Yamamoto? Sure 'nuff did! On one of them islands, shot 'im right outta the sky. No hospital ship for him, that's for sure."

Suddenly a scene came forth, as real as the logs of this cabin. Magnetizing hazel eyes, a voice like a brook, the smoothest touch this side of Heaven, and a necklace that caught the sun from a porthole… Jesse heard himself spilling his guts to a nurse.

That nurse—oh, she knew how to listen. Instant emotion overwhelmed him. Aboard that hospital ship, he had fallen in love.

On this pleasant autumn morning, sunshine mottled the path to the hospital. As a worker, I might have used the back entrance, but rarely did in the mornings. Something about passing through the rather regal entryway, with its tall ceiling and long windows, added to my sense of purpose.

Often, I interrupted a cleaning lady busy buffing the wide floor tiles, but she didn't seem to mind. Her greeting in Spanish had become a part of my going-to-work routine, and I sometimes stopped to practice my limited vocabulary.

Turning down a hallway and up the stairs at any given time

of day, one was bound to meet someone, often a visitor. Sometimes they shielded their eyes, but most often glanced my way. Only a smile was necessary to loosen their lips.

"Ma'am. D'you work on the sixth floor? Got our son up there."

By now, I dressed in my uniform at home, and before the small mirror in my room, pinned on the white cap that distinguished me as a *bona fide* caregiver. My new room provided a real closet all to myself. After Judson left, Miss M went into a frenzy, cleaning and re-painting his room. She insisted I move in, since it was twice the size of mine.

Yesterday, after six months of training, Dr. Graham called the staff together for a small ceremony. He presented each of us with a pin to mark our progress.

Such a busy man. How did he manage to think of these things? Turning off on fourth floor, I touched my pin with a deep breath. Who knew what challenges faced me today, what pain and suffering in the bodies, minds, and spirits of the young men arriving day-by-day?

Something about touching my pin strengthened me before opening the door to the ward. My training would stand me in good stead, surely it would, for Dr. Graham left nothing to chance.

And there he stood, leaned over a set of papers at the nurse's counter. He glanced up with the usual glint in his eyes. "Another day, another dollar, Kindred?" His grin said more than words. "Well, another day, at any rate. I've got a job just made for you. Follow me."

A job made for me? How could I ever have considered a life's work buried in words, in literature? Greeting new patients like the one Dr. Graham led me to, supplying what I can in encouragement despite his circumstances—had I not been born for this?

I still work with words, I guess, but words in action, living words. Like Rosita in the hospital kitchen, sending nourishment in a never-ending supply, nurses make a different offering. The words we hear, all too often a patient's last ones, surpass the literary. These words are holy.

One day Rosita said, "I don't know how you can keep on, with so much sorrow. Every day you have to say good-bye to at least one soldier."

"You keep on with your work, too. It's the only way."

Before I know it, half of the day has flown by. Hours have passed—no time to go home for lunch. No time for anything. We had four Codes today. Three of those boys needed someone to listen silently beside them, close their eyes and remove their dog tags.

Thank goodness Helen came on duty this morning, too, so we could work together. At day's end, she walked with me part way home, both of us too weary to talk much. We have shared lifetimes already—no need to verbalize on a day like this.

At my turn, we said good-night and went our separate ways. Thankfully, Walt would share the evening with her.

Me? I peeked into the kitchen and seeing that one of the boarders was helping Miss M in the kitchen, headed straight for the alley. Not much more than a path that sprouts grass in spring rains, this lane grows nothing at all during summer's heat.

Packed hard by wagons over the years, and by tribes and explorers before that, the history here plays a tune of its own. This was where Elwyn trod back-and-forth when he could still walk.

This insignificant treasure, a back way to nowhere, known only to me and Miss M now, grows dearer and dearer. Once, before the carriage house was built, she says it served as a passageway to the neighbors' fields, but still has much to offer.

On this late afternoon, what better gift can I give myself than a solitary walk, unnoticed by anyone? Each step, though I've taken so many already today, brings the inner quietude I need.

Those young fellows who died still linger with me, but within this space, I make peace with the loss. The war's horrors, evident every day, might sweep me into despair, yet this solitude helps.

Though evening will soon claim the light, the Texas sun still sends a message…to my arms, bare and exhausted, to my shoulders, where rays penetrate through cotton fabric. Steady as the sun, in spite of the war, this world goes on. My private hopes and fears for Jesse meld with the longing I've seen shining in the eyes of the wounded. In a strange way, these boys and my son have become one. Somewhere, if he is hurting, may someone provide exactly what he needs. Lifting them all up together transforms the burden.

There's no explanation for this sort of healing, and no need to explain. Miss M knows its power, as did Elwyn. And so do I.

Walking forms a kind of prayer, she says, though not the fold-your-hands type we all learned as children. No, this amounts to elevating others' sorrows and worries along with our own, to a place and power Who can cope with them far better than we.

In this maddening war, the vast weariness that clutches our entire nation weighs like a yoke on us. Today as I walked, I opened myself to see the ones prayed for with new eyes. This walking-lifting renewed my strength.

Chapter Eighteen

Lil Wall shouldered a scuffed army-green duffel bag and reached for another pack loaded with food for the road. Seeing the bag, Jesse's mind went wild.

"Puke green," the men called their uniforms, the duffels, even the paint in the basic training barracks. The bag L'il Wall carried was army-issue, and from it, he took Jesse's pills. The revelation hit Jesse like a punch. Why, he must have been issued this bag. He must be a soldier!

As Jud directed, Jesse and L'il Wall had waited three days, and each day included several short walks. Jesse's leg cooperated, growing stronger with each stroll around the cabin. His gait would never enter him in the Easter Parade, but got him from here to there.

L'il Wall went back and forth from tending to the wounds-becoming-scars on his shoulders and neck to preparing for their journey. On the second day, he took his patient outdoors.

And then like a beacon out of nowhere, that duffel spoke to Jesse. The message could not have been clearer. The Army issued the duffel to him on Day One of basic training, and they'd been together ever since.

Somehow, staring at its muck-colored stains and mars and ripped canvas brought back a chunk of his recent past. Better yet, he knew where he'd hidden his papers before loading the duffel onto the truck bound for a ship. *The* ship that would reunite him with his unit.

He almost cried out with this fresh knowledge…his papers would solve every possible enigma. But for the moment, he focused on the ship. Yes, a ship had once waited for him in San Diego harbor.

That vessel would've carried him back to the Pacific Theater. His unit in…*Guadalcanal!* He yelled it aloud. Until this moment the word had escaped him, but now blazed like a torch, and L'il Wall's eyes burned, too.

"So that's where you fought the Japs?" He let out a low whistle. "Jud said it'd all come back t' y'. When that feller wraps his heart roun' somethin', it's bound t' come t' pass."

"I am Private Jesse Kline, U.S. Army. That bag…I sewed my papers into a hidden pouch."

Scrambling for the bag, he broke several stitches to free his documents. Holding them in trembling fingers and reading the details of his life over the past months unearthed even more facts. Kentucky…ah. Those gorgeous, lush hills and back woods, his cousins Beau and Pearl, Thomas, Aunt Annie and Uncle Winn and their older children gone off to lives of their own.

Let's see…Polly and Trey and Owen. Information pulsed within Jesse like a blood infusion. Recalling his cousins' names brought such satisfaction, Jesse could hardly let a question pass. He'd moved to be with them when he was eight. Before that, he lived in Texas on a ranch.

For now, it seemed enough to stop here—no more inner searching for a while. The knowledge of where he'd signed up for duty, even the name of the sergeant who'd broken him and his buddies into army life, spread through him, sweet as honey in warm butter.

Knowing his place of origin gave him a destination to return to. Somewhere to go, people who would always take him in. Now he could write to them, let them know where he'd gotten to…once he landed somewhere with a name.

As L'il Wall and he trekked an ancient Indian trail running parallel to a new highway constructed for the war traffic, Jesse's thoughts cascaded with his feelings. Not that he let the tears fall.

He'd been through war and back again, after all. Yet no words suf-ficed to describe this sensation. He'd been lost for a time, but now was found. He'd survived, like the time he and Beau had taken a wrong turn in a cave they thought they knew well.

Beau, such a bright-eyed, lively pal, said Uncle Winn showed him a spot they could hike to without getting lost. Jesse hadn't been in Kentucky long, so he trusted Beau and figured this exploit would be safe enough. But they'd gotten confused and spent anxious hours as the subject of a search.

Uncle Winn's face when he found them, his expression and hugs meant the world. Right now, this scene returned in such a vivid wash that the hardscrabble terrain around Jesse turned more intense.

He'd come this far, through battle and being wounded, recuperation and a terrible accident that took the truck driver's life. But he'd survived. He lost his bearings for a time, yet they had returned. He had become a person again, a person with a history.

Up ahead, as determined as an ox on this trail a century ago, L'il Wall led the way. So far, Jesse called this route *the way to Jud,* since he'd promised to meet them.

According to Li'l Wall, Jud had given him his nickname, back in Texas where they worked on the railroad together years ago. His hackneyed grin accompanied the tale.

"Somethin''bout me bein' like Li'l Abner, I think it was. Jud saw Li'l in the comics and liked the name. Guess other folks did, too, so it stuck."

Just like that, Jud had re-christened this fellow. The Wall part seemed apparent, since Jesse's guide stood solid as a stone fortification.

"Did you give Jud a name, too?"

Li'l Wall's eyes widened as if Jesse had struck him. No. Of course not. Only Jud possessed the power to name folks.

But soon, Li'l Wall lapsed into a story. "Oh, them days Jud n' me worked on that road, son. Why, ev'ry day I sweat hard 'nuff t' water a buffalo fer a week. Tho't I's gonna c'llapse at times, but

Jud, he kep' on goin', and sure nuff, by the end of the day, the end of the day come."

Panting, L'il Wall tackled a steep rise. "Might could use some water right now. How's 'bout you?"

"Yeah." They found a half-boulder that had been split rolling down from the heights and sat for a while.

"'Nuther few miles and I'm thinkin' ol' Jud'll show up. Did we tell y' we headed out West t' work in a mine? Jud fought in the last war, n' once his buddy passed from this world, waren't nuthin' could stop him from goin'. He jes' pulled me 'long."

"His buddy?"

"They come outta them trenches in France t'gether. Jud waren't goin' nowhere's till his buddy passed. Took care a' him since the war, all them years, right up t' the end."

There went Jesse's eyes again, smarting like all get-out. Willie's countenance appeared before him, and Joe's. Yes, war buddies… he knew all about them, and all about losing them. If only he had a buddy left to watch out for.

Staring out over this desert land, Li'l allowed him time, and the mass in his throat finally dissipated. Li'l picked up his pack and started off.

This time, Joe and Willie kept Jesse company, and the itch to get back to his unit nearly overwhelmed him. The Allies must put an end to the Japs once and for all.

At their campsite that night, Li'l tended the fire, and Jesse nodded off. Some time later, he woke to two voices. Jud had found them.

"How d'ya know? He's jus' been talkin' in his sleep."

Jud, as usual, waited a while before answering. "That's it. He said *chicken fat* in his sleep. Jus' like…"

The fire's crackle obscured the rest of his statement. Then, "'Sides, they both got green eyes and red hair. Don't happen much."

Beyond the fire a distance, Jesse pondered. *Chicken fat?* He had said that in his sleep? Where had the saying come from?

Green eyes and red hair—Jud meant him, for sure. But who else?

*March 1944*

"Yes, Sir!" Ignoring the seething inside, Jesse forced his voice to cooperate. Holding back a white foam of rage took all the self-control he could muster.

As if to solidify his thoughts, the Major re-stated his decision. "You will proceed to Letterman General Hospital in San Francisco for further recovery. They have the newest equipment, something called X-rays that can see right through your skin."

As he stared straight ahead, his back as stiff as he could hold it, Jesse's vision blurred. And the Major caught this unintended display of emotion.

"You don't want to end up with big problems later in life. That's what our docs say will happen if you don't get your shoulder fixed while you can." He reached out but came short of patting Jesse's forearm.

"I'm well aware how much you want to get back to your unit, but you've already been wounded twice, and now this shoulder injury. Besides, who knows what will happen in the Pacific and when? Rejoining your unit may still work out. Right now, though, you're no good to the Army in your condition."

"Yes, Sir." Even as Jesse consented, the calendar on the wall defied him. Nearly summer's end. He'd never make it back into the battle. He just knew the war would be over before they pronounced him healed.

Everything he'd been through turned into a maze, a series of mishaps and unexpected curves in an unpredictable long road. To his chagrin, the Major painstakingly read the details out loud, including Philip kidnapping him from the hospital in Van Nuys.

Under the officer's scrutiny, heat flooded Jesse's face.

"Kidnapped?"

"In a manner of speaking…another soldier used a gun. But

he was wounded, too, and only trying to get us to a doctor who could help."

The Major's eyebrows did a two-step, but he kept reading. "And from Henderson, the truck taking you to the coast veered off… Driver killed on impact, you were thrown out…?

Jesse's nod did nothing to ease his puzzlement.

"Thus the shoulder injury added to your leg wound."

Jesse set his mind. No matter how crazy this all sounded, it rang true. But he wasn't about to give up. Things changed in the Army. Heaven knew they changed, often overnight. Hadn't Mr. Somerset warned him about that before he left home?

"I've assigned an orderly to make sure you end up where I'm sending you, Kline. Barring any unforeseen bandits attacking the stagecoach, I expect you to be in the hospital and properly cared for by this evening."

The officer's sideways grin made Jesse grimace. "You've got quite the story, but believe me, I've come across even more peculiar twists and turns. Be thankful you've hung on. And from now on, how about concentrating on getting stronger?"

Almost like his high school football coach, who had a way of softening disheartening blows. The night Jesse bobbled his extra-point kick in the final senior football game had to be the worst. With the game tied, he'd wanted to leave for the war in a glow of glory, leading his team to the district championship.

But such was not to be. Though that game replayed in his head a million times, he still couldn't pinpoint exactly what went wrong with his kick. The shame, though, hung on like sap to a maple.

This Major liked to hear his own voice, it seemed, but on that cool Kentucky night, Coach Harding had offered the same type of advice. With far fewer words, he swaddled the disappointment in the packaging of the future.

"Soon you'll be facing lots worse. Things like this either strengthen or weaken us, depending on our attitude. I'm counting on this one to make you a better soldier, a better man."

Looking back, Jesse figured Coach had been right. Paying attention to every single detail of each shot he had fired in the Pacific paid off. Except for one thing. He'd still lost Willie and Joe.

And now, another hospital. Another set of docs. And might as well be honest…likely some pretty nurses.

But first, two men waited for him outside the building's entrance. What could he possibly say to Li'l Wall and Jud? They'd taken all these extra weeks to care for him and see him back to where he belonged.

Thankfully, Li'l spoke first. "So, y' know where you're goin' now?" His tone made Jesse smile.

"Yeah. To a hospital first, then hopefully back to the Pacific. Thanks to you two for getting me here."

"Not in trouble with the gen'rals?"

"I guess not. Somehow, they believed what I said."

"Well." Finally, a word from Jud, who slowly shook his head. "Life's got some surprises, don't it?"

"That's for sure." Jesse bit his lip as an orderly came toward them. "I can't thank you enough for how you've…"

Jud's chin rose. "After the war, go down to Waco. Someone's waitin' for y' at Miss M's Boardin' House, south side of town."

Quite a speech from this silent helper who sat up night after night dressing his wounds. Jud's eyes blackened even more. He turned prophet now, and words fell like the benediction the preacher had intoned over Jesse and Willie before they left for the war.

"You'll get there one day. Sure 'nough, and she'll be waitin'."

Jud gestured to Li'l Wall, who waved his hand. Then they hoisted their supplies and went on their way, two giant vagabonds out to do good.

"I'm driving up to Sandtown, along the Brazos. There's been a surge of influenza there, and I need to see firsthand what's going on. Anybody want to ride along after your shift?"

When no one else stepped forward, I did. This day had seemed extra long, so an outing would be good for my spirits.

"We'll leave right after four, and it'll probably take a couple of hours. You might want to let Miss M know."

"Right." Leaving for a quick lunch, I hurried. Maybe I could do something to help with dinner now.

When Miss M heard the news, she scowled. "Sandtown? Influenza? That man! As if he doesn't have enough work at the hospital already!"

Taken aback, I waited. It wasn't like her to permit such an outburst, and the violence she put into rolling out the rolls spoke just as loudly. I had almost finished peeling the potatoes by the time she continued.

"I shouldn't have said what I did. Doc has the right to go where he wants, and who am I to judge, after all he's done for us?" Her heavy sigh filled the room. "I just don't want him catching something. Now that he's finally stopped driving back and forth to the hospital in Gatesville, I thought…"

"Sounds like he's concerned about a real outbreak."

"Hmm. I suppose so. But what if he catches it? So many people depend on him. The V.A. grew from 300 beds to more than 900 before the war, and now there's nearly 2,000—over 500 acres of buildings. Isn't that load enough?"

I dried my hands and found my purse. "Some people seem to have an extra capacity, don't you think? I mean, they have more endurance than the rest of us. I'd say Doc's like that.

"Besides, there's probably not a germ in the world he hasn't contacted, especially after his Great War service and the influenza epidemic back then. Plus taking care of all these men who've fought all over the globe."

"Mmm. That's for sure. Judson was like that, too. Maybe what I'm really worried about is *you* catching the flu. That's the last thing we need. I know it sounds selfish, and you're a dedicated nurse, but…"

Miss M threw her hands up in the air. "Oh, for heaven's sake! I'm being a regular worry-wort instead of practicing what I preach. Guess I'd better quiet down and pray you stay safe."

Avoiding her gooey bread-dough fingers to give her a hug took agility, but I made it work. "Yep. And keep in mind what an old toughie I've become. We deal with patients who have the flu often enough. No doubt I'm immune."

Just before opening the screen door, I glanced back. Frowning at her bread dough, Miss M could have looked far more convinced. Just that morning, I'd read the word *unstinting*, one of my favorites. She was so generous—she never stopped giving to her boarders.

A few hours later as we drove through the downtown area, Doctor Graham pointed out the sights. "Did you ever see the Cotton Palace? Quite the attraction in its heyday."

"No, Mama and my sister and I stuck close to home."

"I remember as a kid thinking I must have been dropped into the World's Fair, there was so much going on. Seemed only right to celebrate Texas being the king of cotton, and Waco the center of it all."

"Those were the days here in town. We rode the Ferris wheel and a wooden roller coaster, too. My brothers and I should've been thrown out, we were so rowdy. But my dad thought we deserved a little fun once a year. Not a bad thing in the long run."

The streets rolled by, filled with shops and larger stores, including Cox's, where Miss M had taken me for a new dress when I first came. Seeing the front entrance brought back a good memory.

"We used to shop at Sanger Brothers Department Store, right down here in the heart of the city on Austin Avenue. Mother took us once when school started, since we all had outgrown our pants and shoes over the summer, and once in the spring, so we'd look our best on Easter Sunday."

Doctor Graham stopped at a stop sign. "Funny how things like that stay with you, isn't it? My mother felt sad when the store closed down back in '31, though we only went shopping two times a year."

A pleasant breeze cooled the car as he stopped for another sign and rounded a curve. Seemed like ages since I'd sat here in this same seat with him on the drive into Waco, a lifetime ago. So much had changed, and my prospects had turned so much brighter, with a new challenge every day.

"Remember when you picked me up that first time? Have I thanked you lately for doing that?"

"Can't say that you have. We've both been way too busy." His wide grin belied the tension of a long day in the wards. "But I'm sure glad I did. I'm not sure what we'd do without you at the hospital these days."

What had he seen when he first looked at me? Did he have any inkling what precipitated my showing up so destitute by the side of the road?

Tempted to ask, I left it at that, and soon we arrived at our destination. It was easy to see how Sandtown got its name. Sand from the banks of the Brazos spread everywhere—not an easy place to live. Homes here seemed meager, but I got the feeling people cared about keeping things up.

A box of flowers outside a window on the shady side…curtains tied back in neat bows declared that somebody cared. As he parked the car, Doctor Graham looked around.

"This is one address. Rosita has met the wife, she said."

From inside, we could hear Mexican music playing, and in the side yard, two children with sticks made figures in the dust. Such intelligent black eyes, and I took the little girl's smile as meant for me alone. How good to be in a neighborhood where little ones played.

They ran over as we approached, and I wished I'd brought one of Rosita's cookies for each of them. Oh, those dark eyes! They tripped me up inside…so much energy and potential.

"You came to the right place, Private. Your X-rays show us all we need to know. There's a healed fracture in your leg from shrapnel hitting the bone, but it's mended fairly well already. Unfortunately, you're going to need surgery to re-align the bones in your shoulder."

"Surgery? No, that can't be. I've been getting better every day!"

"Do you ever want to be able to shoot your rifle again?"

"Sure."

"Well, the way this break is repairing will preclude that. The bone needs to connect here…not here. See how it's askew?" The doctor, a colonel, held up a filmy paper with a murky image of arm and shoulder bones.

"This is an X-ray. Your skin shows up as transparent and the bone shows as a shadow."

A shudder ran through Jesse. These newfangled X-rays were making things even more complicated than before. He'd figured it would take a few weeks to get back to the field, but with exercise and enough ointment, surely…

"We've had a number of successes with shoulders just like yours. It's a matter of reducing the scar tissue and redirecting the…" The doc glided his pencil over the X-ray. "We'll schedule you for surgery first thing next week."

Back in the ward full of men in worse condition, Jesse gave

himself a talking-to. "You oughta be thankful. At least they're not amputating."

That brought Phil to mind. Another war buddy, now minus an arm. Would he still be in Henderson by now, or had he finagled a way to stay in the military? One day, it would be worth finding him to thank him for the kidnapping.

Then he settled on Jud's mysterious comment. What a puzzlement, that he should go to Waco. But there was no way of getting to the bottom of this without following his instructions. Instructions? Actually, they seemed more like a gentle command.

He should have asked more at the time, but the orderly had come to take him to San Francisco and everyone was itching to leave. What a mystifying fellow Jud was. Probably wouldn't have answered, anyhow.

*…come to the right place…* Had the colonel been right? Finally, he'd gotten to where he ought to be? He'd been tossed around so much, Jesse had no idea. But once again, he really had no choice.

Since Judson left, several evenings often passed without listening to the war news. So on October twenty-third, I planned to read in my room until I fell asleep. These days, that usually took a matter of minutes.

But when I circled the dining room one last time to check for crumbs from dinner, a war correspondent's voice crackled from the parlor, where several boarders sat together listening. Miss M, too, had her ear to the radio.

"It's the Battle of Leyte Gulf in the Philippines," she whispered. "I've been thinking so much about your Jesse lately, and a big battle has started there."

> *"General MacArthur has returned to his beloved Philippines at last. It's looking as if our forces have achieved their objective, folks, but with heavy casualties on both sides…"*

I clapped a hand over my heart and sank into an armchair. So strange to hear someone else say Jesse's name, although every few days Miss M asked if any word had come yet.

How did I ever bear this anxiety without telling anyone? Despite my wild tears and cries that night out in the yard, I'm glad Miss M knows. She's praying for him, too, and that thought eases my heart. Surely her prayers must mean more than mine.

So far, the answer is always *no*. No word yet. Sometimes, words seem like the enemy rather than a friend. Annie's latest letter arrived just yesterday. She went to her local Red Cross office to submit a request for information about Jesse, but it will take time.

Of course. War has a way of making everything require extra time.

*The U.S. Navy landed four Sixth Army divisions on Leyte with Japanese aerial counter-attacks damaging the USS Sangamon (CVE-26) and a few other ships, but without hindering the landings. Later in the day, General MacArthur gave his "I have returned" radio message to the people.*

Did I want to hear the rest? My best instincts tell me it might be better not to know. Lately, I've been learning more about quieting my soul, as a recent sermon admonished.

*Be still, my soul* amounts to far more than the words to a hymn. These days, each of us must find ways to conquer the fears that would destroy us.

And one method might be by allowing only a certain amount of news from the war front into my mind. Perhaps Helen is right. Reading her copy of *The Portable Dorothy Parker* might be the best choice tonight.

A few weeks ago, she introduced me to this author. "Dorothy always seems to find something witty or hopeful, even in the midst of trouble. Her stories make me forget the war for a while."

"I don't think that's possible for me." I jerked on the edge of the sheet we were using to remake a bed. Should I tell her about Jesse?

"Well, it can't hurt to try."

"True. I will."

Almost Doctor Graham's exact words as we returned from Sandtown the other day, where he cared for five people in various stages of influenza. He left pots of soup at the homes, compliments of Rosita, along with his usual positive outlook, and promised to return.

"We've done what we can. I'll be back in a few days to check on them. Let me know if you want to come along." He wound our vehicle through evening traffic, and I took in the lights of the city, like droplets of hope speckled everywhere.

October had arrived…soon cooler air would blow in, and we'd need sweaters at night. My thoughts meandered to the South Pacific. Shining blue-green salt water, once-beautiful islands ransacked by the fighting.

There would be a field hospital…an evacuation hospital most likely, a bit further from the actual battlefield, where docs and nurses worked day and night trying to meet impossible needs.

And one of their patients might well be Jesse. Every passing automobile seemed to sigh, "Oh Jesse, where are you?"

Chapter Twenty

*Autumn Valentine*

> *In May my heart was breaking–*
> *Oh, wide the wound, and deep!*
> *And bitter it beat at waking,*
> *And sore it split in sleep.*
>
> *And when it came November,*
> *I sought my heart, and sighed,*
> *"Poor thing, do you remember?"*
> *"What heart was that?" it cried.*

Today, Dorothy's wit failed to divert my attention from the war. Hers was not my reality, but did I even understand what she meant? Was her heart fickle? So *easy come, easy go* that by November, it had forgotten the love it lost in May?

Or was she saying that she lost her heart itself in losing a loved one? Something in me voted for the *easy come, easy go* style of life she'd perhaps become accustomed to with her husband, Alan Campbell. With a Hollywood contract to write for Metro-Goldwyn-Mayer, the couple seemingly had it made. They enjoyed a world of opportunity and ease, with breezes blowing in from the Pacific on hot nights.

"What difference does the war make to them?" Even as I spat out the accusation, I knew better. Who was I, wide-awake and grumbling in my bed, to judge others? People always have more challenges than you can see on the surface, and I'd read about Miss Parker's unhappy life.

"Just take the book back to Helen…that's all. Reading it helped her but isn't right for you."

I closed that door and tried again to sleep. As I did, a gift Rosita gave me earlier in the day came to mind.

*"Dios es esta en el presenta, no en el pasado ni en el future. Dios esta donde estames ahora."*

That was the gist of her statement when she'd seen my gloomy face in the kitchen. After a full day that I felt good about, I had let myself slip into conjecture before I even left the hospital.

"Where are you?" Rosita's question, was I in the past or the future, stopped me short. I had stolen back to the past…or flitted back and forth between unchangeable regrets and projecting to an unknown time when Jesse came home.

As direct as a ray of sunshine, Rosita roused me from the wasteland of my thoughts several other times, and I'm so glad. How wonderful to have someone be able to *read* me and nudge me back on track!

*God is where you are now*—her final sentence lingered. I so often stray from that reality. How can this be so difficult? But Rosita agrees that staying in the present can be a challenge.

It's as if I were born to travel from past to future. I get ensconced in the present only to start thinking of my errors with Clyde or what I might do for Jesse some faraway day. But lying here in bed, I vow to discipline my thoughts. I have power to restrain them from constantly following my emotions. I simply must practice.

A vagrant breeze, nothing like those Californians would be enjoying right now, teased my curtains. By morning, perhaps it would gain strength—and the same might be true of me.

*Late fall 1944*

"At ease, Private Kline. You ever heard of Manzanar?"

"No, sir."

"Most people haven't. It's an internment camp in the Owens Valley between the Sierra Nevada on the west and the Inyo Mountains on the east. The government has scattered nine other relocation camps for Japanese-Americans over the West and South.

"They keep these locations relatively quiet—hush-hush, you know. No use riling up the population." Something flickered in the Colonel's eyes but disappeared as he continued.

"The danger's over now, but these folks sold or gave up their property early in '42 when they were labeled enemy aliens and forced to leave the coast. So for now, they need to stay put until the war ends. The Army keeps a low-profile guard at the camp, just to make sure life there goes smoothly.

"Living conditions aren't the greatest. Tight quarters and… Well, let's just say we need to keep incidents to a minimum for the duration."

An itch started under Jesse's collarbone. Why would Colonel Marks be telling him this? He'd been on the shooting range, where he oversaw sniper training every morning and afternoon, when the message came. Once he'd gotten out of the hospital, the Army had assigned him to supervise this training, despite his frequent reminders that he wanted to get back in the thick of things.

Weeks had passed…months. And now this. A sigh escaped Jesse's lips, longer and more heartfelt than he wished. The Colonel squinted at him before glancing down at a file in his hand.

"You've been doing excellent work on the range, Kline. No doubt about that. We're aware of your performance during battle and that you desire to re-join your unit, but you've already served in an exemplary manner. Now that our troops have invaded Mindoro, we're needing fewer snipers.

"We've made progress in victories on Guam, in New Guinea, and the Mariana Islands. You've surely heard that called a Turkey Shoot, haven't you? "

"Yes, Sir."

"These days our big B-29s do a lot of the work." The Colonel peered at Jesse as though trying to read his mind. "You may be thinking of Burma and Luzon and Manila. You're right, still plenty of battles to be fought, but…" He studied a paper from the file.

"The doctors' consensus cannot be ignored. Your injuries have healed well, and if it were a year ago, we would most likely consider sending you back. As it is, we've decided you'd be most useful to the war effort as a guard at Manzanar."

Screaming was no option, but Jesse's frustration ached in his throat. Oh, what he would say if only he could!

*A guard! Watching over people who offer no threat whatsoever! Stuck in the middle of nowhere while the war's still going on—I can't believe you'd do this to me. Can't believe you'd waste my skills! What kind of commander are you, anyway…?"*

He could go on and on. But of course, he employed the only utterance possible. "Yes, Sir."

As he returned to his barracks, burning zigzagged through his gut. He wanted to slam his fist through the flimsy wooden walls, but where would that get him? Back in the hospital, no doubt.

The unfairness struck like a blow to his midsection. He'd done everything he could to serve well, but things spiraled out of his control. All kinds of thoughts sped through his mind.

He could go AWOL—they obviously didn't appreciate him, anyhow. Wouldn't be tough to simply disappear over the Sierras and make his way back to Kentucky…and then what? Find a cabin back in the hills, farm a plot…hide out, essentially, for the rest of his life.

"Argh!" How could he ever live with himself, even if the Army never caught up with him? Fortunately, the barracks lay empty right now, fully able to receive his yells.

His bunk caught his weight, and as he flopped down, the most intense dark eyes bored into him. Jud. It was almost as if he'd somehow entered this building and with a mystical power, pierced Jesse's soul.

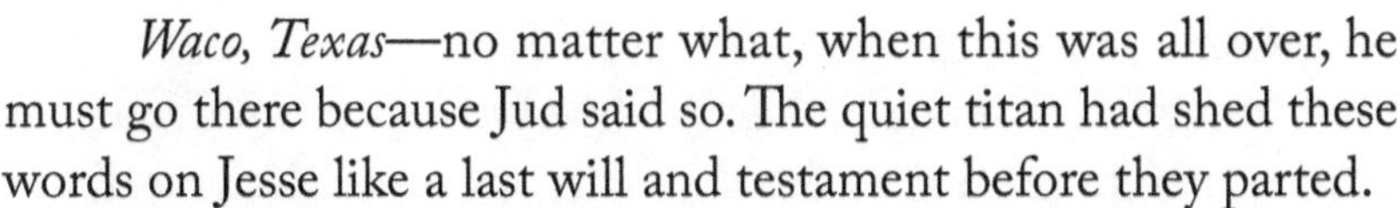

*Waco, Texas*—no matter what, when this was all over, he must go there because Jud said so. The quiet titan had shed these words on Jesse like a last will and testament before they parted.

He had to go because Jud felt sure somebody waited for him there. Mama, he guessed.

But Mama or whoever it was, their prayers seemed worthless right now. He kept getting stopped from what he believed to be his destiny. Surely someone would intervene, so he would be able to avenge the deaths of Willie and Joe.

Staring out the barracks window at nothing, his temper finally cooled somewhat. So many unplanned events had occurred. Maybe more would, too, and he would still get to rejoin his unit.

This place called Manzanar, between the Sierras and… what had the Colonel said? At any rate, the camp perched out in the middle of nowhere like a turkey buzzard on a lone tree. Mountains—that definitely meant a few short months of summer and in winter, bitter cold and storms.

Scenes passed before him…blizzards, unheated barracks, miserable, angry prisoners staring from behind barbed wire fences. Japanese-Americans, but the word *Americans* dissolved. Only black hair and slanted eyes venomous with hatred remained in Jesse's image. They would be just like the enemy who had killed his buddies, the enemy he so longed to fight again.

Surely what the Colonel said could not be true. Surely someone would change his orders. But even as he entertained the idea, doubts rose like ashes in smoke.

"So what did you think of Miss Parker's writing?" Making a bed with Helen always led to short conversations, a welcome break. At these times, we reminded each other that another world existed outside these hospital walls.

"Well, I liked some of it. Some not so much."

"I know what you mean. I couldn't relate to certain parts at all."

"Really?"

"Sure." Helen angled her head. "Like that poem about Valentines in autumn. She's a different sort of woman than me, that's for sure."

"Hmm. I felt the same way. Maybe if someone lives on a special scale, a Hollywood-type life, your heart can grow cold. You can have a romance and six months later, forget it entirely. Maybe in that world, there's plenty of romance around for everybody to have more than one."

Talking with Helen about this felt good. I'd just given back the Parker book and was glad some of the writing struck her the same way. Since the other day when she shared about her miscarriages and I told her about Jesse, we'd become even closer.

"But *love*, a mother's love, for certain, runs much deeper. How could a mother ever forget her child?" Helen replaced a pillowcase and gave the pillow a good punch before setting it in place.

"My sentiments exactly. Not a day goes by but Jesse's little-boy face reminds me how precious he is. How irreplaceable."

An alarm sounded, so we hurried off to our next task with some American mother's son fighting for his life. No, a mother cannot forget this love. Especially if her only son seems lost to her right now, claimed by this awful war.

Yet another disappointment. Studying the papers issued to him, Jesse's heart turned to ice. He would never be able to reunite with his unit, never again see the ones he'd been with from the start.

Looking back, he would bet that despite their bravado, they'd all been as jittery as he on their first day of basic training. Everyone put on their bravest face, though—sometimes a certain amount of bravado can carry you through to the next stage.

He'd been looking forward to getting back with them so much. Now he would never know who made it through the war and which ones didn't.

They had pledged their all to each other. He'd made his vow to Wilder, Howell and Barkley, Robinson, Lewis and Smythe, Daniels and Benson, Kendall, Michels, Pierce, and all the rest. At least he remembered most of their names.

They'd determined to stick together no matter what. But because of the Army's latest arbitrary decision, they had vanished from his life.

*The Army gives and the Army takes away.*

Almost like a verse from the Bible—something Aunt Annie said, probably after Uncle Winn's funeral. When they got home that day, they went inside the house and suddenly realized how empty it had become.

Far too soon, Winn had been taken from them. Grandma Kline came to stay for a few weeks, another change. She kept her tears to herself, but the hurt on her face made Jesse wince. So pinched. So full of pain.

So he had looked away and tried to keep Beau and Pearly busy outside. But everywhere they went, Uncle Winn met them… in the wooden swings he had made for them, in the barn he had built, in the horses and fields of grain he had nurtured.

This *giving and taking away* stung. And no less all these years later.

Chapter Twenty-one

*January 1944*

Just another slant-eyed girl with Jap blood flowing through her veins… At first, she looked like every other young woman in this camp. But from the moment Jesse noticed this internee standing by the gate in a nasty north wind, holding a small child's hand in hers, he couldn't look away.

Here at Manzanar, the internees lived in barracks set apart from the guards and administrators. He'd determined to have as little as possible to do with them, preferably nothing at all. Ever. His assignment, to stand guard in the towers, fit perfectly. From that distant vantage point, internees appeared like miniature toys one might shove out of the way with your foot instead of real human beings.

For Willie, Jesse made his decision to ignore them, for Joe and for all the other guys who would never make it back home. Honor-bound, he made this choice also for those who had left a leg, an arm, or some other body part in the Pacific Islands.

Not to mention the other soldiers in certain hospital wards filled with screaming, locked off from the main areas. He'd never ventured closer than a hallway, but after surgery when he felt well enough to take walks, their desperate voices reached him at times. Needle-bearing nurses sometimes ran toward these men, sent home, fighting for their sanity.

At Manzanar, all of these people around him were Japanese, despite the *American* in their official title. Maybe the soldier who killed Willie had a brother or cousin here. Who knew?

The first days of this assignment passed like a slow engine on a long, long track. Jesse did his duty and remained aloof. When he did have to mingle with the prisoners, he chose duty with older folks.

Japs or not, the children tugged at his heart. Youngsters ought not be so somber, so…self-controlled. They ought to be running through Kentucky meadows, splashing in a creek or playing baseball instead of shivering in this fierce sand-blowing mountain wind.

But then one morning, a girl with her yellow skirt blowing in the usual sharp wind and a red scarf bunched at her neck, caught his attention. Perhaps it was the way she held the little one's hand.

He knew better than to make eye contact with internees yet broke his own rule. Not that she even realized, being so far below him.

No hazel eyes this time. No kind nurse like the one he'd fallen for aboard the hospital ship. But something about this girl's posture struck him. Amidst all of the rules and humiliation she retained her dignity.

Every line of her profile proclaimed that she knew who she was and where she had come from. Perhaps not where she would end up, true, but still, she held her head high. When the bus came for the child, her son or younger brother, Jesse assumed, she stooped to his height and whispered something to him.

Then she waited until he boarded. Quietly, without moving. Obviously, she took responsibility for the lad's safety. After the bus traveled out of sight, only then, she turned and walked back toward the central barracks area.

Jesse never entered that mile-square blocks of barracks, a mess hall and small recreation center, but his training taught him how the internees lived. The Relocation Center had thirty-six residential blocks separated by streets and firebreaks. Each block had fourteen twenty-by-one-hundred-foot barracks typically divided into four twenty by twenty-five foot apartments.

Blocks also had separate men's and women's latrines and

showers, laundry and ironing rooms, and an oil storage tank. Each apartment was furnished with a single light bulb hanging from the ceiling, an oil-burning stove, and up to eight cots. One outdoor faucet provided water for each barracks.

Now, he would gladly take a mission that required entering the living area. Trying to get this girl out of his mind was like swatting flies back in Uncle Winn's barn on a hot summer day. For every swat, two more flies landed. Something about her touched him, despite her remoteness from the tower.

Strange. He would never see her again in all these masses of folks, more than ten thousand. This camp operated like a small city, but that meant a large city for a guy from the Kentucky hills.

But the next day, there she stood again, distinctive in the small gathering at the bus stop. This time, she and the boy waited as the temperature dropped even farther to the low teens. Ice began to pelt the area. Did she stand out because of the bright colors she wore? No, something else about her mesmerized Jesse, yet he couldn't say exactly what.

Like everyone else, she was short. Tidy, he had to say, like most of the women internees. But otherwise, her physical appearance revealed nothing remarkable.

All afternoon, as the weather worsened, he kept thinking about her. "Somehow, I'll work things out to be down there when that little fellow returns."

And he did, against his better judgment. He took a position at the far end of the gathering so he could observe the reunion of children and adults. In a population of black eyes, this girl's still drew him. In a sea of looks veiled by shame, loss, and fighting the bitter cold, hers managed to retain a certain glow.

With a smile and a hug, she greeted the boy and tightened his scarf around his ears. Then she gave him all of her attention. He bubbled over with news, most likely from the school on the other side of the camp.

The next morning Jesse watched again, and the next day. For

the entire week, the girl's radiance registered as from the heart. No matter what she'd faced in being forced to come here or what she had to leave behind—probably her childhood home—somewhere along the way she must have chosen to see the bright side.

After all, her own government had sent and was holding her here against her will. He had no idea what she had been doing when the feds apprehended her—maybe she'd been in college.

Whatever her situation, she refused to allow these circumstances to thwart her smile. Her deep-set dimples accompanied him to his bunk each night, and during the day, he could not get her out of his mind.

Little-by-little, some distinct observations came clear. She must be about five feet tall, about to Jesse's armpit. Always neatly dressed, she arrived at the same time each day, about seven minutes before the bus.

In the mornings, she spent those minutes engaging with the child. Nearly always, he gestured with his hands and arms, sometimes his feet, with her eyes fixed on him. It was as if they shared a world all their own.

Dressed plainly in a brown woolen coat, a scarf that matched his guardian's, and today, a wool hat with ear flaps, the child appeared serious and obedient. They sat on the benches, and he nestled close to her. If they stood, his hand always found hers.

If the bus came late, the girl showed no signs of impatience. Unless you looked up to the guard tower, one of eight at Manzanar, and spied a military policeman looking down, you might not even realize she and the child were imprisoned.

The red scarf always circled her neck, and on the coldest day, nearly hid her clear skin. She kept her black hair chin-length, meticulous despite ever-present winter gusts.

One day she dressed the same, but wore mittens, as did the little boy. Down to the black rubber boots over her shoes, she created an image of carefulness. Thoughtfulness. Restraint.

In the afternoon, if she found one of the wooden seats

unoccupied, she pulled a small volume from a side pocket in her wool coat. *Poetry?* The thought created a stirring—how long had it been since Jesse had read real literature?

The jacket, too large for her, reminded him of a Navy pea coat. Probably the internees had little choice about clothing here, especially when the weather grew this cold, often below zero. Before the war, most probably had no need for heavy coats at their coastal homes, but now were forced to pick garments from the community clothing room.

Where had this young woman lived before the war? Was the boy indeed her brother, or perhaps her son? And somewhere amidst this ocean of Japanese faces, did her parents and husband live here, too?

Fortunately, standing watch at the bus stop offered no other attraction, so the guard who traded duty with Jesse seemed glad to continue their exchange. At least the towers' walls offered some relief from the cold.

On Friday after the bus dispersed its young passengers, the young woman gave the boy his normal welcome hug and headed toward the barracks with him in tow. Over the weekend, the boy would not go to school—not until Monday.

With each step they took, heaviness descended around Jesse. This high desert country appeared stark, stripped of all but meager signs of beauty, nearby peaks excluded. But those snow-covered peaks remained inaccessible, only to be viewed from afar.

Winter had entered into the land like a parasite and pared it away, sharpening the indistinct crags to the east. In the night, icy gales shrieked through canyons there, giving the coyotes and wolves some competition. In his barracks, so much sand had blown in through the floorboards each night that they'd added linoleum.

He'd heard it was even worse in the family barracks. Someone said they'd seen the lids of tinned goods nailed down to cover holes or internees stuffing them with whatever they could find to ward off the wind.

Even as Jesse scanned the distance, an odd hunger nagged at him. He would return to Kentucky after the war, he supposed, but that time seemed a world away. So did his unit.

At the same time, a persistent truth surfaced. His English teacher would call for synonyms now, and *loneliness* would surely come to mind. He'd never felt this way before, but here, the word suited. Eleven thousand people total in this place, but he had met none of them, and no one except his commander knew anything about him.

In essence he had no one, although Jud said someone in Texas waited for him. Could that truly be Mama? Possibly…probably, but right now, she seemed like a figment of his imagination. At certain times, meeting Jud and L'il Wall did, too.

Aunt Annie's family in Kentucky would be glad to see him, and so relieved when he got there. But things would never be quite the same, especially with Willie gone. After these long years, could he settle down there again?

But this particular sensation didn't revolve around settling in this place or that. Seemed more like what he had felt with that nurse on the ship, and about as hopeless.

With relationships between guards and internees forbidden, no guard in his right mind would seek one of these women, anyhow. When he first arrived here three months ago, he would have agreed.

*A Jap is a Jap is a Jap.*

What normal American guy would fall for a woman of Japanese heritage? Yet now, this girl… Ruminating caused his thoughts to go deeper. The assumptions that had developed during his tour in the Pacific lay exposed.

For all he knew she'd been born in this country, just like him, but because of something she couldn't control—her bloodlines— her life had been interrupted. She'd been coerced to come here, forced into accepting her fate. Yet in the middle of what must be a nightmare, she possessed a certain dignity. *Aunt Annie would call it serenity,* he thought.

Something about this girl reached out to Jesse, beckoned him, and he'd never even met her. Climbing back up to the tower, he grappled with what this might mean.

When a siren signaled the end of his shift, he dawdled. The next crew signed in. At last, he descended the ladder. Time to hit the mess tent. But supper would not satisfy what ailed him. Without putting his yearning into precise words, he knew one thing.

He must speak with her. He had no idea how, or if he could even discover her name, or what on earth he would say. But he felt as sure about this as when he had signed up for the Army. There simply had to be a way.

"Drop this by Major Zier's office on your way to chow."

Jesse took an envelope from his commander and mulled over this week's events as he headed toward the office. It had been a quiet Friday in the bus stop area, but he gained a new insight into Yuko's personality.

He'd taken to thinking of her as Yuko for lack of a real name. Seemed as good a guess as any. But his recent thought about her had to do with books. She had been reading a rather thick one while she waited for the child in the afternoons but brought a different one today.

This probably meant she was one of those people, like Aunt Annie, who always had a book going. At one time, so had he.

*Crunch…crunch…*the sharp crushed rock here made for noisy walking in any season. At least frequent snowfalls muffled the sound a bit. All weekend, he'd pondered his situation and come up with no ideas at all.

Wouldn't look right for a guard to go asking around about an individual woman. Social lines between guards and internees had been drawn tight. His barracks, a distance from the women's and children's compound, had little to offer by way of inspiration.

The other guards, almost all members of the Military Police, played poker in the mess in the evenings, but the game failed to interest Jesse. So it was take to his bunk or take a walk—not much else to do.

When he knocked on the assistant camp director's door, he expected someone to take the report from his hands and be on his way. But no one answered. He knocked again, louder, and something like a groan issued from inside.

Finally, a dull-sounding, "Come in." Had he really heard this, or imagined it?

Set in the back of a barrack-like building, the office did little to impress, with a desk, a long table under a window, a couple of chairs and a row of wooden files that covered the longest wall. Seated at the desk, a uniformed officer—from his decorations, a major—spoke with what appeared to be a permanent scowl.

"Set it on the desk. Thanks." He barely looked up, so Jesse obeyed and started to back out.

"Say, wait up." The officer scanned Jesse's uniform. "You wouldn't know anybody who can type, would you? More than ten words a minute?" The Major eyed him under bushy raised eyebrows.

"Type? I can, Sir—forty words a minute in high school."

"Well, I'll be. Been tearin' my hair out tryin' to find somebody." He scraped back his chair. "My assistant had some kind of accident last week—fooling around with a gun or something. Has to have surgery, and they've shipping him out to a hospital.

"So I'm stuck with…" He gestured to several piles of forms and letters. "We've got a real mess here, and besides, the Army's reinstated the draft for Japanese-Americans now. They call it the 442nd Regimental Combat Team. So you know where that paper-work's gonna come…"

He pointed at his chest with an enormous sigh. "You say you can type forty words a minute?"

"I could a couple of years ago. My trigger finger might be a little rusty by now."

"Sit down right here."

Jesse did, and the Major slid a typewriter in front of him. A black Royal, just like he'd used in Mr. Somerset's class. He put in a sheet of paper and adjusted the tabs. The keys, grimy but all in one piece, felt cool and right under his fingertips.

"What do you want me to write?"

"Anything. Something you've memorized. Write a letter to your mom."

"Okay." Jesse let loose. If only he could use this instrument to write letters all the time, he'd be sending a lot more because the writing flowed so fast.

After a minute or two, Major Zier bawled, "Lemme see what you've got there!"

He read some of the letter and took a deep breath. "Well, I'll be. If I was a prayin' man, I'd say I just got myself an answer. Son, I hope you like doing this, because your job's just been changed. Where are you posted now?"

"Guarding in the towers."

"Hmm. From now on you'll be my assistant here."

Stunned, Jesse stared at him.

"That all right with you?" With a lop-sided grin, the major gestured with his arm at piles in every direction, sending a bare light bulb swinging from the ceiling. A gold Great War medal on his uniform flashed in the light.

"Lots of work here, just waitin' for somebody with magic fingers."

"Sir—it's fine."

"All right. I'll inform your commander. See you in the morning at seven sharp. And don't let anything happen to your fingers between now and then, hear?"

*The Army gives and the Army takes away.*

Right now, the *give* part stood out. The Army gives an office a whole lot warmer than a guard tower. Linoleum had even been installed to keep out the sand.

And the Army gives some meaningful work and a system to learn. The only *taken away* was the opportunity to watch Yuko and her young companion every day. But what opened up—oh my! As Major Zier guided him through the various tasks performed here, Jesse could not believe his good fortune.

The Dewey Decimal system. Thanks to his high school teachers, he already knew his way around that. But as he made progress through the files, an astounding realization struck. He had obtained access to names…each guard and each internee in this entire installment. Every day, he would be thumbing through files to find certain individuals and their locations.

Another part of this job, delivering letters and notices, provided a closer look into unexplored areas of the camp. He would have a chance to meet people face-to-face.

Each morning, hope energized him as he headed for the mess, ate breakfast, and took off for the office. Surely one day he would run across Yuko or her parents…or someone who knew her.

He'd never been given to speculation but had no doubt—finding her was only a matter of time.

Spurred by her reading and his new opportunity, he searched out the camp library. People donated these books for the prisoners, he figured, and the small space actually smelled like the library back home. Still, he felt a little guilty when he made off with a well-read copy of one of the *Miss Marple* series.

Reading Miss Christie's mysteries out of order wasn't the best idea, but at least they held his attention. He liked Hercule Poirot best…maybe one of those copies would be turned back in the next time he stopped by.

As for Yuko, he hadn't yet determined her rightful name but daily narrowed down the possibilities. About twenty years old, with a son or brother of elementary school age. This amounted to more information than some amateur detectives received when they began their investigations.

Over Jesse's lunch times, a long list grew of the young women in this place. He kept the full compilation in his duffel for safe-keeping, and each day, found a little free time to extend his search.

The boy wouldn't be taking Bus B unless he qualified for public school, so he must be at least four years old. Rooting out his name might prove easiest, since children received much less attention around here than adults.

Chapter Twenty-two

The injuries we're seeing these days make me close my eyes, but grim reminders still fill my inner vison. In '42 and every year since, the word has been "By Christmas, the war will be over."

Well, it's not over, by any means. And the stream of casualties certainly has not decreased.

On Christmas Eve, Helen gave me the best gift ever, a book. It's pretty new and written by Betty White. Such a plain-Jane name for an incredible author. I don't recall getting quite so involved with a character, although years ago I did shed some tears over Jane's plight in *Judith and Jane*.

Must have been about 1925 when Mama wrapped that up for me at Christmastime. Looking back, I realize the simple tale of a poor, happy girl becoming friends with a rich, snooty one has been replayed many times, but still, Jane's situation touched me.

Now, I'm getting to know Francie, the narrator of this story, who is about eight at the beginning, and I can tell she'll be with me for a long, long time. When I began reading, it was like I had suddenly moved to Brooklyn, New York, and begun following this girl around.

She keeps no secrets. Tells the reader what she's thinking and how she feels about everything. Her life has mixed with mine. Some days, I half-expect her to pop out from one of the recesses in the hospital halls. Or more likely, her mother, Katie, with her mop pail, dust rag, and broom.

Katie's little girl nudges at a spot deep in my being, and getting to know her detail-by-detail opens the space a bit wider.

Ragged clothes, dirty face and all, Francie bares her heart and invites me to try on her life. She shows me her Mama's workworn hands, her brother's hunger, her father's impossible need.

A pretty life it is not. When Helen gave me *A Tree Grows In Brooklyn*, she warned, "I had trouble putting this down to go to sleep at night."

Not me, I figured. I usually was half-asleep before getting in bed. But Helen was right. In a flash, the woes and worries, trials and small triumphs of a child growing up in dire New York City poverty enveloped me.

Some of Francie's experiences mirror mine, at about the same time in our childhoods. Having run away with Mama years before, I knew what it meant to feel out of place.

Though Francie's father was a drunkard, he could be so tender with his children, and her mother never left him. In spite of his brokenness, Francie always felt her Papa loved her. But with someone who had two personalities living right in her home, she never knew which one would crop up, and had to be forever on the watch.

She loved this parent—loved her Papa beyond the telling and would do anything to make him happy. But happiness seemed far out of reach for him.

At life's challenges, he shrank back, leaving her in charge. Mistaken in thinking she could rely on him, she always felt uncertain.

Katie and her children lived this way from day to day. Though Mama and I never even visited a big city, Betty White makes the streets of Brooklyn so real, I can almost smell the rancid garbage or the chestnuts roasting on sidewalk grates come winter.

Every page exudes the tension they lived with each day. Would Papa come home drunk or in a good state of mind? Would he delve out his paycheck for booze or pay part of the rent this month? Would he find an odd job to carry them through? If not, what would they eat?

The volunteer tree that grew near Francie's fire escape served her well. She climbed out on the metal extension to be alone, to read and watch the neighborhood goings-on. Here, she observed the milkman wash his horse, the neighbor women throwing out their wash water, and teenaged girls across the way getting ready for Saturday night dates.

Against all odds, this tree somehow got a start and somehow, it grew, a small oasis of green in a sea of dingy gray. Something alive where bricks and paving reigned, a living plant that signified hope.

At the ranch, the wildflowers had served as my tree. Spying a few of them near the tumbledown fence always heartened me. A few sprigs in a pint jar to brighten the table became life-giving. Sometimes even the tiniest petals, what most would label a weed, seemed to reflect the sunshine.

"Kin, are you all right?" Today, Helen's voice startled me during lunch. On this rainy morning, I had brought a sandwich so I could read straight through the forty minutes.

"Oh, hello!"

"You're in another world."

"Yes, and it's all your fault! The *Tree in Brooklyn* has invaded me, heart and soul."

"Ah. So that's it. Don't you just love Francie and want her to make it?"

"I sure do."

"I finished the book a week ago and am still cheering for her! I have to find something new to read. Things here are getting so…"

"Hard to find the right word, isn't it?" I had settled in an alcove off the front lobby to see something different for a while, and so had Helen.

"Such severe cases." Her shudder made complete sense to me. "I give thanks every day for the training Dr. Graham insisted on. Without that, I would never be able to cope."

"Me either."

"Nice to have this area to come to, isn't it?" She squeezed my arm. "So many people in the main lobby, and some of them were here before I came this morning."

"I guess you could say nothing happens fast here if you're waiting to see a loved one."

Just yesterday, Annie's letter contained another photo of Jesse, and the image returned to me now. Could he be a patient in some hospital at this very moment, with no one to visit him?

*Let him be all right…please keep him healthy.*

"Well, I'll let you read some more. See you in a few minutes."

Getting to sleep would be a challenge tonight. After all, this had been a momentous day! For weeks now, Jesse told himself, *Surely Major Zier will send me on a delivery to the school area some day.*

In the meantime, he bided his time and made the most of opportunities right here in the office. And then this morning, his afternoon list of courier duties included delivering a notice to one of the teachers at the boys' school.

Once there, it took only minor reconnoitering to find the child. Out on the flat rocky space that served as a playground, small black-haired boys played quietly. Jesse waited and watched until one stood out, perhaps because of his red scarf.

His immense black eyes focused on some creature on the earth where he squatted. Seeing no adults around, Jesse decided to risk a foray—what could it hurt to approach and ask his name?

"Hello. What do you have there?"

The little fellow's dark eyes sparked. "A tarantula."

Such clear pronunciation, despite missing one of his front teeth. Jesse squatted down to his level. "Really? But it's daylight. He should be in his burrow, shouldn't he?"

Those black eyes became torches. "I know. Papa always used to read to me about them. He would ask, 'Kenji, why is this one awake in the sunshine?'"

"That's a great question. I don't know the answer, but I can try to find out."

The boy nodded soberly. "My sister will, too."

Jesse's heart leaped. "Your sister?"

The child nodded again, as if he expected her research to produce results quite soon. But with Jesse about to ask his sister's name, a teacher stepped from the doorway.

"Come, Kenji. Everyone hurry. Recess is over."

Ah, Kenji! And so close to knowing his sister's name, too! Jesse considered. Major Zier would be expecting him, with no lack of typing still to do. He ran a somewhat laid-back office, but that was no reason to take a risk.

Still…what if this teacher could tell him what he longed to know? A middle-aged woman with pulled-back hair, the picture of order and authority, she eyed him askance as the children hurried inside.

No, maybe another time. At least he knew what to call Yuko's little brother and where he spent his days.

"Kenji…Kenji." A name that rolled easily from one's tongue.

Kicking out a cramp in his bad leg, Jesse stood up. Just before Kenji entered the building, he turned and waved. Those intense eyes had a way of latching onto the heart.

Hours later as Jesse lay in his bunk, in addition to replaying all he remembered about Yuko, Jesse recalled every feature of today's meeting. Kenji's clean white shirt, his dark blue jacket and pants, the careful part in his shiny, well-combed hair, his scuffed but polished leather shoes.

This earnest fellow was no orphan, by any means. Obviously, someone watched over him with great care.

A week later, on a day Jesse least expected it, there stood Yuko. He'd gone to deliver a message to someone in the men's barracks, and an MP went inside for the recipient. While he waited, someone walked up behind him and stopped a respectful distance away. All of this, he saw through the corner of his eye, but thought nothing of it. When the internee came forward to accept the message from Major Zier, Jesse allowed him time to read before asking if he'd like to send back a reply.

"No. No, I need some time to think."

So Jesse turned to leave and almost ran into the girl who had begun to fill his mind. A sudden break in all-day cloud cover made an aura of her hair, but she kept her eyes lowered.

He took a couple of steps toward her and stopped. What on earth could he say? *"I'm Jesse Kline, and I've been wanting to meet you. I saw you from the guard tower a few weeks ago, waiting for the school bus and…"*

How could she possibly answer? A guard had been watching her? The exact way to frighten her unnecessarily.

So he continued on, but only as far as the fence between another unit of barracks and this one. *Building 23. Memorize. Who is she visiting? Wait and watch.*

Someone emerged from the building as if expecting her. She and the older man talked quietly right there in the yard. The man's hair showed white above his ears. Surely too old to be her husband, could this be her father or an uncle?

As if his life depended upon the answer, Jesse gaped. After a few minutes, some head shaking and a few last words, Yuko turned. Her steady approach sent a shiver through Jesse. And then she paused near him as if deciding whether to turn left or right.

"Ma'am?" He lurched forward from the shadows. "Do you need help?"

Her intake of breath gave him fair warning. How often…if ever…had a guard spoken directly with her?

"I…no, not really. I need to pick up my brother from the bus stop, but not quite yet."

What would happen if he asked permission to walk with her? Launched into his story? Would it sound far too incredulous?

Would she think he was stalking her and flee in terror? Worse, would she report him?

But if he didn't do something soon, then what? Every day, circumstances here changed. Many male internees had joined the new regiment, others got whisked up in the night and transported elsewhere.

If she were transferred, how would he ever find her again?

As if she could see his whirl of conjecture, she angled her head. "Sir? Do *you* need help?"

Jesse's voice failed him. Something in his throat blocked the normal air flow. He bit his lip so hard it must be bleeding.

"Are you all right?" She stepped a little closer, so the sun flamed in her eyes, creating a golden display.

"Not really. I mean, yes, I'm fine, except..." Jesse threw up his hands. "I've been trying to find out your name."

"Have I done something wrong?"

"No, no. I used to work in the guard tower above the bus stop, and every day, I saw you with your little..."

"My brother?" She paled. Her expression sickened Jesse. He reached out a hand but stopped short of touching her hand. Now he had done it—she was worrying about Kenji.

Clearly, she would do anything under the sun to protect him. In a flash, a mother's fear, a sister's rage, and a guardian's protective strength flashed through her otherwise inscrutable eyes.

"He's such a bright boy."

"Oh." She let out a long breath. "Yes. It's just that he is all I have now, and he only has me. But how do you know about him?"

"I saw him at school one day."

"You have talked with him?" Her tone rose at the end of her question and tension narrowed her eyes.

"A little. I delivered a message to the school, and he had found a tarantula out in the yard..."

"Yes, I remember. He said he met a man...tall. That must have been you?"

"Yes. I meant no harm." The lines in her forehead remained, and Jesse's voice trembled. "I mean, he already knew so much about the species… And I…"

Still no change in her expression. "At the bus stop you always look so…" Dare he say *pretty* without offending her? "You and your little brother seem so close, the way families should be."

She angled her head a fraction of an inch.

"Seeing you together made me homesick, you know?"

The worry lines in her forehead relaxed the slightest bit, almost to neutral. He must sound like a madman but had to try again.

"Maybe we could walk toward the bus stop?"

She fell in step, and Jesse's hopes soared. On the other hand, a thousand what-ifs could occur…

"Please. I don't want either of us to get in trouble. You know the rules."

"Yes."

"But I…I've been thinking about you." He almost stumbled on a rock. "… and wondering how I could get to know you."

"Oh." Just one single syllable. No emotion whatsoever.

"Maybe you'd rather not…"

"I'd have to consider. I know nothing about you."

"Yes. Of course. I'm Jesse. Jesse Kline. If I could possibly know your name…"

She stared off into the distance. So much in a name. Finally, she whispered, "Miko. Miko Yoshida."

"Miko Yoshida." Incapable of moving, Jesse could only repeat what she said. "Miko Yoshida, thank you so much. Did I say I'm Jesse Kline, from Kentucky?"

Not a flicker in those eyes. After what seemed forever, she glanced toward the bus stop, where several people had gathered. "I'd better go."

"Yes."

She took two steps, and Jesse's heart sank. How could one short conversation have turned out so badly? But then Miko turned.

"My Grandmother used to quote a wise old proverb. 'One kind word can warm three winter months.'"

Leaving him with those words, she hurried away.

The urge to call her back almost overcame Jesse. But as she joined other short, slender, black-haired, black-eyed women waiting for someone, clarity prevailed, and a sense of peace.

After all of his speculations, lying awake at night thinking of her, being on the look-out every day, allowing thoughts of her to consume his life, what he longed for had finally happened. Whatever came next might remain a mystery, but so far, his prayers had been answered.

He had met Miko. He knew her name. This was, at least, a beginning. *One kind word can warm three winter months.* Surely this positive statement must be a good omen.

Chapter Twenty-three

*Miko Yoshida. Barracks seven, unit thirteen. Registered nurse student, San Diego State University, 20 years old. Mother: Sakira, deceased; Father: Takashi, died at Manzanar of natural causes, September 1943; volunteer at camp hospital.*

Jesse slammed the record book shut. The clock testified he'd spent his entire lunch break reading. For all he knew, looking into personal statistics for a private cause might qualify as a criminal act.

On the other hand, he had learned so much more about Miko. She had lost her mother not long ago, and her father only last year. *Natural causes*…in circumstances like this, what was that supposed to mean? Before that, she had lost her home and been transported to this godforsaken place. So much change, so many reversals.

Surely this must cloud her eyes at times. Sorrow upon sorrow, and all in such a short period. Her story, repeated over and over among these internees, had an effect on Jesse. She had become an individual.

Then, little Kenji. He found himself missing the boy, wanting to speak with him again, to hear what his bright mind had discovered lately. Through all of this chaos, the light in his eyes had not dimmed, his desire to take in all he could had not altered. Strange, the listing under Miko's name had not included him.

Mulling the facts about Kenji and Miko led to one clear realization. Although he still knew very little about them, what he had discovered only made him hunger to learn more.

*Dear Mama,*

*I'll start with exactly what's happening right now. I'm in an Army office, taking a typing test. The officer wanted to see how many words I can type per minute and said to write to you.*

*So I am.*

*I've been thinking of doing that anyway and should have sooner. It'll take a couple of pages to even begin to explain what's been going on with me.*

*At least I'll get started and hopefully will be able to finish later. It's probably okay to write the word Guadalcanal now, since our unit has long since moved on from there. That's where I was wounded—nothing serious, but shrapnel landed me in an Army hospital in California, and then another one, where the docs saved my leg.*

*Can't say how grateful I am for that, every single day. I do still have a limp at times but not often. Then on my way back to my unit, I was in a truck accident. I had a bad shoulder injury, and amnesia for a while. I had no idea where I came from. Some men from Texas found me and long story short, my memory finally came back.*

*For weeks, a giant of a man named Jud and his buddy, L'il Wall, nursed me in a desert cabin. This fellow Jud—he knows things, and he knows you, I think.*

*When he and his buddy left to work in the mines, he said after the war I must visit Waco—the south side of town—Miss M's boarding house. Before that he had hardly spoken a word, but he said I need to go there because someone is waiting for me. Is that you? Do you know this guy?*

*Jud's parting words gave me plenty to puzzle over. What does he know that I don't?*

*I have to believe he's talking about you and have often*

*wondered where you are. I'm using the address Aunt Annie sent and hope this reaches you.*

*I will wait to hear from you. Please use my latest address on this envelope. It may sound strange, but it's a camp for enemy internees in the High Sierras.*

*I'm a guard here now, and probably will be till the war's over. One more thing I must say before I close. Through all of these experiences, I have thought of you over and over.*

*Thank you again for saving my life.*

*Your son always,*

*Jesse*

It was the *always* that undid me. But of course, *always*. Once a son, forever a son.

However, Miss M had more to teach me. She'd been with me when Jesse's letter came…handed it to me at the door after work one day. I started to tuck it in my pocket, but she had a fit.

"You've already waited forever—open it! Forget about the kitchen for once and enjoy this moment."

"Okay, but you come with me." I pulled her to the porch swing. Somehow, having a witness seemed right.

Before opening the letter, I took another few seconds, and regretted it right away. "What if…" I began, and Miss M's eyes widened.

"Don't you dare! Don't you *dare* doubt this after all the prayers I've prayed for you and Jesse! Can't you see the positive side of things and accept this as a gift?" By now, her normally ladylike cheeks flamed.

My gulp must've echoed down the porch. She was right, and I knew it. But chastising myself did nothing to change my ways. I needed a scolding from someone who knew me well and still cared about me. Someone who believed changing might still be possible.

"Go on, then. And hurry up!" She so rarely raised her voice, I almost went into shock.

So I read the letter aloud. Almost choked on *always*. Miss M let me have the first word.

"He wrote *always*."

"Of course he did."

"But I…"

Her eyes warned me to stop right there. "Kin, you must alter your way of thinking. Just because you've turned down one rutty road in your mind for a long time doesn't mean you have to keep on choosing that route."

She didn't have to say another word—all of a sudden, I remembered her childless state. She'd never had the gift of a son or daughter, not even one.

Yet she knew more about being a mother than I did. She acknowledged the depth of the bond between a mother and her child. Hearing her remind me made my chest hurt.

But she hadn't finished: "You have let shame smother your joy for so long. To protect Jesse, you sent him off to a safe place, but you still listen to those demons inside that say you did the wrong thing.

"He wrote, *Thank you for saving my life.* Don't you see? *That's* the road you must take from now on. Tell that other voice you've had enough of its lies—tell it to be quiet!

"Hasn't shame stolen enough of your life already? With your wonderful son wanting to see you, are you going to let it take even more?"

Like a child, I sat there sensing my chin pucker. Then I realized Miss M's was puckering too. She was paying her own price for speaking up. Still, we silently agreed. A choice had to be made when I sent Jesse to Annie, and I had managed to live with the terrible loneliness after he left.

A choice had to be made now, too. And only I could make the decision. Once again, she'd hit on the truth…a certainty hard to hear but conceived in love and wrapped with courage.

We said no more, but before Miss M went back inside, she

gave me a hug full of warmth, a gesture that said more than words. Oh, what great loss she had known with Elwyn's health and never having the chance to be a mother.

She could be living such a lonely life, but how did she react? She reached out to people like me every single day. Suddenly I saw her life through a larger scope. It was as if this house created a stage for her to meet people and provide what they needed.

Childless, she still knew the meaning of a mother's love.

Across the yard a dog barked, and a neighbor's big old Tom cat raced up the steps, pummeled the length of the porch and leaped off. Obviously, he knew this area well.

Judson had held this particular feline in low esteem and shooed him away many a time. The hound, a bit wiser than the feline, skipped the porch and raced across the yard to the next jumping place. A scuffle broke out, snarling and snapping— hopefully no eyes would be clawed out.

Meanwhile, the swing invited me to rest a minute more. Its slight sway reminded me of simple realities. Fights like this went on all of the time. Around the world with this war, and all across the country, everyone had battles to fight.

Some of them might be entirely unseen, but oh, so real. In fact, the inner, unadvertised skirmishes might take a greater toll than the overt ones.

From now on, I needed to claim new strength to say *no* to the barrage of cutting words so often whirling inside my head. Say *no* instead of letting them continually crush me. *No* to their dogged focus on the past.

And strength to say *yes*, too. To turn away from self-pity and say *yes* to my son. A resounding *yes* to now and to the future.

All because quiet, dignified Miss M cared enough to help me face reality.

"What addlepated idiot ever signed his name to these orders in the first place?" Major Zier threw down his pen and scraped back his chair.

A few feet away in the far north corner of the room, Jesse looked up while keeping his fingers moving. Today he had so much to do, and whatever conundrum the major tackled had nothing to do with him.

*Brrrl…whizz…brrrl…whizz…brrrl…whizz…brrrl.*

The Major was dialing his boss again. This occurred several times a week lately and though Jesse sympathized, he could only observe.

"Major Zier here. What's going on over there in your office? I keep getting these fouled-up papers—somebody doesn't know what they're doing!"

The voice on the other end of the line sounded relaxed and collected, which made the major's left heel bang on the floorboards even faster. *Rat-a-tat-tat-tat…*

After three more exchanges, louder each time, he smashed the receiver into its cradle. Jesse finished typing a paragraph and flipped back the return.

"Didja hear that?"

"No, Sir."

"He says, 'Just retype the report without the error and re-sign it. Honestly, that's the quickest way to fix this.' So that means a couple hours' more work for you, and where will we be? We still won't know if the next man up will sign off on this."

Not knowing how to respond, Jesse kept typing.

"Are you listening to me?"

"Sir? Yes. They think we should retype the report."

For the tenth time this morning, Major Zier lit a cigarette. "How're we ever gonna dig ourselves outta this paper mountain?" He gestured wildly to the table separating their desks, barely missing the light bulb swinging from the ceiling. With each pass, morning light from the east window caught on its gold casing, creating a *wink.*

"It gets bigger by the minute, right? And there's only so many fingers on your hands, exceptional as they are."

Jesse's shrug did nothing to mollify his boss. He might have suggested overtime but was already working fourteen-hour days. No other suitable reply occurred, so after stretching his fingers into the church-and-steeple Mama had taught him when he was little, he started the next paragraph.

Major Zier paced the office, coming within inches of Jesse's desk. Back and forth, back and forth. By now, his path showed on the gray and white linoleum. Finally, he stopped in front of a window looking out on a walkway between two units.

"I've got it! Betcha there's somebody in this camp who's typed their whole life and can help us out. Some internee…some woman…yeah. Some of 'em had to be secretaries before the war, doncha think?"

"I would think so, Sir."

He drummed his fingers on the windowsill. "Course, we'd have to watch out. Gotta remember this is all hush-hush and make sure nothin' top-secret gets into her pile."

He rushed to Jesse's desk, the flare of brilliance in his eyes. "But you could help sort it all, right?"

A nod sufficed—better let him ruminate on this some more. Everyone knew measures taken to solve hitches in Army work sometimes led to even more challenges.

But the Major had convinced himself. With a vengeance, he rubbed his cigarette stub in the ash tray.

"Never a problem without an answer, my daddy used to say. The Army sometimes makes me doubt that, but usually I come full circle."

"Sir. Your father sounds like a wise man."

Reaching for his cap, the major stopped short. "Oh, he's always saying something he thinks sounds bright. Sometimes he hits it, other times we have to shake our heads."

"So he's a guy who thinks out loud?"

"Maybe so. Anyway, I'm going to see what I can do about this, and right now." Major Zier grabbed his jacket and headed out into a bitter February wind.

Alone in the office for the first time in a while, Jesse stepped out to marvel at the mountain range to the east. Between Kings Canyon and Death Valley National Park, the Manzanar Relocation Center boasted a crude, U.S. Army-constructed campsite. In other words, something could go wrong at any time.

Today, some electrical workers scaled a light pole just across the way and swayed above the camp as they made repairs. Below them, rings of wire waited to be sent up the pole by their helpers. A wonder the light hadn't gone out yet, since this happened more than once a week, and high winds were often the culprit.

Down the road, people in winter wraps went about their daily errands. A few doors west, the newspaper editor entered his domain under a sign dripping with irony: *The Free Press*.

At first glance a visitor would think this *Anytown, USA*, except for the presence of uniformed Military Police. Manzanar offered schools, a hospital with real nurses, doctors, hundreds of babies born here since 1942, and churches where people worshipped, celebrated weddings and held funerals.

About ten thousand internees made their homes here, way bigger than any town in Aunt Annie's county. Ten thousand people who had been rounded up against their will, brought here by truck and told to make the best of it.

Who had named their newspaper *The Free Press?* The sarcasm struck deep. Jesse considered writing Miss Stewart with this perfect example for her Senior English class.

If a visitor took a closer look, they would see families assigned to shoddy military-style barracks. *Crammed into* was more like it. Living in Army shacks built of one thickness of pine planking covered with tarpaper sufficed for a GI, but these families included old folks and babies.

This high country froze in winter months, and these folks

had been allowed to bring a bare minimum of comforts from their homes. Besides that, most of them resided on the California coast, where winter brought rain and much milder temperatures, not snow and ice.

Until now, Jessie viewed this camp through one spectrum, but getting to know Miko made a vast difference. Even in their brief walk, he had learned so much. She could never again be just one more Japanese internee.

Early in life, Mama had taught him not to judge folks by their looks or their color. They'd been in a town at some type of celebration, and older boys were taunting a tribal man. Mama had pulled him aside and whispered, "We must never treat others like that." Most Americans had been taught this, he figured, but the war skewed their perspectives.

When the war ended, then what? Would we go on hating the Germans and Japanese forever?

Chapter Twenty-four

The office could hardly have held another desk, but Major Zier found room somehow. Jammed even further into his corner, Jesse attacked his first sorting task, and the pile on the new typist's desk quickly grew.

"Make sure there's nothin' anybody could use to inform a spy, all right? No references to operations here or the military anywhere else, no descriptions of specific tactics or mention of the Jap side of the war at all. You know what I mean—about like the instructions they gave you about writing home from the Pacific."

"Mmm," underneath his breath. Jesse added, "I'll do my best, Sir."

"Hold aside whatever's questionable, and I'll look through it. The rest will go to our new assistant. They've found us a woman—didn't I tell you? Used to work in an office as a stenographer or some such. They're doing a thorough background check, so it might be a week or so before she gets here."

Major Zier ran nervous fingers through his thinning hair. "And remember, her being here is all about work…just plain work, got it?"

"Yes, Sir. Work it is."

"Might seem like a waste of time to sort through all of this, but in the long run…" He glanced around at the hodge-podge of furniture over-filling the room. "Sure hope it helps. If it don't, I'm fresh outta ideas."

At this rate, the major's hair might not make it through the war. Besides rubbing his scalp, he also picked at a scab on the crest of his right ear when something made him anxious. And it seemed that recently, quite a few things had that effect. The first week Jesse joined him, he explained, "I was in the last war, and felt sure I should sign up for this one. Couldn't help myself—thought with my experience, they might send me to a training center to work with recruits.

"Been in road construction in-between but figured everything I've learned along the way might help." His shrug accompanied a heartfelt sigh. "I sure didn't plan on ending up in a place like this, but then, neither did you, right? So here we both are, and we'll make the best of it. At least we're doing something for the war effort, although my wife has her own thoughts on that subject."

"Sir?"

"Oh, nothing. She's back in Pennsylvania, without the least bit of accurate information."

At this mention of his family, Jesse maintained silence. Better to err on that side of things. Abraham Lincoln knew what he was about when he said, "Better to remain silent and be thought a fool than to speak and to remove all doubt."

Lincoln came to mind often these days, since the intact copy of *The War Years* Jesse had found in the library was keeping him up till all hours. Such a task Carl Sandburg undertook when he set out to research this complicated President—someone said Sandburg read over a thousand books in just his first year of research for the four-volume set.

What a convoluted era President Lincoln had to embrace. Such knotty problems involving millions of human lives, with so much at stake. All of that hatred between North and South—living in Kentucky, Aunt Annie had mentioned tinges of it still alive and well.

Some of those hill folks had grandfathers and great-uncles who fought for the South, and they weren't about to forget. During this present war, it seemed good to remember a time as thorny as our own.

The *War for Southern Independence,* as some Kentuckians still called it, had changed the face of the United States forever, and so would this war. Despising the Japs and Germans had roots in the deep past.

Jesse walked around his desk. Now, what could he do to keep from feeling hemmed in? Move his desk a little closer to the window? After a few minutes, he gave up. If anyone might feel trapped, it would be the new typist.

Maybe he'd finally accepted that he'd never rejoin his unit. He could honestly say that working here was better than being caught in an enemy ambush. And far better than languishing in a POW camp, either Japanese or German, where so many soldiers found themselves.

But for some reason, news reports had more to say about the war in Europe than in the Pacific. With the USAAF and RAF's all-out bombing of Germany's aviation industry and the Luftwaffe the third week of February, reporters spoke of nearly nothing else. British RAF bombers attacked aircraft, engine, and ball-bearing plants by night while the Eighth and Fifteenth Air Forces carried on the same program by day.

"Big Week," they called it, with four thousand heavy bomber sorties dropping more than twenty million pounds of bombs. The USAAF lost more than two hundred heavy bombers with over 2,500 casualties.

You could bet some of those aircrews who made it to the ground alive were captured and taken to POW camps deep in Germany or Poland. The thought brought an involuntary shiver. Who could complain about a cramped office safe in the High Sierras?

They would make the best of it, but the paperwork burgeoned with each passing week. Major Zier's smoking doubled, and that spot on his ear became a sore. If only this new helper would fit in well and be able to do the job.

One thing about it, they'd been so crazy busy that there hadn't been much time to think about Miko. At least not during the day.

At night, though, her voice came drifting into the barracks. The little he had heard her speak replayed in Jesse's mind like a spring breeze. What she said about a word in winter had the feel of poetry. Her blissful whisper in this windswept camp designed for isolation and punishment carried a message: beauty still exists. Beauty and hope.

Relief arrived in the form of Mrs. Sato, the new assistant. She had no Japanese blood but had been born in Thailand and married into her enemy-alien status. Besides her husband's heritage, his work as a deep-sea fisherman had alerted authorities that he might have more connections out on the Pacific than met the eye.

All of this Major Zier shared in confidence from the files, and knowing a little about her helped. A few days later when Mrs. Sato arrived, she mentioned none of this, of course.

With typical Asian dignity about personal matters and an expression as unfathomable as the Pacific's greatest depth, Mrs. Sato knocked on the office door. When Major Zier opened it, she announced only her name.

"Welcome, Mrs. Sato! Can't tell you how glad we are to have you step into this…" Major Zier swept his hand over the office, which looked as if some huge seagull had dropped piles of white paper everywhere.

"We've heard you've had office experience. We're trying to make order out of this paperwork and appreciate any help we can get."

She fingered the edge of her scarf as she studied the room. Her first impression remained known only to her.

The Major showed her the coat hooks and ushered her to her table. "For starters, I've made a pile of forms to be typed and folded in thirds into these envelopes. If you have any questions, ask either of us."

Noticing Jesse at his desk, he added, "Oh. Mrs. Sato, meet my assistant, Private Kline."

She bowed to Jesse, revealing a delicate trail that looked

like white ink dribbled on her hair just above the part line. He nodded back.

"Nice to meet you, Ma'am. There's extra paper over here when you run out, and some razor blades if you make an error."

With a nod, she hung her coat and took her seat. She perused everything on her table, the erasers, pencils and pens Jesse had placed there, along with a glass of water.

He went back to work, as did Major Zier. In minutes, Mrs. Sato clacked away on the Royal as if she had worked here forever.

Eager to please and an outstanding typist, she slipped right into her duties during the next days. Her speed put him to shame, and also to her credit, she rarely made a mistake.

At this point, sorting paperwork took up hours of Jesse's day. Sometimes, figuring out what information qualified as *safe* required research. Deliveries filled a share of the late morning and early afternoon, and he typed only two to four hours a day.

This new hire reduced fourteen-hour days to ten or twelve—something to celebrate. But where do you celebrate in a camp like this? For internees, with their natural contacts and networking, gatherings might be possible. For guards, though?

Going to the library more often, Jesse acquired a stack of books-in-progress or put them on his to-read pile. Since most of the MPs gravitated to their own kind, the evenings provided plenty of reading time.

Not a bad thing. That's how life had been back at Aunt Annie's, where the most commotion of an evening arose when a fox neared the hen house. After Beau and Pearly went to bed, Aunt Annie read to him, and in later years, if he had trouble sleeping, he pored over the classics in the family bookshelf.

After leaving Texas, it had taken a while for sleep to come easily. His chest hurt so, missing Mama, and Papa's accusing gaze often found him in the night. He hated to bother Aunt Annie when that menacing face lurked in the darkness, so *The Secret Garden*, *A Tale of Two Cities*, *The Hardy Boys*, and *Les Miserables* kept him company.

"Your Mama has always written about what a good reader you are, even as a little tyke, but now I can see for myself. She's so proud of you, Jesse!"

Some nights, he would pull out a notebook and write Mama secret letters…many of them he never sent. As in a journal, he detailed what was going on at school and at the farm. What had become of that notebook? Probably at the bottom of the old trunk Aunt Annie gave him for treasure-keeping.

One rainy Saturday, she pointed out the trunk and said, "This is yours now. Our grandmother—your mama's and mine—brought it from the Old Country aboard ship. If wood could talk, this trunk would tell you tales about the crossing from Liverpool to Ellis Island.

"Grandma brought her favorite books along, and some of them sit on my shelves right now. There's nothing I'm prouder of in the whole house."

So…despite Papa and having to leave Mama to join Annie and Winn's family, Jesse acquired a legacy of sorts. The trunk, for one thing, and books, plus a history with reading that both Mama and Aunt Annie shared.

After an hour in the world of *Les Miserables*, Jesse got up to walk around the barracks. Such a crisp early March night, but a few stars peeked through the clouds. On a night like this nearly a hundred years ago, Civil War soldiers would be reading *Les Miserables* by firelight.

In the distance, muffled lights shone from the other barracks. Thoughts of Kentucky meandered through Jesse's mind, such a quiet, back-country place to grow up.

He supposed it would be a perfect spot to settle down after the war. Doing what, he wasn't too sure, but getting a degree under the GI Bill seemed possible.

He could become a teacher like Mr. Somerset, teaching kids to type and keep business records. Or history maybe…

One light went off and flashed again a few seconds

later—probably meant something to somebody. Even with no idea when this war would be over, he couldn't help thinking about what to do afterwards.

The guys in his unit most likely enjoyed no such leisure. A pang ran through him at the thought of them still slugging it out, always with the grim reminder of an eventual Allied attack on the Japanese mainland.

Most military commanders accepted that the Japs would never give in. Each island's defenses convinced them of this, along with the growing number of *kamakazi* attacks. Nothing in the Pacific came without a struggle.

With each invasion, news reports claimed the Navy had gleaned valuable lessons for the next island, but it seemed each one had its own instruction to offer. And the reports could not disguise the terrible cost in human life.

Of course, Jesse had no idea where his unit had gotten to, but wherever it was, he ought to be there with them. They were his second home.

At this point, though, the Pacific war had taken on new dimensions.

After Pearl Harbor, the government proclaimed Italians and Germans enemy aliens too. By now, most everyone knew how Giuseppe Dimaggio, Joe's father, had been banned from working in San Francisco's coastal wharves in 1940.

Though he'd been living in the U.S. for forty years and over a million Italian-Americans were fighting with the Allies overseas, the government saw his kind as a threat. On Columbus Day, 1943, the President finally removed Italians from the enemy-alien list, but the war would have to end before the same would occur for the internees here.

What about Mrs. Sato and Miko's stories? He'd heard plenty of scuttlebutt among the guards about Japanese-Americans losing their fishing boats, homes, and land. Would they even have homes to return to after the war?

As far as Jesse knew, Miko had lost everyone but the older brothers she mentioned and Kenji. Her papers listed her as a nursing student in San Diego when the war began…would she continue studying afterward?

The weeks kept slipping by without any glimpse of her, but *one kind word can warm three months of winter* stayed with him. Hopefully that meant she wouldn't mind seeing him.

"Sure would be nice to talk with her again." The cool night received Jesse's plea, a prayer straight from his heart.

On Friday morning, Major Ziers always attended a meeting at the HQ building. A few weeks after Mrs. Sato started working, early in the morning, he asked Jesse to stay in the office until he returned.

"Just in case, you know. Don't want to take unnecessary chances, although Mrs. Sato has worked out fine thus far."

"Yes, Sir."

"You have any complaints about her?"

"No, not at all."

"Good. Well, see you sometime before noon, then."

As usual, Mrs. Sato had begun typing before her starting time. Her determined countenance and flying fingers created a music of their own that accompanied Jesse in his work.

But then the typing stopped. He glanced at Mrs. Sato, who sat quietly with her hands in her lap, watching him.

"Can I help you?"

She studied the door as if a malevolent might suddenly appear. Her deep sigh left Jesse concerned. But she said nothing.

"Ma'am? Mrs. Sato? What is it?"

Bowing her head, she squeezed her nose between her thumb and forefinger. Alarmed, Jesse slid his chair back.

"Please, tell me what is wrong?"

She pulled something from a pocket of her sweater—at least Jesse thought so. Nothing to see, but she made a fist with her left

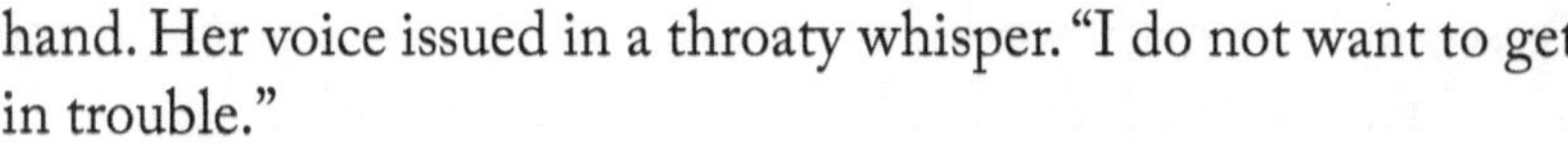

hand. Her voice issued in a throaty whisper. "I do not want to get in trouble."

"Ma'am?"

A tear lined her lashes.

"Ma'am, I can't imagine why you would get in trouble. You're doing a fine job here."

"It's…I have a message for you."

"A message?"

"Please. The Major…"

With no idea what else to do, Jesse stood and waited, hovering between her table and his desk. A nasty knot formed in his gut—something like what happened when enemy fire paused for an indefinite time.

A strange sensation descended, as if what happened next would change his life. The way he'd felt when he ran off to search for Uncle Winn after he didn't come home for supper, or his premonition just before he leaped out of the bus from the troop train at basic training.

Mrs. Sato let out a sharp breath. "Forgive me, but Miko Yoshida, my friend, asked me to deliver this to you. Please do not tell anyone." Mrs. Sato stumbled from her chair and thrust a damp folded paper into his hand.

"Miko? She's your friend? Why, I…"

Without thinking, Jesse unfolded the paper and read:

> *Hello Jesse Kline,*
> *I have been thinking about what you said. I wonder if we might write letters to each other? Also, I visit the library often, almost always on Monday and Thursday evenings. Perhaps we could meet there?*
> *Yours sincerely,*
> *Miko Yoshito*

Poor Mrs. Sato. Her hands shook as she awaited her fate.

Jesse couldn't help breaking into a grin. He patted her on the shoulder and tried to think how to handle this…what to say.

"Ma'am, you have done nothing wrong. Thank you. Thank you so much."

"But the Major…?" She twisted a wisp of hair that strayed from her victory roll.

"He will never know. This is not Major Ziers' concern. You don't need to worry. You have only helped your friend. As for me, I see your actions as very kind."

She wiped away a tear, so he handed her his handkerchief. "You have done your friend and me a very kind and brave favor."

Chapter Twenty-five

"Ma'am, have you read this little blue book?" Henry Darwin, the long-time occupant of Room Six, squatted before the refrigerator and called to Miss M.

"Absolutely. I don't think the seal is broken, because I checked it with a piece of paper, like it says on page 26. I couldn't pass the paper along the edge, so that isn't what's wrong. I looked at the gasket, too, but can't see that it's worn out."

"Hmm. Well, I cleaned the condenser, although you already had it spic and span. Only so many things can go wrong with these Frigidaires, y' know."

"So this is like solving a mystery?"

Henry scrabbled to his feet and scratched his head. "Maybe so. The motor don't need oil, since there's no belt." He studied the distance between the fridge and the big iron heating grate in the floor. "I wonder…just a thought, y' know…if it's sittin' too close to the hot air when the furnace is on, and to the oven."

Miss M, who had just lighted the oven and was about to bake a cake, put her hands on her hips. "Could that be it?"

"Might could. Another thing, the sun shines directly on this wall most of the afternoon, don't it?"

"Why, I suppose so. I've never noticed."

"Check tomorrow. If it does, we'll need to figure out another spot for the fridge, and I'll get somebody to help me move it after work tomorrow night." He dusted off his pants and left through the side door.

"Inventions sure make life easier, but they can also cause a person worry." Miss M opened the oven door and slid in the cake. "Of course, this would have to happen when it's hotter than blazes."

"But Henry sure seems to know what he's talking about, don't you think? I wonder if it is the sun, since this has never happened in winter."

"Good point—so far we haven't had to call a repairman. Remind me to watch tomorrow."

"I will, if I remember." I slit the tops of three pie crusts. Mine never turned out as professional-looking as Miss M's, but I enjoyed trying on my day off. Today I used peaches and apples straight from the trees out back.

"Talking about the heat reminds me of the summer of 1916—school had just let out for vacation, and the war hadn't started yet. My friends and I felt foot-loose and fancy-free until graduation day, even though most of us already had jobs.

"But in the evenings, we ran around downtown, and the night before Jesse Washington's lynching, we were all there at the courthouse. Oh, was it hot!"

"Jesse Washington?"

"Yes—you haven't heard of him? The Klan was there, all decked out, and I imagine the poor fellow never had a chance. The Klan was in cahoots with the law back then, and if they wanted a prisoner, they got him." Miss M scrubbed the counter with a rag before starting her potato peeling.

"He'd been convicted of a crime?"

"I'm not sure about *convicted.* Accused of raping and murdering his boss's wife over near Robinson. They said he confessed, but who knows? They chained him around the neck and dragged him out, stabbed and beat him while they paraded him through the streets. Then they castrated him right there in front of everybody."

"Glad I didn't live here then."

"Oh, people here were used to things like this, since McLennan County was a Klan hotbed. The crowd got involved. They cut off Jesse's fingers, soaked his body in oil and hung him over a fire.

For two hours, they raised and lowered him over the fire. My parents witnessed the beginning, but even Daddy had to leave after a while. Years before, his daddy, Grandpa McCain, had been a big somebody in the Klan."

"And your father wasn't a member?"

"Well…I wouldn't say that. Almost everybody joined at one time or another. Even some of the preachers in town, truth be told. If you didn't, you had hell to pay."

"*Whew.* So you watched all of this happen?"

"Part of it. Washington was only seventeen, my age. And our family knew some Negro friends of his, so we could only take so much." Miss M shook her head.

"Yet people got so excited, like when a carnival drove into town. A professional photographer took pictures of the body hanging over the fire, and somebody made postcards of the scene.

"A pretty dark part of Waco's past, although that photograph traveled to other cities and states, and word got around. Waco's reputation suffered, so people took note. I expect the main business owners got together to demand change, because within a few years, the lynchings stopped."

Waco had always had a wild reputation, according to Clyde, but since I came to town, I hadn't heard much. The Klan was alive and well in our little ranch town too. And Clyde had been one of them, I was pretty sure.

"I'm sure glad things like that have gone by the wayside for the most part, although you can be sure the Klan still lives and breathes. Hatred doesn't die easily." Miss M shook her head.

"Trouble is, no one will ever know for sure if Washington killed that woman or not. Even though they say he confessed, if you were a Negro back then, they considered you guilty. That was the law, more or less."

"Such a bleak story. I can't imagine how miserable it must have been for his family. Do they still live around here?"

"I've never heard. Hopefully they left, but it's hard to move far when you've got nothing to start with." Miss M's peeler had made a huge dent in her pile, and I found a paring knife to help.

"At least, since much of the nation saw those photos, everyone could see what things were like here. Nothing like disapproval to change behavior."

With the potatoes ready to boil, Miss M left, and while I waited to take out her cake and bake the pies, I leafed through her little blue refrigerator booklet.

*Wartime Suggestions to help you get the most out of your Refrigerator.*

*How to store food, how to make the most of the freezing compartment, what to do with food left over, how to get variety in lunch box sandwich spreads…peanut butter and honey, minced meat spread, mushroom filling, eggs and ham, olives and nuts.*

Someone put a lot of energy into compiling these recipes and typing them. If only the human race had a handy little blue booklet describing exactly what to do when things go wrong between nations.

In the meantime, war breaks out. And war, by its nature, creates barely believable circumstances.

Several times, Miss M had marveled over the way Judson found Jesse. We ran out of words to describe this stunning coincidence. How could Judson and his buddy have stumbled upon the precise road where Jesse had been thrown out of a truck?

Depending on the day, we reached various conclusions, each including divine guidance. The circumstance resembled the way Dr. Graham found me, lost and walking to I-didn't-know-where.

Always, we agree that the truck accident had kept Jesse off the battlefield, much as he wanted to return. "So what looks like a bad thing turns out to be the best that could have happened."

Who could disagree? It's fun to speculate, and sometimes I added a miraculous story I've heard at the hospital.

Now, my Jesse guards Japanese-Americans in a prison camp on American soil.

Just last week I heard of another camp called Crystal City, southwest of Waco. The government built this one for suspicious German-Americans.

Were most of these citizens even guilty of any crime? I had to wonder. At least we have done better during the past twenty years, and my son's generation, coming out of this horrendous war, will too. Surely they will shun anything that even hints at the terror the Klan forced Jesse Washington and others like him to endure.

The barracks' radio blared the nightly news, and for some reason, fewer men went out to play poker tonight. Concentrating on *Les Miserables* became harder than normal. The normally quiet room gave way to laughter, smoke, and a few arguments.

Jesse opened the window closest to his bed to stir up some fresh air. He kept thinking about President Lincoln and all the dilemmas he faced seventy-some years ago. Had he read Hugo's masterpiece during the war?

When someone turned on the news, the men got even louder, and Jesse gave up the fight. Instead, he imagined the scenes the reporter described.

> *June 23, 1944*
> *American GIs have spent this day hacking their way through French hedgerows to flush out long-ensconced German oppressors. Since the June 6 invasion of Northern France, their progress has been steady, but slow and costly.*
>
> *In fact, through French Resistance efforts, one ancient city, Bayeux, experienced liberation even before the Allies entered. Famous for its tapestry depicting the Norman Invasion of England in 1066, we can be sure its citizens await their treasure's return from hiding.*
>
> *Since that liberation, our troops have set several small*

*towns free, with more to come. We can only imagine the relief and joy of these French people, who have been controlled by the Reich for years.*

*Our GIs keep the ultimate goal in mind, to invade the German homeland and put an end to the war in Europe. At the same time, we turn toward the Pacific, where we wage war against a treacherous enemy entrenched in islands that must be taken for our cause to succeed.*

*A few days ago, our troops initiated the Battle for Saipan. This attack, another D-Day invasion like the recent one in Normandy, provoked stiff resistance. Of the four Second Marine Division's battalion commanders involved in the initial assault, none escaped injury or worse.*

*And why this particular island? Why now? Saipan must be taken for a strategic base from which to attack Japan directly. From Saipan, our long-range B-29 bombers can reach Tokyo. Enough said.*

*Operation Forager, as this invasion is otherwise known, breached the Japanese perimeter in the Mariana Islands. Carrier-based air raids began in February, destroying several fuel-storage facilities and most of the enemy warplanes on the island.*

*However, General Yoshitsugo Saito's thirty thousand soldiers still awaited our marines. On day one, Allied casualties topped three thousand, but despite the tenacious resistance, our men fought their way ashore.*

*During the past two days, our Navy's Fifth Fleet has engaged the enemy in the Battle of the Philippine Sea, winning complete victory. This success has deprived the Japanese of troop reinforcements, supplies, and air support.*

*With Saito's men withdrawn into the island's interior, our warriors continue the fight. One more island, but this one will prove absolutely essential to final victory over the Empire. So, with battles on every front, we continue to pray for and support our brave men in harm's way.*

*Now let us turn to…*

Jesse's own snore wakened him. Silence reigned in the barracks, except for the usual snoring, of course. He rolled over into a shaft of moonlight coming through the dirty window.

Here he was, safe and secure in the wilds of California. *Ha!* What a joke of a soldier he'd become—falling asleep in the middle of the war report.

If ever a library depicted the word *shabby*, this one did. A smattering of tall shelves, not enough by any means, and a few lower ones. A meager check-out desk manned by one of the internees, an older woman whom Jesse might have mistaken for Mrs. Sato. Just inside the entrance, she kept busy reading when not helping patrons.

Since he'd been here often enough, the woman hardly lifted an eyebrow at his entrance, and he proceeded to his usual haunt. This section, if one could call it that, revolved around historical titles, mostly biographies, with a few romance novels thrown in for good measure.

Thumbing through a book or two, he waited. Miko had said nothing about timing, except that she came here on Monday and Thursday evenings. With an eagerness he could scarcely pacify, he'd walked over as soon as mess ended.

What if Miko didn't arrive tonight? That would mean nothing, since she had used the word *usually*. A word might warm winter months, true, but a word might also complicate a situation. Ah well, he had nothing else to do anyhow, and reading here worked as well as in his bunk.

Situated in the back of a barracks, this trifling space gave insufficient deference to some of the authors represented. Always on the look-out for something by Hugo or Dickens, Jesse took advantage of his height.

Most patrons stood about Miko's size, so why had the

builders set the shelves so high? Probably had to do with the smallness of this obscure corner—no other way to go but *up*.

Clearly, comfort played no part in the planning of this camp. *Enemy aliens*…did they deserve comfort of any sort? As for light, the single glass bulb, like the one Major Zier kept hitting with his hand, could definitely use some help.

The general rule was to take no more books than you'd brought back, so tonight, three became Jesse's magic number. A copy of *A Tale of Two Cities* lurked way back on a shelf, so he grabbed it and found a seat near a wooden table much like the one in Aunt Annie's kitchen.

If he had to choose an object that signified the warmth of her home, the table would win. A round oak top set on a thick pedestal perfect for resting your feet, the piece had been marred by knives, ink, crayons, pencils and who-knew-what-else over the years. Here, everyone did their homework. Here Aunt Annie rolled out her pies and cut her ultra-high biscuits.

That got him to thinking…where did they find the furniture for this place? Setting it up and especially arranging for trucks to haul everything here had to be one chaotic job. And who donated the books, obviously second-hand?

Aunt Annie wrote about knitting like crazy, making sweaters and socks for soldiers, and said Mama was hard at work caring for wounded young men. Not too hard to imagine…she'd always had such a tender heart for the ranch animals.

Probably women like Annie and Mama had launched an effort to send books here like the fundraising drives back in Kentucky. *So many war bonds for so much…support the cause!*

Even though he'd read *A Tale* before and his English class discussed the themes, the fate of poor Doctor Manette during the French Revolution drew him in. Such a struggle between sanity and madness. Maybe like what some GIs now in Japanese or German POW camps would experience if they survived till the end of the war.

"A prominent moral threads through this story. *Things are not always as they seem.*" Miss Stewart said this back in their literature class. "Somebody who appears to be no-good and downright disreputable can transform into the most upright person imaginable. On the other hand, those who seem to seek justice may turn out to be cruel and bloodthirsty in the end."

Miss Stewart summarized another fitting theme for a warring time. "In this story, we visualize the power of forgiveness and the all-too human desire for revenge."

He could almost hear her now, hands clasping her literature text, intent on every word. Mr. Dickens had toured the United States more than once, and his book had gained popularity here. But the success of *Les Miserables* touched Jesse even more. The image of Civil War soldiers passing around sections to read by firelight highlighted its value. Hugo conveyed them to another time, far from their present distress.

Three years had passed since those easy high school days when studying words seemed like a game. At that time *revenge* meant little…now it had become a throbbing reality. Not a day passed without Jesse craving to get back to his unit to wipe out the enemy soldiers who killed Willie and Joe.

No doubt those Nips had become casualties by now, but it seemed only fair to take out other Japs in their place. For a moment, Willie's face appeared, and hatred for all things Japanese flooded in. Lately, this occurred less often, perhaps because nearly everyone in this camp seemed harmless and looked back at him through dark, earnest eyes.

An hour quickly passed, with the world of 1795 England and France inundating his consciousness. Dickens' magic transported him into such dire scenes…the dreaded Bastille, the overall state of Doctor Manette when he left that despicable dungeon, his daughter's shock at discovering him alive. Each passage took on life.

Then once again, Willie's countenance, in vivid color, paraded before his mind's eye. Just as he reached to his throat to stifle a familiar choking sensation, the door opened—and there stood Miko. Fresh-faced, eyes bright, and thoroughly Japanese.

She spotted him as he stumbled from his chair but held up her hand. As she returned her books and skirted the counter, her feet *tap-tapped* on rough floorboards toward the back shelves.

She had a plan. His heart pounding, Jesse meandered toward the back as if nothing extraordinary were happening. After all these weeks, were they truly coming so close?

Pretending to peruse the volumes before her, Miko gave a furtive glance his way. Then she held up her mittened hand. His gulp seemed louder than the door opening.

From her fingers jutted a folded paper. Close enough to see the lines of concern on her forehead, he stopped, and trance-like, reached for what she offered. For the merest moment, his hand nearly touched hers, enough to sense her warmth.

In a quick nod, her chin dipped into her red scarf as if to say, "Read it!"

So he did.

*"Hello Jesse Kline from Kentucky. If you leave soon, I will follow a few minutes later."*

She might have been his commanding officer. Saluting occurred to him, but instead he met her eyes. Dare he smile? But she already bent to one of the lower shelves. Time to go.

Oh…what had he done with Dickens? Dumbly, he returned to where he'd been sitting and retrieved the book. Except for the two of them and the clerk, only one other person had entered the library. Good.

Outside, evening shadows altered the harsh landscape. Gentle twilight shades, purple against a now-ochre desert, tempered its daytime brashness. The closest mountain peaks revealed themselves only as dark shapes hulking in the night.

For the most part, stillness had fallen over the camp. With no wind, night sounds came through…doors opening and shutting, people speaking to each other on the path ahead. Probably most children were asleep—perhaps Miko engaged Mrs. Sato to watch Kenji.

A quiet, dark world. Not so very different from the night Doctor Manette reunited with his daughter.

Imprisonment had a way of changing perceptions, amending certain viewpoints and converting what Jesse once took for granted. For certain, time had altered things. Or maybe it had changed *him*.

This evening, for nearly an hour, Dickens' detailed descriptions of the revolutionary era had worked in Jesse's mind. As with any good book, the effects lingered.

During this short wait for Miko, he stepped back and studied his situation. Here at Manzanar, captives surrounded him. Prisoners. And Miko qualified, though she had done nothing against the government. The injustice of her captivity wedged into Jesse's heart.

At the same moment, a wayward gust blustered into camp from the West, driving shivers down his back. Had she been wearing her navy wool coat tonight? He hardly recalled anything except the expression in her eyes. Taking the paper she held out, he had noted more meaning in them than in the whole world around him today.

Dark as coal, but so full of feeling, those beautiful eyes attested to her trust. Beyond that, so did her actions. She had taken her time, since they met before, considered what to do and risked meeting him here.

In deepening dusk, desert bareness received a soft shadow covering. Clothed now in curves and sweeps unseen during the day, the land appeared almost friendly. The difference revealed itself gradually in this time just before full dark.

As an American G.I. sworn to destroy our enemies, he guarded internees deemed enemy aliens. But along the pathway that eventually led back to the barracks, he still waited for one of them—a young woman named Miko.

Such an unlikely situation, from noticing her at the bus stop to that day they first spoke…from her poetic encouragement to the note Mrs. Sato had delivered… Anyone looking on would say this attraction would never amount to much.

But the truth was, nothing could have kept him away this evening. Again, Miss Stewart's words from way back in Kentucky informed Jesse. In both fiction and life, things are not always what they seem.

Chapter Twenty-six

"It shouldn't be so hard to write to Jesse. After all, he's my son!" I'd been at the dining room table for half an hour, starting a letter and crossing out every other word, starting again…but nothing sounded right.

Miss M had gone off to do the week's shopping, and the house sat so silent, I figured now would be the ideal time. I kept putting this off, for some reason. Hearing from Jesse had been a dream come true, but sending him a reply had turned into hard labor.

"It's because you're so wound up in him, Kin." Helen's encouragement buoyed me yesterday as we walked from a long day of bandaging and bathing and whispering words of hope to boys lying in the ward.

"And you two have been separated for so long…maybe it would help if you just keep it simple. Like three short paragraphs."

I must have looked interested, because she continued. "Something like, I'm so glad you wrote me, and can hardly believe you'll be coming here. I work in a hospital and do a lot of overtime, so I'll save up to take time off. I've already asked. Just let me know your plans, okay?

"Then you can ask what it's like at that camp. Say you hadn't heard places like that existed. How many people does he guard? Say you'd like to hear more.

"That would be enough, but you could tell him about your nursing courses and that you've almost completed your R. N. degree. If all else fails, you could ask about the weather in the Sierras."

She made it sound so straightforward, and at the time I felt invigorated. Tomorrow I'd get that letter ready to go!

Most of what she said stuck with me, so I started again and followed her outline. At the end, I wrote:

> *I haven't heard from Annie since Beau signed up for service. I'm sure she's waiting to see where the Navy sends him. It must be lonely for her and Pearl now.*
>
> *Some day when the war ends, I hope we can all get together again.*
>
> *Thank you so much for staying in touch.*
>
> *Love you always,*
>
> *Mom*

There. I did it! The clock showed only twenty minutes had passed but following Helen's guidance had made things easier. Before I could change my mind, I folded and sealed the letter, stamped it, and walked it to the post office.

I hadn't been there for months—on weekday mornings, the mailman usually took our letters from the mailbox out front. Seeing so many workers scurrying around on a Saturday reminded me that other occupations had to work overtime, too.

The rush of voices coming from the back room sounded a lot like the hospital. Everyone intent on a mission, all-hands-on-deck, as they say, to speed the U.S. Mail on its way to our boys 'over there.' Those letters meant so much to each recipient, like golden chains connecting far-away loved ones to their families.

My job, on the other end of all this, tied up the loose ends of lives torn apart by the war. Doctor Graham literally tied up some of those ends in surgery, but so much remained. Each serviceman entered our wards with unique needs.

Helen and I, with a raft of new nurses, worked to make sure they stayed put in their beds to recover. For some, that became quite a challenge. One guy insisted on traipsing the hallways

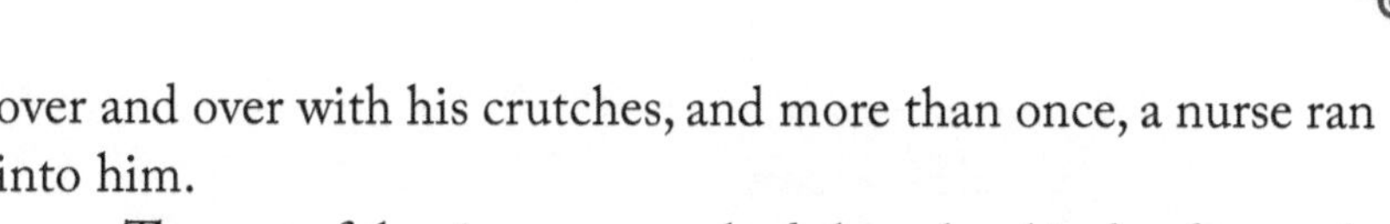

over and over with his crutches, and more than once, a nurse ran into him.

The rest of the time, we soothed the other kinds of wounds they bore. These, no one could see, and if they felt comfortable enough to talk a little about them, we felt we'd won a medal.

Turning a corner near home, I almost crashed into a group of boys on their way to a sandlot baseball game. A couple of them held ragged leather mitts, one dragged a bat, and they all chattered about their game.

Had Jesse ever played with other boys like this? Certainly not when we lived on the ranch, but in Kentucky? *Yes,* I thought, *with Annie's family and their neighbor children.*

"And you gave him that chance."

This voice taunted other messages that normally rose from deep within. "*You* gave him that chance."

Yes. I did—what a concept to savor. Now, my grown-up boy wanted to see me, wanted to hear from me, wanted to come here. And oh, how I longed for him!

All at once, a rare afternoon breeze shook the cottonwood branches. The sun caressed my shoulders like a benediction. One day, Jesse would be coming back to me! I pinched my wrist.

"It's really true. Jesse, oh my Jesse!"

Keeping my mind and body busy worked most of the time, made it possible to force this excruciating desire way down inside. In this way, I could function without uncontrollable emotion taking over.

But today, I let loose and ran down the path as far as I could. Like a woman obsessed, I ran and cried and laughed. Nearer home, an old tune erupted.

The song? Why, an old Kentucky melody from childhood. The words sprang from the past, somewhere deep down, about Kentucky hills, about lush grass and stretches of woodland. And hope.

*I'll hold you close.*
*You'll cling to me.*

*Whate'er may come,*
*Where'er we roam,*
*We shan't forget*
*Our sweet old home in*
*Ken…tuck…ee."*

*April 1945*

Clanging bells could have several meanings, so you had to wait until the source clarified. But on such a hot afternoon in the stifling office, Jesse's curiosity peaked. Mrs. Sato gave no sign of noticing, and the Major, yelling into his phone, probably didn't even hear them.

One whiff of outside air would have alerted anyone…fire. Uncle Winn's instructions for discerning its origin would have served well, had any trees grown here. But only mesquite and other smaller bushes and plants had the tenacity to survive.

After what seemed eons, a small plume of smoke rose from the southeast side of camp…the direction of the school. Jesse backed into the office and made a sign to Major Zier, who wiggled a nonchalant eyebrow as if he had bothered to tell him nature was calling.

Jesse took out for the school as if a battle's outcome depended on getting there. On this sultry afternoon, the camp came to life slowly, but as he ran, signs increased that others were thinking like him.

Somewhere, a driver gunned a truck engine for all it was worth. The vehicle slowed, ground gears at a turn—most likely headed toward the huge water tanks to the east of camp.

At times like this, instructions from Uncle Winn often surfaced. He tried to cover every possible situation that might occur in his children's lives.

"You can gauge a fire's intensity and direction by the degree of damage to fuel. It's really simple. Vertical objects like trees will burn more on the side of the approach, so the most damaged side faces toward the fire."

A bit further, the cindery smell became evident. Burning wood, for sure, not the powder-laden metallic odor that lingered even days after a battle.

Now, close to the schoolyard where he'd first met Kenji, the smoke increased. After his first walk home with Miko some weeks ago, and several similar treks from the library to the edge of the women's barracks' property, he understood why the boy meant so much to her.

Her baby brother, born late into the family, could have been her child, and when their mother died, Miko promised to care for him. Then here, at the camp, she and Kenji also lost their father. With two older brothers, one practicing law in California before the raids of '41 and '42, the other serving in the European theater, Kenji meant everything to Miko.

As she said, "You see a child like all of the others, but my whole world revolves around Kenji. He will grow up to make a big difference in this world, to make my parents proud."

"I'm sure he will. If my mother had believed one child didn't matter that much, she might not have risked her life to save me."

"She saved you?"

"Yes. My father lost his self-control when he drank too much, and one night, he almost killed me. The next morning, Mama put me on a train from Texas to her sister's house in Kentucky."

Even as smoke swirled from the schoolhouse chimney and Jesse raced forward down a steep hill, he recalled how cleansing that talk had been, like the one with the nurse aboard ship. But when he mentioned Mama to Miko, it seemed as if the barred doors of his heart flew open.

Telling her about his father's brutality, and how his mother had stepped in, worked a sort of magic in his soul. He couldn't put it into words, but he could see better, even hear more clearly after that. His desire to reunite with Mama only intensified.

As he gained on the school building, with a ramshackle fire engine pumping nearby, one goal claimed him.

Kenji might be inside—he must save this precious child.

Officers would keep family members away from here—already, they'd constructed a barricade on the side from which Miko would arrive. To cross to the other side, situated on a high rise, would take at least a quarter hour on foot, and he doubted the authorities would allow it, anyway.

He could almost see the tears glinting in those enormous, beautiful eyes and hear the throb in Miko's voice. She simply must not lose Kenji.

"You! Grab this hose while I try to get another one going."

Jesse obeyed the other guard who took charge and put his full strength into manning the heavy, pulsing rubber pipe. Then, from the corner of his eye, he spied a speck of red in the schoolyard. Even though winter had fled, for the most part, this scarf still encircled the boy's neck.

He'd asked Miko about this, and she said the scarf belonged to their father and had become a symbol, like a blanket to a baby. When she hid it away, Kenji asked for it as she dressed him for school. What harm could it do?

Indeed. Today, this sight of scarlet set Jesse's heart afire. He'd been praying for a way to know Kenji was safe. And there he stood, in a far corner of the schoolyard with his teacher and the other children, all aghast at the flaming building.

The impulse to run to him nearly overcame Jesse, but he'd been given a vital task. The other guard had disentangled a second hose and stood ten feet away, spraying water in a steady stream. Between the two of them, little progress had been made.

And then another truck lurched to a halt on the school's other side. Two guards leaped out. Another two hoses went to work and the fire began to cough and sputter rather than rage and flare.

"We've done it!" Jesse's partner moved forward into the yard to douse the conflagration from closer range.

"Yeah. Hope all the kids got out okay."

"Oh, I think so. But keep in mind, they're still the enemy."

"These little kids? You really believe that?"

"Of course, don't you?"

"They don't even know what the war's about. Can't blame them for the mess the world's gotten itself into."

"Hmm." The other fellow kept working, and so did Jesse. But when another guard came along and offered to relieve him, he started toward those priceless little people still hovering a distance behind the school with their teacher.

He hadn't gone far when he noticed a group of internees near the fence, a swarm of bees against the high desert's barrenness. Their agitation showed in talking more than normal and gesturing toward the clump of students.

Standing in the strong wind, several held handkerchiefs to their noses. Before Jesse could pick out Miko in the crowd, a woman ran along the fence toward him. Now her fingers clutched the wire fence, her eyes red and swollen—Miko.

"You will find Kenji?"

"I see him, thanks to his scarf." Jesse's answer came out in a pant. "Maybe they'll let me bring him to you."

"Oh, Jesse!"

Two succinct, sober words, but oh, what they ignited! Contorted with worry, Miko's expression reminded him how dear she had become. He would do anything—absolutely anything within his power—to smooth the deep wrinkles slicing her lovely forehead.

> *Dear Sis,*
>
> *I can only manage a note today. We've heard some news about Beau. His ship has been on dangerous missions in the Pacific Theater. His business education teacher helped us piece this much together since Beau's letters have so much crossed out that they tell us almost nothing.*
>
> *Yesterday a telegram came saying he's missing in action. I don't know what to do, Kin, and can't think of anything besides praying. I know you will, too.*

*Mr. Somerset is keeping in touch with the Red Cross for us. That helps a lot. Our boys have always been favorites of his, so I know he'll leave no stone unturned.*

*It's just Pearly and me rattling around this big old house now, and she's growing up so fast. She looks a lot like you when you were her age.*

*Trey joined the Navy, too, so his wife and children moved in with her parents in Indianapolis for the duration. Polly and her family have moved to Alabama, where her husband has been hired to supervise factory workers.*

*Owen works in San Antonio now, as a civilian attached to the base there. Then there's Thomas…the last I heard, his unit was headed across France toward Germany. I hate to even think of him over there!*

*Honestly, I've been thinking of moving closer to you. There would be just too much sorrow in this place if we should lose Beau or Thomas. My whole family has scattered hither and yon.*

*I imagine there's not much available housing in Waco, like a lot of places. Is that true? Polly says that's how it is in Alabama, though she'd like us to move down there.*

*Enough for now. I miss you, Kin, more than ever.*
*Love always,*
*Annie*

Astounded, I set Annie's letter in my apron pocket and hurried to help Miss M with supper. Annie truly wanted to move here? Why, I…

As Miss M and I stacked platters with chicken and filled bowls with string beans and mashed potatoes, I barely breathed. Something about Annie wanting to come here, wanting to be with me, opened an unfathomable inner chasm.

Annie, the bridge to Mama…to all of the past before I married Clyde. My big sis, who helped care for me when Mama set off from home—she wanted to live near me? The thought produced almost more emotion than Jesse's letter about returning here after the war. What did all of this mean?

Somehow, I held my feelings at bay until Miss M and I washed the dishes and set the kitchen to rights. She seemed extra quiet tonight, or extra tired, so I went upstairs to my room.

In one of the southwest windows, the rows of medicine jars I'd been collecting from the hospital, mostly green and yellow and gold, cheered me as always. Nothing like sunshine through glass to brighten a room as the day wanes.

Without really intending to, I'd gathered quite the collection from trash cans in the wards, so many that the evening janitor had noticed me carrying them home. I'd been surprised when he offered to help.

"You want just these three colors? I kin pick 'em out when I spy 'em and save 'em for y'."

"Why, thank you," I'd said, only then realizing someone had noticed. With no specific idea how to use them, I washed and dried the bottles on the weekends.

At first, I kept them in a box beneath my bed, but then one evening, inspiration struck. Why not let them play with the light, like the leaded stained-glass windows in the hallway and down in the dining room? Often at the hospital, these bottles still reminded me of the magic that one small bottle had worked for me as I fled the ranch.

My rows had grown until they filled nearly the bottom half of the window. Sitting on my bed with them filtering light my way, I pulled out Annie's letter. With so many people in her life, why should she choose me out of them all?

I didn't know, but something in my chest eased. In a primal way, Annie represented life—my life from its very beginnings. She and I shared the same parents, the same losses, the same memories. She knew what I felt when I recalled Mama—Mama's voice, her touch, her scent, her very being.

Even my sparse memories of Kentucky, Annie understood. When a whiff from a certain tree or flower took me back, I could count on it affecting her the same. Way back then, she probably took a turn at rocking me to sleep herself.

Like no one else on earth, she *knew* me, knew my moorings and all about my childhood silliness. She recalled my growing up years, and we had lived far apart for far too long.

My bottles made a final mosaic of the day, multiplying sunlight into a hundred small spectacles before my eyes. Remembering the glass bottle and the contents that sustained me on my journey, I clutched Annie's letter and found my pillow. Sleep overtook me, such a healing, strong, all-embracing sleep.

When I wakened at the sound of Miss M next door, starting a new day, I knew exactly what to write Annie. Exactly the sentiment Miss M echoed as we worked in the kitchen.

*Oh, do come! Please come! We have room for you. We have colleges…we have everything you need.*

Chapter Twenty-seven

"Some of the parents are over there." Jesse pointed Kenji's teacher toward the serpentine fence where Miko and the other parents clung to each other. On enough of a hill that they could see everything, yet not get near their children, his heart went out to them.

"They must be terrified. I think it might be safer to take the students there. The building will keep smoldering for some time, and this smoke can't be good for them." As if to support his opinion, some of the children coughed or cleared their throats.

"Do you have authorization?"

"No. I'm Private Kline. I work in Major Ziers' office."

Her shrug displayed her exhaustion. "I have no authorization for keeping them here, either."

"It can't be harmful to move them away from the smoke, can it? And if other parents arrive, they can still spot their children as we're walking."

Owl-necked, she glanced all around. "And if the bus comes?"

"We can hail the driver from there—it's right along the road. No use holding the children here, so close to the scene."

Her terse nod implied all that lay at stake. Young children in danger, parents aghast with worry.

So they started out, a gaggle holding onto the teacher's skirt, older students taking the hands of the youngest. Just as Jesse started to search for Kenji, the child ran to him and tugged at his jacket. He held up his arms and Jesse squatted down.

"Remember me?"

"Yes. You saw my tarantula."

"I sure did. Want a ride, buddy?"

Kenji nodded, so Jesse scooped him up. Such a light load, like carrying a twenty-five-pound sack of flour.

"Put your arms around my neck, okay?"

Kenji obeyed and oh, the warm rush! Having him snuggle in felt right.

"The fire…"

"Yes. There sure is a fire."

"…came so fast." The words trembled out on shaky breath.

"That sounds scary."

Kenji burrowed into Jesse's chest.

"But you're safe now. I won't let anything happen to you."

A tiny nod. A muffled sniff. Kenji's neck-hold tightened.

A river of emotion engulfed Jesse. A few times, he'd carried Pearly home when she wandered along with him and Beau to the creek. On the way back, she always wore herself out and begged her big cousin for a ride.

But Kenji's distress ran much deeper than everyday weariness. He'd been afraid for his life and with good reason. Jesse gathered him even closer, if that were possible. This little fellow needed human touch…he needed Miko.

The fire's scent rode the wind, adding to the smoke trapped in Kenji's clothing. Somewhere along the way, the children spotted their parents, and their teacher encouraged them to hurry. Jesse had meant to ask her name, but…

From a narrow-leafed cottonwood, rare in this area, a conspiracy of ravens cawed their contempt. As Mama used to say, "There's a reason someone named them a *conspiracy*. Some folks call them an *unkindness*, too."

These massive winged creatures, stony-eyed and shiny blue-black, had always sent trepidation up Jesse's spine, but not today. As they passed directly under the tree, Kenji trembled at their raucous caws.

"It's okay, it's okay. They won't hurt us. Maybe in their own way, they're cheering us on."

Several other vehicles bore down on the scene now, and from the school rose firefighters' shouts. An investigation would surely begin soon—the Army would see to it.

But right now, only one thing mattered—the well-being of this peerless small person in Jesse's arms. Though the entire journey amounted to perhaps ten minutes, each step of the incline emphasized a solitary goal.

*Get Kenji to Miko.*

Her quietness would banish the boy's fears. Jesse could already see her obsidian eyes fill with tears at the sight of her baby brother—such a deep love they shared.

Kenji's breath grew more regular, and even as the way steepened, the sound of his heartbeat so close to Jesse's created an incomparable truth. Two heartbeats nearly entwined…what could a man exchange for such a treasure?

This boy's breath, now in sync with his…how could anyone place a value on this sensation? Given the choice, except for handing Kenji over to Miko, Jesse might never have let go.

Looking back from July's stifling heat, this had been a spring of headlines. First President Roosevelt's death on April twelfth, after such a long, long fight, both the war and the President's battle with disease. Then the Allies announced the end of the war in Europe on the Eastern Front. The Third Reich's Unconditional Surrender on May 7—the news reports declared this fact.

Across the nation, joy and disbelief became bedfellows. Could the war truly, truly be over?

Surely, the government would be closing down that camp in California soon, although technically the Japanese were still enemies. When it did close, would Jesse come straight here?

I re-read his letters, the latest one hinting about a new friend he had made. He described a little Japanese-American boy, bright-eyed, intelligent, and well-mannered. The child had obviously won his heart. Later, like a good storyteller, Jesse added more about the child's older sister.

Would Miss M's house be receiving three new occupants instead of one? A mixed marriage would be tough these days. With every report of more bloody island battles *en route* to final victory in the Japanese homeland, hatred of the Japanese increased even more.

From the moment Admiral Yamamoto succeeded in the horrendous attack at Pearl Harbor, he had been classed with Hitler. The *yellow peril* became evil incarnate. Now, that theater of the war dragged on, and more of our boys died.

What a celebration there had been around the country about a week after the President's death when some Navy pilots intercepted Yamamoto's plane on his way to encourage his men somewhere in the Pacific! To think, our troops had avenged the deaths of so many Americans caught off-guard in 1941!

Besides this, tales of terrible conditions in Jap POW camps kept growing. Once the soldiers from the Bataan camp in the Philippines were liberated, word got around. The Japanese were inhumane, capable of atrocious treatment. Who could say *Jap* without wanting to spit?

The depth of this revulsion could not vanish any time soon. At the same time, I was learning more about Jesse as a man. He had been through so much during the war—and as a child—I could easily visualize him handling just about anything.

Now that some airfields were already closed, with others being made into airports, things had changed so rapidly here. Companies needed workers for dismantling and renovating, but thousands of men would be returning, each one searching for reliable labor.

If Jesse found a good job with someone like Doctor Graham in charge, what could stop him? On the other hand, I quietly hoped he would use the GI Bill of Rights President Roosevelt signed into law last year—a perfect opportunity to make up for missing part of his last year of high school.

All of this conjecture got me nowhere, and I knew it. But I was born to speculate. When I admitted this to Helen, she giggled. "I guess somebody's gotta do it. But don't you sometimes just want an empty brain?"

"Absolutely! But it's not possible, so I'm stuck." We'd taken a Saturday afternoon to go to a movie. "And I bet watching this movie won't help one bit."

"Oh, come on! What's a little murder and mayhem—I've heard this is Joan Crawford's all-time best performance."

"Me too. But I'm just saying…you know how my mind works." Our discussion took place while waiting for tickets. On the way home, the movie's intrigue still gripped me. I could think of nothing else.

"See? It took your mind off all of your questions about Jesse."

"True. But now I'm thinking about Joan's daughter killing that fellow who rejected her."

"Me, too, but that's the trick, Kin. It's just a movie."

"Right." Just a movie, but closer than Helen could know to some of my worst memories.

"How about I treat you to an ice cream?"

Soon we were licking rich chocolate and feeling like school-girls. Well, Helen, anyhow.

"It's so nice to get out. I feel like I've shed ten years."

"Yes…relaxing, even though tomorrow, we'll be…"

"No! We're not going to mention the hospital—we agreed, remember?"

We took our time window shopping and making our way home. People's faces seemed brighter since May eighth. On that day, there'd been an End of War festival in the streets, but Helen and I had been on duty.

Still, Doctor Graham and Rosita folded paper hats that he passed out in the wards. He turned up the radio all day so we could hear reports of the huge gatherings in Times Square and elsewhere. After that, patients started talking more about going home, more about what lay ahead.

Dr. Graham even made a short speech. "With the war so heavy on everyone's mind for so long, it's time to turn a corner. We've come through a dark time, and for those in the Pacific, it's not over yet. But soon it will be. Congratulations, everyone, for we've all played a part."

Helen and I said good-bye at our usual spot, and when I got home, Miss M was deep into preparing the evening meal. "Tell me all about the movie."

Perspiration spired down her face, and I felt guilty for leaving her with all the work. As usual, she read my mind.

"Now, don't feel guilty. Next week, I might go to the movies myself. They say this one is so good, but I really like Loretta Young. Maybe I'll wait for *Along Came Jones.*"

Then she slapped her forehead. "Oh, I nearly forgot. A letter came for you. Go read it—it's in on the piano."

From Annie…but awfully thin. Usually she filled three or four pages. I tapped the edge on the piano top, as if that action might change something, for the heaviness I'd felt when Annie first wrote about Beau going missing descended like a heavy mist.

*July 31, 1945*
*Dear Sis,*

*Seventeen years. That's the time Beau received here on earth…and barely, with his birthday just a couple of weeks ago. We'll have a funeral for him next week, along with several other boys whose families have heard the same news.*

*This time, the telegram felt like fuzz in my fingers, as if it would disintegrate any second. Mr. Somerset came along with the deliveryman. I don't know how he arranged that, but I couldn't have been more grateful to see him.*

*We women are strong, that's for sure, but something about*

*having him there to keep me from falling meant so much. He stayed until Pearly got home from school, helped me tell her and did the chores for us.*

*By then our neighbors heard the news and came over. Even though there's nothing anyone can say, it helped to have Marie set to work in the kitchen to feed everybody and Elmer offer to do the chores for a few days.*

*No word about how Beau died, but an enemy submarine sank the USS Indianapolis after the ship delivered something vital to the war. Mr. Somerset is betting it was a bomb. What I hear about shipwrecks makes me not want to know the details.*

*I can only hope Beau was spared fighting sharks in the ocean. Mr. Somerset found out that of nine hundred sailors who survived at first, only three hundred made it through until they were rescued.*

*Why, oh why, did I sign for him to go so young? I'll be asking myself this to my dying day. Why, why, why?*

*Now Pearly and I really do wander around this place. The rooms seem like strangers. Honestly, like I mentioned before, as soon as she graduates, I'm ready to move somewhere else.*

*Tell me about Waco. Would it be possible to find a small house there if I sold the farm? I could work in a store or bake goods for folks or do something else to put Pearly through college. And we should have extra money left from the farm sale, too.*

*You do have colleges nearby, right? Pearly has always wanted to become a teacher, so I want to be sure she has a chance. Polly says they're staying in Alabama and we should come there, but something about Texas is calling to me.*

*You and I have been away from each other so long. Maybe we can take care of each other in our old age. Please tell me honestly what you think.*

*For now, this is all.*

*Love,*

*Annie*

*P.S. Would you please let Jesse know about Beau? I don't have the heart to write him.*

*August 15, 1945*

On second floor, Dr. Graham turned the radio on so loud that Rosita heard it from the kitchen and ran up to check on things. Seeing them together under any circumstances always thrilled me.

Just recently I'd heard their love story, and with *quick-start* romances all around us due to the war, what a joy to hear about one that came later in life for both of them. The closest I could figure, their acquaintance began somewhere around the time Dr. Graham gave me the most consequential ride of my life.

Of course, it would be many months before I started working at the hospital, so by that time, they were well ensconced as a couple. Dr. Graham, a settled bachelor, had finally realized the love of his life waited for him every morning at work. He entered the hospital through the back door of the kitchen, with Rosita always there to greet him.

Married when she was young and having recently lost her son, Rosita kept her love for Doc under wraps until he made the discovery. Her old-fashioned, long-suffering attitude set her apart… she knew some things were worth the waiting.

I could picture Rosita early every morning, way before dawn, opening up the kitchen to create fresh pie crusts, biscuits, and her top-of-the-line homemade bread for the patients and staff. Someone told me once that if the only reason to have taken a hospital job would have been the food, it might have been enough to persuade them.

Each day, somewhere between deliverymen, Doctor Graham arrived, hung his hat and coat on the hook just inside the door, and bade her good morning. He might have shared a word about the weather, but not much else.

Throughout the morning, the promise of hot buttered bread

drew him back. Their romance began a few years back just before Christmas when he came for bread and noticed Rosita more than usual.

She looked troubled. He felt certain she needed help with something, and when he inquired, she told him she worried about the children in her neighborhood missing out on Christmas. So many parents and grandparents worked nearly round-the-clock in the war effort, who would prepare *La Posada* for them this year?

He offered to help her with the meal and she accepted. As simple as that, and voila! A love story developed. Better yet, a Christmas one. So today, even though they spoke only a few words to each other when Rosita came to the second floor, the love between them shone out to Helen and me.

After Rosita left, Helen whispered, "Such a lovely couple, don't you think?"

My reply issued from the depths of a grateful heart. "The very best."

Doc turned the radio so loud because today was *The Day* we had long awaited. We couldn't get enough of the reports.

> *The final surrender papers will be signed in a couple of weeks, but today will forever stand as a memorial day to the end of the war in the Pacific. After the bombings of Hiroshima and Nagasaki on the sixth and ninth of this month, we knew this moment would finally arrive.*
>
> *Still, it's as if the world has suddenly halted its flow in one direction and changed course in a rather abrupt turnaround. Though we have longed for this turn of events, we need time to take them in and fully appreciate what has occurred.*
>
> *More than four years at war…four long years of sacrifice for our nation. Seemingly endless years of leaning into the nightly news, hoping for word of loved ones far away. Fifty months of grief…an unbroken season of loss.*
>
> *The stories that arise from this war will go on and on, for*

*its evil has been unparalleled. Its malicious hand has touched nearly every corner of the known earth, and shattered lives everywhere.*

*So we pause to take in the news today. We relish the scent and taste and touch of victory at last. Our young people have risen to the challenge and in the rising, their generation has forfeited much.*

*But the Japanese Empire has finally signed an unconditional surrender. This weary old world now stoops to pick up the pieces and find its way to peace once more.*

*Personally, I must say that meeting with you here has filled and energized me in ways impossible to explain. Perhaps later, words will come.*

*But for now, those of us in the news media salute all of you who have so bravely weathered this catastrophic period. We share our fondest hopes that no other scourge like this will ever return to alter our lives and loves.*

"It's over!" One of Jesse's bunkmates switched off the radio. "I suppose we ought to raise a glass, but I'm too tired tonight. How 'bout you?"

"Agreed. There'll be plenty of time to celebrate tomorrow."

"Those in the know have already been talking about dismantling this camp. Guess that'll be the next thing."

"Yeah." Jesse put the letter from Mama he'd been reading on the table beside his bed. Such a lot of change today, some of it the kind that made you sick to your stomach.

"The war is over, but Beau…" This, he whispered to himself as he lay down. "Poor Beau. So close to the end of this mess."

Someone turned out the lights, so he sought comfort in his pillow. Mama'd had an awful time writing him the news, she said, but Aunt Annie just wasn't up to it. He could imagine how crushed she must be.

Hopefully, Thomas would make it home safe from

Germany—losing one son was far more than enough. With her family all over the country now, Mama said Annie was considering selling the farm and moving to Texas.

*Wouldn't that be something?* Jesse's next thoughts circled around Miko and Kenji. Would she go back to the California coast where their home had been confiscated? How could one go about retrieving property lost to the government, or would that even be possible?

Maybe her brother could help. Or maybe she never wanted to see California again.

"Where are you going when we leave here?" The question rose from the bed next to Jesse's.

"I'm not sure. I've got family, but they're all over the place now."

"Yeah, me too."

This would be a rough night for sleeping. The clock ticked away the hours, with various scenarios arising. Some memories from times with Beau surfaced. Had this younger cousin died instantly or been one of those sailors fighting the oil-slick sea water for days?

But always Jesse's thoughts returned to Miko. Would Mama agree with him taking her and Kenji to Texas? But first things first—would Miko go with him?

They'd become so much closer since the fire—not close enough to show outward signs, of course. Last April, another guard had been dismissed for spending time with an internee. Would those two get together again now?

No one must notice him and Miko, not yet. But yet, Jesse knew he didn't want to live without her.

He had spoken with that guard before he left, and his parting statement still rang. "I didn't come here to get a girlfriend, that's for sure. But she got sick in the middle of the night, and I took her to the hospital. Then…well, we just kept running into each other. I know it'll be rough if we ever marry—people won't accept her back home. But how do you deny what's happening inside?"

Keeping his own secret, Jesse had commiserated. "This war has made lots of things so much more complicated." That was the best he could say to encourage the fellow as he packed for his unexpected departure.

"They're sendin' me all the way back to Connecticut."

"Do you think you'll ever see your girl again?"

"Don't know how. But my granny always said, 'Time heals all.' The guard shrugged into his jacket. "I guess we'll see if that's true or not. At least I get to go home a little early."

Connecticut sounded like the end of the earth—unless he were really determined, what with all the troop movement across the nation, a trip like that might never come to pass. As this soldier walked toward the transportation depot, Jesse tried to put himself in his place.

If he were told he would never see Miko and Kenji again, what would he do? The thought of living without their smiles, never hearing their voices, stopped him short. He could not conceive of that lonely world.

Amidst snores and grunts from the others in the barracks, his answer came as clear as the noon lunch bell. If it were his to choose—that is, if Miko were willing—he would find a way for them to be together.

"They're closing Blackband Air Field in October." Doctor Graham settled his pencil behind his ear, where the fringe of his hair had all but turned white. "Seems like yesterday they worked on it day and night. Remember?"

Another doc nodded. "Hmm. In some ways it seems like twenty years, with all the extra facilities they've created, and all of the casualties."

"True. Things'll keep changing around here for the next few months, but the brick and mortar the Army has put into this place will still be here."

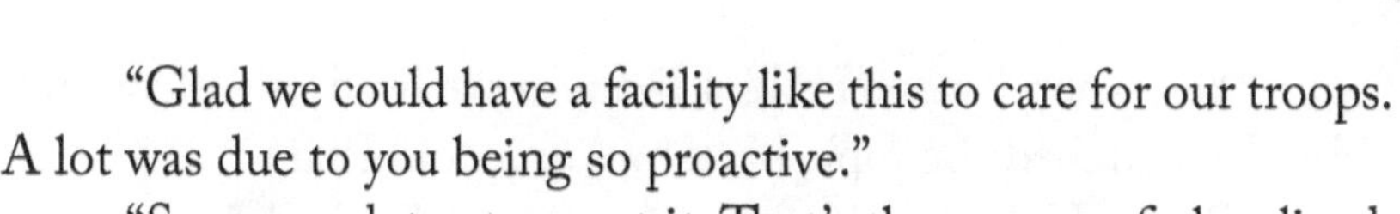

"Glad we could have a facility like this to care for our troops. A lot was due to you being so proactive."

"See a need, try to meet it. That's the way my father lived, and I guess it rubbed off."

Walking behind them down the hall, I happily eavesdropped. At the same time, a good share of my mind rummaged through the latest letters from Jesse and Annie.

Miss M encouraged me to give Annie a warm invitation and even added her own note to one of my letters. A couple of boarders would be leaving at the end of August, making room for Annie and Pearl. Later, after the house quieted down for the evening, Miss M pulled me to the porch swing for a longer talk.

"Seems strange with no one gathered around the parlor radio, doesn't it? It's like the war stole our lives for a time, and now we've gotten them back."

In the last shafts of light from a golden-orange sunset, we plopped down, each with our own thoughts. And then Miss M said, "You know, I really do believe God has a way of working things out, Kin. I no more than start worrying about something when the answer shows up. Back in the late Thirties, I wondered how we would find enough boarders, and I could ask the same right now. But it sounds like Annie might be the answer."

"Hmm. Can't say the same for me, exactly, but I do think I'm getting a little better at praying."

"Of course you are! If you sat down and wrote out a list of the answers you've received since you came here, I bet you'd fill a few pages."

From the main road, a car honked, and further west, a motor revved. Seemed like the number of automobiles in town increased by the week, many of them driven by young GIs home from the war.

"There's talk of a new concrete highway through the southwest part of town. I hope it's at least a mile from us, so we can still hear the quiet in the evenings."

"Me, too. I suppose this house used to be out here all by itself?"

"Yes, when I was a child. I thought we lived in the country." Miss M switched the topic back to Annie and Pearl.

"Baylor University's advertising their fall schedule now, and I noticed the education courses. Why don't you send a telegram to Annie? While she finishes the farm business, Pearl could register and come on ahead. That way she can get right to her studies and not miss out on anything."

"You're sure?"

"Sure as sunshine. By the weekend, we'll have two empty rooms upstairs. When you came, God gave me the sister I never had, and now I might get another one! And Pearl—well, I'm hoping she'll become like a daughter."

Miss M seldom sported a look of longing, but her voice almost broke. "I so wanted to have children, you know. So did Elwyn, but after the war…it wasn't meant to be. Still, we got to know some of the girls at church and tried to remember them on special days.

"But with you and Annie and Pearl, I will feel even more like I have family again. It's one thing to inherit a big old house like this, Kin, but another not to feel lonely in it."

She'd never opened up this way before, and I had no words. I'd never imagined I'd be thankful for those three graves in my past, but at least I'd been able to name those babies, and then bear a living child. The Great War, though she never gave specifics, had robbed Miss M of even that.

"I've also been thinking about Jesse. What would you think if we offered him—or for now, Miko and Kenji, depending on how things go—the carriage house? It still needs a bathroom, but that's about all.

"Oh, what a perfect idea. I could make some curtains for the windows and…" My mind whirred with possibilities…*a tie-back yellow check or calico, maybe…*

"Jesse's hinted at bringing them here but doesn't know for sure. Miko might want to go back to her home on the coast first, just to be sure. He said in his last letter that he's also considering using the GI Bill."

"Makes sense. I haven't even met that son of yours yet, but he already reminds me of you."

"How is that?"

"He knows his mind and seems determined. Taking advantage of the GI Bill couldn't be a more common-sense idea, and we have plenty of colleges around here. I'm sure he realizes there might be some push-back to marrying a Japanese-American. Waco's never been known for being overly tolerant, but…"

Ah. The stories about the Klan and Jesse Washington came to mind.

"But if we all unite and put our best foot forward as a family, we can pave the way for Miko and Kenji. I can't imagine our church *not* accepting new members, and the elementary school principal's a good friend. He used to board here, you know, back when he first came to town as a science teacher."

"I didn't. So many people started out here with you!"

"Well, that's true. I always felt God put me right where I am for a reason." Miss M's sigh hovered—perhaps she was recalling all of the people who had rented rooms and eventually left to start families. After a while, she continued.

"Sounds like Jesse truly loves Miko and her brother. He's young but has your tenacity. Besides, the war's made people older than normal, don't you think?"

"I do. They've had to grow up fast."

"Anyway, I can see our place becoming even more like a real home. With your sis and niece here, Jesse and Miko…"

"You really are one of the most generous folks I know. Of course, everyone will pay their way."

"We've been blessed so much throughout the war. I've saved a lot of the rent money, enough to add that bathroom in the carriage house and maybe even another one in here. Wouldn't it be nice to have two big bathtubs to choose from?"

"Ooh, my aching feet. With all of these women, especially, it sure would!"

"Well, I'm putting in a work order first thing tomorrow with a friend of Judson's, and Mr. Darwin may offer to help out, too. Hopefully if Pearl travels here in the next two weeks, we'll be all ready for her."

As I leaned back in the swing, the first evening star appeared. "Oh, Miss M, I can't believe it. Annie wants to move here…and Jesse! My people are choosing to come to me!"

"No surprise to me, dear. And just so you know, I see them as *our* people. They're coming to make us a stronger family. Elwyn would be so very pleased!"

"There's nothing left for me here. They took everything." Miko let go of Kenji's hand and he ran to Jesse. From the walk they took along the shoreline this morning, he held a conch shell.

"Come with me for a minute, buddy. Let's see what we can build with your shell." Jesse guided him a few yards away so Miko could say her good-byes. Such a strong girl—she would most likely never see her childhood home again.

"Let's build a bridge!" Kenji's bright eyes filled with excitement.

"A bridge it shall be." Scooping and digging with the shell, the project began.

Soon Kenji was mimicking Jesse in a rhyme he'd learned from the engineers on Guadalcanal. "Cheers! Cheers! We're the Engineers!"

Miko took her time circling what once had been the family home. She and her older brother, the lawyer in Washington state, had received word about their other brother's death in the march into Germany. What remained for her in here?

Jesse thought she might want to return to the university in San Diego, but she had no desire to stay in California. Her brother felt the same way. When she received word from him, she read a paragraph out loud.

"I'm going to settle in Seattle. If that doesn't work out, I may move on to Canada."

Such a trying time…at first, Miko hadn't wanted to return to her home at all, but someone traveling that way offered them a ride. It seemed more than unfair that the government shoed her family to this desolate camp up in the hills and refused to even offer transportation back to the coast.

But that was the least of it. On the trip, camping out one night after Kenji went to sleep, Miko explained more of what happened to her family. "We had heard of trouble, but my father couldn't believe anyone would hurt us. Then the government froze our funds, so the bank wouldn't cash his paycheck.

"Our grocery store would no longer let us shop there, and we had only a small garden. As long as my father could still fish, we had food, but then an officer came and forbade him to go out in his boat.

"We had two days to sell the boat, our furniture, everything. A friend of my father's said his son could live in our house and he would send us rent, but that money never arrived. I'm afraid to see what has happened in the meantime…"

Ah, well. They were here now, and Miko had been right. Animals had taken over the ransacked house. Seeing the jumble inside, Jesse thought maybe they shouldn't have come after all.

When he and Kenji had a truly impressive sand bridge underway, Miko slowly turned their way. All Jesse could think was, *She'll make the best of things—she always does.*

"Oh my! What great engineers you are!" Her eyes shimmered, but she kept her voice steady. "What will you call this bridge?"

"I think…*Shiny Bridge.* Because of the mica in the sand… see how it sparkles?"

"Hmm. I do, and that's a perfect name." Miko exchanged a look with Jesse, acknowledging his commitment to teach Kenji through their play.

"And do you know where we get to go next, Kenji?"

He scrunched his forehead. She hinted, "Starts with a *T*"

"Oh…Texas, the biggest state! Does it have an ocean like this?"

"Well, not one near the part of the state where we'll be going, but there'll be cowboys and cattle with long horns."

Jesse shouted, 'Yippee-ay-kayay!'

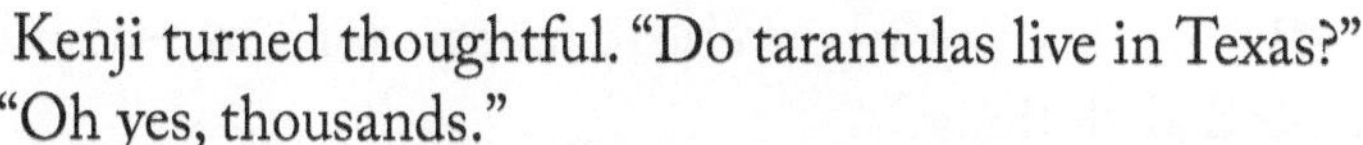

Kenji turned thoughtful. "Do tarantulas live in Texas?"

"Oh yes, thousands."

"We'll have a yard with flowers and live in a house with Jesse's family." Miko clasped Jesse's sand-crusted hand. Something about this touch communicated more than a litany of words.

She had said her farewell to this home. She was ready. And she was saying *yes* to his proposal. He squeezed her fingers as the glimmer of a smile appeared on her lips.

"Oh Kenji, my mama can't wait to meet you. She's your grandmother." Jesse studied Miko again. "Miko and I will get married, you'll go to a new school, and some day Miko will earn her nursing degree."

Miko angled her head. So few words needed in this relationship, when her eyes spoke so well for her.

Jesse tousled Kenji's hair, sand and all. "And I'll…well, we'll see. I'll work somewhere, and Texas has colleges where I can study, too. Maybe one day, I'll become a teacher. What would you think of that?"

Kenji clapped his hands and squiggled sand between his toes.

"From now on, everything will get better and better."

"No more war?" Kenji's chocolate eyes requested—no, required—an answer. Jesse let Miko do the honors.

"No, Kenji. No more war."

"Sleep well, Kin. You've had a long, long day, but the carriage house is looking mighty fine, more like a home every day. With the new bathroom, I can already picture our new little family living there."

Today had been long, but I enjoyed it. We drove the old truck out to a swimming hole with plenty of clean sand and loaded up the back. By the time we returned, Mr. Darwin had built and painted a good-sized sandbox. Like Judson, he could do almost anything.

Filling the sand box took some time, and picturing Kenji at play filled our conversation.

"It's hard to know how else to prepare for him—wish I knew if he needed clothing."

"Surely he will, and maybe a bicycle? But we'll have to wait till they get here. I haven't even seen a picture of him yet, so there's no telling what size he wears. But little boys wear out shoes and outgrow pants pretty fast, in my experience."

"Do you know his birthday?"

"No—I really don't know any more than I've told you. We'll have a lot of catching up to do." Then I recalled something Jesse had written. "Oh! Jesse says Kenji loves to read, so I can shop for some books. Maybe we can fix up a little desk just for him."

"Hmm." Miss M tossed in the final shovel-full and leaned against our old cottonwood. "I've got an extra colander he can use for sifting, and some old measuring cups to bring out here. At least he'll know we thought of him when he sees this, right?"

"He'll know. I'm sure of that."

We went inside to make the noon meal and spent the next few hours getting ready for supper. When the dishes were all put away, Miss M yawned.

"I'm headed right to bed. Can't believe Pearl arrives tomorrow evening, and Annie in a couple of weeks."

After she left, I couldn't settle down to sleep. Sitting out in the porch swing with a glass of warm milk didn't seem to help, so I wandered the alley. Mr. Darwin had covered Kenji's sandbox with a canvas tarp to keep out the neighborhood cats, a sign of his thoughtfulness.

One came sneaking up like a snake, so I hissed it away. Only fresh sand for little Kenji!

He may have begun his young life in an internment camp, but from now on, he would be our special boy. I was almost as anxious to meet him as to see Jesse for the first time in so long. His last letter had something to do with that.

*For a long time now, I've felt as though I'm Kenji's father,*
*and now that Miko and I are officially engaged, that feeling*

*only increases. I feel responsible for him, but that doesn't weigh on me at all—it makes me happy.*

*You're going to love this little fellow. He's extra smart for his age—Miko's father read to him a lot and taught him as much as possible before he passed. He's also just plain sweet—his smile could break a guy's heart.*

So Jesse had learned through his Uncle Winn how to be a father. Tears sparked as I considered the beauty of everything working out. Annie and her family would be joining an exodus from the Midwest to Texas and the coasts.

The path ahead seemed so bright, so exciting. Why, then, did such a tumult arise in me tonight? Walking it out helped as much as anything, so I continued beyond our property.

Half an hour later, when I turned back toward home, what had been troubling me came front and center. Just like that, I knew what I must do.

~

"Over there! That's where you and I met. I thought this old corncrib might could've fallen down by now, but there it stands…or sags."

An enormous mound of fluff in my throat threatened to suffocate me. Riding with Doctor Graham had seemed light at first, almost like a picnic outing. In fact, Rosita packed a lunch for us, since she was taking her usual Saturday meal down to the Sandtown community today.

She and Doc had made their offering into something far more by enlisting others to join in. Our church got involved, and whole families made the trip now, taking children along to play with the Sandtown children.

But I had dedicated today to stopping the old voices…stopping them once and for all. Now, the turn south lay not far ahead. The road took us through dried-out farmland or pastures with hungry-looking cattle nosing uncooperative earth.

From time to time, Doc engaged in his own banter, and I supplied perfunctory grunts and *m-hmms*. I had hoped Rosita might come along since I rarely got to see her outside the hospital kitchen. But here we were, Doc and me, just like at the beginning.

Before I expected it, the limestone rock where I rested on that long-ago trek took shape in the shade of a tall cottonwood. If I were to stop, would a bottle be lying there to greet me? I might have told Doc about that life-saving drink, but the condition of my voice box and the motor's roar made the story impossible at this juncture.

Half an hour farther, I sensed the next turn coming, the one toward the west, toward my old life. Toward that death-in-life I had left behind.

Right then, truth be told, I wished I'd have ignored the inner prompting—no, nagging—that kept urging me to make this trip. What could be worse than re-visiting the past? Yet something in me would not rest, and Doc had listened when I explained my need for a ride.

"I could take the bus, maybe. But I'd have to miss an extra day of work, and there's no place to stay there."

"What about Saturday? Actually, I've been meaning to ask if you might still own property where you came from. A young man back from the war has asked me about buying land in Texas. He wants to seek his fortune in cattle."

"Property?" The thought hadn't occurred to me. "I guess so. Yes, though the cabin and barn are nothing to shout about. And Saturday would work. The office I need to visit is open on Saturdays…at least it used to be."

Sheriff Stringham's office. I could see him now, blue eyes steady from under his hat brim. I recalled him telling me the only way to survive was to leave Clyde. And years later, promising to send word when the telegram from Annie arrived saying Jesse arrived safely in Kentucky.

He'd shaken his head that day and sighed but said no more.

I knew he was thinking, *Why don't you go along with Jesse?* Only the heart knows its weaknesses. If only the heart knew more about its strengths! I *could have* left that day. *Could have* built a new life in Kentucky. But that stubborn strain in me… I still had no fitting word for it… something told me I must stay, and I obeyed.

Mistaken loyalty—how many folks have sacrificed even more than I had for this? We think we know what's right and stubbornly stick to that despite hurting ourselves over and over.

Well, then. As Doc pushed the foot-feed, we lapsed into silence. Yes, regret amounted to a wasteland. I had missed out on Jesse's growth to manhood.

*But now he's coming back, and you will watch his children grow up.*

Yes. This voice must become my focus. A wonderful life lay ahead. Besides that, the past few years had fed my soul, given me purpose and the right kind of pride in my work. Given me Miss M and strengthened my faith. For all of this, only gratitude would do.

Before I expected it, the town sign appeared along the roadside. Doc let up on the gas and turned my way.

"Is this it? You've never told me exactly where…"

"Yes," I choked out. Like these environs, the sun had faded the town sign's ragged wood to a pallid dun hue, leaving a scattering of ink scratches on an old board too weathered to reform. If I tried hard, I could make out the H, and a few inches beyond, what might have been a *y* or *g*. And at the end, the bare bones of an e.

"I've never driven this far out here before. Pretty barren country, that's for sure."

I cleared my throat. I must gather myself to be able to speak. Only a few minutes now before the sheriff would ask my mission.

"True. I can't imagine anyone wanting to buy our place, but if it's a GI looking to work hard, he might give it a try."

"After what this fellow faced over there the past five years, I think he's got what it takes to make something out of almost nothing."

*Almost nothing*…that's what he'd be buying.

That town sign's precarious nature stayed with me, perched on a rotting post as if it might fly away any second. A powerful metaphor for everything that took place on the ranch just a few miles from here.

Everything except Jesse's birth. That blessing occurred here, too—that lone, lovely gift. I must keep my attention on him. But the closer we drew to the office, the more I gripped my purse.

One part of me proclaimed that once again, I had trapped myself. At the same time, I knew I must see this through yet would rather be anywhere else on the earth.

Chapter Twenty-nine

Main Street had crumbled even more than I recalled. Though I visualized the most rundown of settlements, even that image disintegrated as Doc shifted his faithful old engine into first gear. "It's the third building down from the corner. The one that's a little taller than the others."

Doc parked in front. My heart lurched, but nothing for it, I must complete my task.

Doc turned my way. "Want company?"

"No thanks. This… I have to do this alone."

"All right, Kin." He patted my hand. "Take your time, and if you need me—"

"Thanks." As I opened the door, my voice squeaked like a hatchling chick fresh from its egg. I tucked in my blouse, adjusted my skirt, and took a step.

Another. My feet weighed tons. I might be on my way to the gallows. Surely any rancher in town today must be observing my slow-motion progress toward the door.

In this late-August heat, it yawned open. The sheriff must have heard me coming, because he met me on the threshold. Behind him sat an old oaken desk, and behind that, the iron bars of a double jail cell rose to the ceiling.

"Is Sheriff Stringham here?" My heart *rat-a-tatted* with each syllable. This man looked about twenty years younger than the one I recalled, and in the shadows, nothing about him seemed familiar.

"No, Ma'am. Sheriff McLeod at your service." Tipping his hat, he motioned me to a wooden chair and took one nearby.

"But Sheriff…"

"He's moved on from here, Ma'am. Lost his son early in the war. Got a call to work with the police in San Antonio and moved his family down there."

"Oh." My mouth went dry. Somehow, I had attached my hopes to one particular lawman.

"How kin I help you, Ma'am?"

"I… that is… I used to live here. Until 1937, that is. Clyde Lovelace…" The Sheriff's eyes narrowed. "We… he ranched a few miles west of here, and I…"

"Jest one minute, Ma'am." He disappeared toward the cells and returned with a manila file in hand.

"Clyde Lovelace. Disappeared summer '37. Suspicious. Case closed one year later, to the day. Investigation revealed a twelve-gauge shotgun round in chicken coop wall. No body, no other evidence, place deserted. Wild hogs? Signed W.L.S."

The revelation took my breath away. Sheriff Stringham had gone to the ranch… found a bullet in the chicken coop… So more than one had been released that night. More to ponder.

The new sheriff peered at me as if answers might be chiseled in my forehead. He flipped through a couple of pages in the file. "Sheriff Stringham was a stickler for the truth. He kept dis'plined records, Ma'am. If he concluded Mr. Lovelace perished of gunshot, that's pro'lly for sure what happened."

"I… yes. I can confirm that, sir."

"You witnessed Mr. Lovelace's death?"

My nod brought him closer on his chair, so that our knees almost touched. I made fists to hide my quivering fingers.

"Where did the shot originate, Ma'am?"

My voice sounded ethereal, as though floating from some radio speaker hidden in the walls. "Clyde's shotgun—he always kept it in the milk house, loaded. I thought…" My chest constricted. Was I closing all doors to a happy life?

"You thought…"

"It was late at night when I spied someone raiding my hen house. Those hens were all I had, so I got the gun and…"

"Where was your husband at this time? I assume Clyde and you were married?"

"Yes. He was in the house. Inebriated."

"Hmm."

"So I confronted the robber. Before I knew what had happened, the gun went off and…"

"The scoundrel had been hit?"

"Yes, but then I realized the thief was Clyde."

"A mortal wound." The Sheriff pronounced this as a statement, not an inquiry. "And what did you do next?"

"I gathered a few things and left the ranch. I… Sheriff Stringham had advised me to do so more than once. My husband was…"

"Ma'am, no offense intended, but this whole town 'members that feller. 'Nother note Sheriff Stringham wrote labeled him *an undesirable.* The Sheriff liked words, didja know that?"

"Why, no. I…"

"Certain sure, he did. Lemme look up somethin' else right quick."

My chest stung. I had always felt Sheriff Stringham to be on my side, but—

Sheriff McLeod returned. "Here 'tis. Some references to Lovelace makin' trouble at the bank. Didja know the Sheriff had t' drive him out of town more 'n once?"

"Drive…"

"Multiple incidents over a ten-year period, Ma'am. Seems as though Sheriff Stringham viewed Mr. Lovelace as an outlaw."

His pause turned into a longer, awkward silence.

"And here…" He looked up, eyebrows spiked like a child making a fascination discovery. "Why, here's a note about the meanin's of names."

I could only shake my head.

"Yes'm. B'lieve it or not, Sheriff Stringham wrote right here in the margin, "Lovelace... *outlaw*. Guess he musta looked up the meanin' of the feller—your husband's name."

*Outlaw?* I had no idea.

"Well, then. As the good Sheriff concluded, case closed. I ain't 'bout t' reopen what he called closed."

Case closed. It took a full minute to take in the finality of his statement.

"Ma'am? You still got somethin' to say?"

My throat dried out. The pool of blood forming under Clyde's shoulder came clear, an image I had pondered far too many times.

"Do you agree with Sheriff Stringham's assessment that Mr. Lovelace's... er... Do you agree that most likely wild hogs consumed Mr. Lovelace's corpse?"

My nod seemed to suffice.

"Any other facts as yet unspoken?"

"No, I... it's just that... I moved Clyde's body." The sheer volume of details I had prepared to divulge weighed on me. But this young man seemed nonplussed.

"Where to?"

"Out in the cornfield."

"Pretty much proves wild hogs took care of it."

"I still... feel badly about all this."

"'Course. Ain't the way nobody woulda planned. But you say the gun just went off. Did I hear that right?"

"Yes."

"No chance somebody else was lurkin' in the darkness and shot him? Jest give me your opinion."

"Why, that thought has never occurred to me. I mean, the blast threw me back a few feet, landed me on the ground."

"Well then, what's done is done. Ma'am, Sheriff Stringham's no fool, and he rightly closed this case. Anythin' else I kin do for y'?"

It took a few seconds to take in his words, the very outcome I had hoped for. Finally, I remembered the property.

"Yes. A returned soldier is interested in purchasing the ranch. I never signed for our land and have no deed."

"Easy enough t' fix. Better you than the gov'ment gettin' paid for it. Land office closed a few months ago. Moved all their records right in here, back in our second cell. Lemme check."

"All right, thank you. I'll be right back—going to get my driver."

"Yes'm."

Busy engaging a passerby, Doc quickly said good-bye and hurried over. "All's well?"

I grabbed his arm. "Yes. He's even got the deed here and…"

"Everything else all right? You look as pale as a bone in the desert."

If only he knew the deep meaning in that image. I caught my breath, and a long sigh escaped. "I think so. I'll tell you everything on the way home."

After the Sheriff asked me to sign a paper, he turned a hand crank to produce a copy of the document, filling the office with a familiar, comforting smell. *Ah yes, the copy room at the university…* I hadn't recalled that basement area for years. Now, the smell of mimeograph ink brought it all back.

Rubbing alcohol, not an unpleasant fragrance and so familiar after my work in the hospital. And methanol, a bit more distinct and sweeter. But oh, the ink! How many copies had I made for my mentor professor? I took to wearing dark blue, since the violet-colored ink always ended up on my hands and clothes.

The Sheriff exchanged pleasantries with Doc and nodded my way. We headed to the car, but before he backed out, Doc launched a question.

"Your papers provide all the buyer will need to find the place. But would you like to drive out there anyhow?"

Sincere concern laced his voice. If I needed to see the ranch one more time, he offered me this chance. A fleeting image of

those three graves flooded me. Violet, Magnolia, and Charles
would stay in my heart forever, but their graves, once so vital to
my well-being, had served their purpose. Now, they only reminded
me of the darkest of times.

"No, thanks."

"Sure?"

"Positive." I settled back in the seat.

"All right. But if you ever do, I know a trusty old automobile
that already knows most of the way by heart."

Nothing like Doc's bright grin to show darkness the gate.
"About the sale. There's no pressure at all. If this doesn't work out,
another property will turn up for my young friend. You don't think
Jesse will want to go into ranching?"

"No. He may go to college on the GI Bill."

Even breathing these words sent a thrill through me. Jesse's
letters recounted the books he's been reading at Manzanar—classics.
Nothing could have warmed my heart more.

Doc shoved a packet my way and a sudden wave of hunger
gripped me. "Go ahead," he nodded. "I got hungry while you were
inside and ate my share."

Thick cheese and Rosita's bread. A lovely apple. A vacuum jug
of hot tea and two thick raison-oatmeal cookies. Rosita knew me well!

Within minutes after I finished, the whole story poured
out to Doc. Facts and feelings exited my lips like molasses from
a bucket.

Halfway home and emptied, I shrank into the comfort of
my leather seat. For a long while, Doc held his peace, as if thinking
through every word. By now, we traveled the new concrete stretch
that led into Waco, and the regular marks in the cement under the
wheels ground in my ears.

"Accidental death, no evidence except an unmatched bullet. I
do wonder about two rounds being dispersed, but stranger things
have happened. Bullets sometimes *ricochet*, you know, and no one
examined the body.

"Of course, even if you'd left Clyde lying where he fell, nature would have taken its course. And then, there's the statute of limitations. I believe it's two years for a wrongful death claim?"

Crisp, clean, legal language. It was too much—hot tears burst forth.

At the first snivel, Doc handed over his big white handkerchief and kept driving. Finally, the eruption died down and he glanced my way.

"Feeling better?"

"I don't know."

"You've held in parts of that story ever since it happened?"

"…so shameful… who kills her husband, anyway?"

"You might be surprised."

"What?"

"The majority of women living with malicious men don't kill them, true. But some do, and it's understandable. As humans, we can take only so much."

"But I didn't… never meant to…"

"Of course not! Do you think after watching you help save so many lives, I would ever think you did?"

Maybe I *had* thought that. Otherwise, why didn't I explain all of this to Doc earlier? At this point I wasn't sure.

"You're not the type of person to plan and execute a murder. It would be all you could do to act in self-defense. I'm sure Sheriff Stringham understood this about you. If he harbored any doubt, he could have instigated a search for you."

"Sometimes I feared he might."

"But did he?"

No answer needed. He hadn't, and in this, I found comfort. The Sheriff would have found me. But he would have believed me, I'm sure he would have. Instead, I let fear take control.

As the outskirts of Waco came into view, Doc put his hand on mine. "I believe the only posse that's been out to get you is *you*. But now, no more accusations, since Sheriff Stringham sealed this case years ago. And as the present Sheriff made clear, there's no reviving it, not ever."

During a shift at a corner, I spoke up. "Now I can face Jesse with a clear conscience."

"What do you mean?"

"In spite of everything, Clyde was his father. I wouldn't want him to think…"

"There you go again. Give me one good reason Jesse would think *anything* but the best about you. Clyde nearly killed him, right?"

"Yes. But I sent him away all by himself. He was so young, just a boy."

"And why?"

"Because of Clyde."

"So. You stood between Jesse and abuse, maybe even death."

"Yes. Still, today helps. I want to close the door on this."

"Well, my strong woman friend, you certainly have done that. I've heard that door bang several times today, in fact."

I wanted to say, *But I'm not strong! If I had been, I'd have gone to the Sheriff right away instead of living like a coward all this time.*

Doctor Graham, perhaps my best advocate, was not to be argued with. I could see it in the granite lines of his profile, the same way he looked going into a challenging surgery.

From now on, I would borrow his logic. I would believe as he believed. This man, of all men living, surely knew the meaning of *strong*.


*December 3, 1945*


You'd think I would have calmed down by now, but not so. On the walk home from work, my mind still swirled. Helen and I talked a little, but not much. This seemed to be a thinking afternoon for us both.

My reverie centered around Jesse, Miko, and Kenji who had

arrived a week ago. The camp at Manzanar closed on November 21, and they'd found a ride to the coast for Miko to check her former home.

Then, they bought train tickets here. Ah. Hard to believe all this has occurred so fast. But oh, the culmination! That unforgettable moment when Jesse stepped off the train.

How can a person laugh and cry at the same time? It's like sunshine and shadows, or rain falling when the sun is shining. One of those unfathomable events that break your heart and mend it all at once. Annie and Pearl went with me to pick them up. Miss M declined to be sure we all enjoyed a royal dinner when we returned.

But before they disembarked, I felt so lost. In a *brouhaha* of train whistles, families trying to spot their loved ones, and the station's general hustle and bustle, I simply took Annie's hand and followed where she led. How wonderful having her with me once again—my big sis.

When she and Pearl halted near a wide wooden platform, so did I. From several cars, people descended one-by-one. So many in uniform, some of them using crutches or canes, some with bandaged arms or heads.

All around us, screams and tears and laughter—oh, what a day! We watched and watched—hundreds of stories here. And then, when we thought one car had fully emptied, a tall soldier emerged with a slight boy in his arms. And Miko, eyes bright, searching the crowd. Of course, this young woman had to be Jesse's beloved.

Honestly, all I remember besides that first sight is being crushed against a strong chest, with Annie right beside me, and Pearl grabbing Kenji as if she already knew him. We hunted for baggage, loading and hauling everything to Doc Graham's borrowed transport.

The ride home became a blur of tears, greetings, questions, and me caught in breathless wonder. Jesse had come! He sat right behind me, with Pearl, Miko, and Kenji smashed in together.

Thank goodness for Annie's presence of mind. She'd driven

their truck on the farm for years, and *en route* from the depot, managed to direct the conversation. Already, Kenji clung to Pearl as though they'd known each other forever. Her necklace had various gems, and she was busy explaining their names to him.

Dinner far exceeded anyone's expectations, with Jesse exclaiming about each dish. Over strawberry shortcake, Kenji fell asleep in Miko's arms, a fitting end to the day. I couldn't get enough of this beautiful child, and Miko's quiet way fit in with us from the start. Seeing Jesse hoist Kenji for the walk home touched me beyond words.

Lighted by the moon, the threesome simply glowed as they neared the carriage house. "Why, look!" Miss M drew my attention that way. "They're walking down Elwyn's Sunshine Alley! Right now, he might re-name it *Moonlight*."

Sunshine… moonlight. Either way, this path, hidden from most folks, lent softness and light to this old world.

Glancing at our group, such gratitude filled me. With Pearl happily beginning her first semester courses and Annie starting a new accounting job at a small gasoline company, what else needed to fall into place?

The answer came a few nights ago at dinner: a wedding. Jesse and Miko explained their desire to marry on the seventeenth, just two weeks from now.

The church women have already taken Miko in—one even offered to sew her wedding dress. Miss M insists on a reception in our back yard.

"We'll have all sorts of guests, and the ladies' circle will provide potato salad and meat loaf. Annie mentioned that's Jesse's favorite. We'll need some Mexican food, too, don't you think?" Miss M took my silence for agreement and plunged on. "I'll talk to Rosita about that, and a wedding cake."

All around us, people revealed fresh energy since the war's end. Now life could begin again in earnest, and Miss M's face reflected that sentiment. Nothing to do but advance full speed into whatever the future held.

"I'm going to have Jesse string some lights from the carriage house to the willow and over to the cottonwood. That'll make a nice big triangle.

"We'll set the tables along the sides, so if people want to dance, they can. Mr. Jeffries has agreed to bring over his piano. He says it's not as heavy as the one in the house, and his wife will play. A couple of her friends will too, on guitar and the cello."

"Cello? This is turning out to be quite an event!"

"A son gets married only once in a lifetime, and you have to remember, I'm living vicariously, too." Miss M's eyes sparkled like they did when she used to share a secret with Elwyn.

"Pearl has agreed to sing a solo during the ceremony. Now, won't that be just the thing?"

My nod rose from unaffected gratitude. The workload at the hospital had grown so, I'd hardly been able to help with the wedding at all. As Annie had on the day Jesse arrived, Miss M was carrying me through.

"I know how busy you've been. Doctor Graham stopped in the other day. He hardly ever accepts my invitation to sit down for a cup of coffee, but for once, he did. He's plain exhausted."

"He definitely is. But we've made it so far, and this influx can't last forever."

"He took pains to mention you and Helen. Said they need to find more nursing recruits, but you two have become his mainstay in the wards."

"Hmm. We make a good team, that's for sure. And I did mention to Jesse and Miko how badly we still need nurses. She had entered nursing school when they sent her to Manzanar, you know."

"Oh my! Doctor Graham will be excited to hear this."

"For now, I'm keeping it quiet. It's up to Miko to decide what she wants to do. She's so intent on Kenji's schooling right now—one thing at a time."

"Right."

"I don't want to be a pushy mother-in-law, you know!"

"No, of course not! But everything's going well so far, don't you think?"

"When you consider all the changes those two have gone through in the past few years, I'd say so. And Annie, too. Thanks to you, we all have a chance to get to know each other. There's nothing like a brand-new start. You have a way of giving that to people."

"Hmm." Miss M's expression, a sort of half-grin paired with… I couldn't tell. I knew she'd always been loath to be singled out for credit and would say she only did what God gave her to do.

But we owed her so much. Our family enjoyed the new apartment, Kenji loved playing in this big yard, and having Annie here paved the way for me to get to know them all little-by-little.

Sometimes I thought my heart could hardly bear more happiness. Before I could say another word, though, Miss M hurried off to the kitchen once more.

Chapter Thirty

*Mid-January 1946*

"But what about your nursing?"

Miko took her time. Sometimes her reply came in lifting an eyebrow, pressing her lips together, or a touch. Jesse supposed her mother had taught her this and didn't mind the wait. *Taking her time* could mean a few seconds, minutes, or half an hour.

But she never left him without at least a clue. For starters, the way she stroked Kenji's hair as he slept carried a message. Not anything he didn't already know. Kenji's welfare came first, and he understood perfectly.

They'd been married only a few weeks, but he felt as though they'd been together forever. He especially liked her serenity and the way she thought things through. Right now, he figured she did just that, while he chopped wood. In their small apartment, she rocked with Kenji during naptime.

To think, he was adding to the wood pile first made by Jud, or Judson, as Mama and Miss M called him. And his new little family lived in an apartment Jud had fashioned. Every inch of careful woodworking relayed its own message about the carpenter.

Everywhere they went, Kenji made friends. Even with the prejudice that still existed, people seemed to make extra effort with him. His teacher used *winsome* to describe Kenji, the precise adjective for their son.

The day after they said their vows, he and Miko went down to the courthouse to adopt Kenji. Even now, that momentous declaration… *Kenji Yoshida Kline…* brought a proud tremble. What a lot this lad had been through already, but he always seemed to adjust.

In the evenings, Miko and Jesse read to him, and he often surprised them with what he'd already learned. Once, when he disappeared temporarily, Miko had found him in the house with Pearly, reading a book.

They ate meals with the rest of the family and the boarders in the big house and spent time there after dinner. But having their own place nearby seemed perfect. And now, something else was working out in their favor.

Jesse had been driving a delivery truck for a friend of Miss M's, a wholesale bread company, with the understanding that once he started college, his hours would be altered. He expected this in a few months, but through a professor friend of Doctor Graham's, he'd been offered a scholarship to begin now—this semester.

The Army paperwork might take some time with the backlog, the professor said, but thousands of other returned soldiers were following this procedure. As long as he could buy his books and pay part of the tuition to begin with, why not get started?

Jesse could think of no good reason but asked him for two days to think it over and get things in order. Doctor Graham must've put a bug in Kin's ear, because first thing after supper tonight, she offered all he needed.

"I have plenty saved up to cover your books, and when the check from the ranch comes, it'll be yours. I'd planned to surprise you then. It's your inheritance, Jesse."

"I don't know what to say."

Mama just smiled. "I'm so glad I can give you something."

"The way I see it, you've given me everything." She wasn't one to cry often, at least that's how he remembered her. He'd been so young, though, and would never know what life at the ranch was really like for her. But this evening, the reflection through the leaded glass parlor window created a perfect diamond in her hair to match the shimmer in her eyes.

From the dining room, Kenji came running. What could fix tears faster than snuggling with him? While Kin buried her face in Kenji's hair and he whispered, "It's okay, G'ama," Jesse took stock.

Ever since Miko said she would marry him, life had started taking better turns. Who would ever have thought he would be grateful for his assignment to guard duty at Manzanar?

Kenji and Miko brought such happiness, he couldn't imagine life being better. With the GI Bill and Mama's foresight, he would be able to graduate in three years. Then he would open up the world of literature to high school students.

As Mama and Aunt Annie said, this career made so much sense, considering his childhood and youth. And all of those long, lonely evenings at Manzanar—without books to read, what would he have done?

After he carried Kenji to bed, a light shone from a second-floor window in the big house, Miss M's room, next door to Mama's. Hers used to belong to Jud, before Miss M's husband passed. She and Miss M still marveled at how he and L'il Wall had found Jesse in the wilds.

He stepped outdoors, and soon Miko stood beside him. Her gentle presence radiated warmth. They walked the alley hand-in-hand in the twilight, back and forth, saying nothing until a shooting star flashed through the sky.

"My grandmother always said that back in Japan, her elders taught her to wish on a shooting star three times, and her dreams would all come true."

"Is that right? What if your dreams already have come true? That's how I feel right now. I'm back with Mama, my life's been saved so many times, and I have you and Kenji."

Miko moved his hands to her waist. "*All* of your dreams? I think there might be another one right here." She chuckled at his reaction. "Jesse, your eyes are going to pop out of your head."

He pulled her close. "A baby? You're going to have a baby?"

"I'm pretty sure."

"Oh man!" His arms flailed as he glanced around. "How will we…? I'd better…"

Her giggle stopped him. "After everything we've been through, don't you think this will work out just fine?"

*July 4, 1953*

Seated in a double iron lawn chair under a canvas awning, Annie and I crooned to the babies in our arms. In a rocker a few feet away, Miss M fanned her face with a hankie. "Whew, what a hot one! But I've always loved parties, and you've brought so many of them to me, Kin. Back when Elwyn was so sick, I couldn't even think of having one, but now…"

She stretched her bare feet out on the grass. "Seems like every month it's somebody's birthday, and then there's Christmas and Easter…"

From the cottonwood, a mockingbird launched his tune a few hours early, and Miss M stared up into the foliage. "Well, what do you know? I thought this afternoon too sultry for a bird to sing. Do either of you want me to take one of the twins?"

"That would be great, but…" I gestured with my free hand toward the food table. "Maybe you could grab little Karen. Looks like she might need some guidance."

Miss M sprang to her feet laughing and soon returned leading a cherubic child with a face-full of frosting and a piece of cake in her dimpled hands. "We were just helping ourselves, Grandma!"

At the far end of the lot, Jesse and some of his teacher friends played baseball with Kenji and other children. Miko perched on a blanket under the cottonwood with Karen's little sister, Hana, who turned three a few days ago. Miko and one of the wives helped their daughters roll a rubber ball between them.

"Oh my! What a great party, Miss M." Annie rocked *her* twin gently back and forth. "These children will grow up with such good memories!"

"I hope so. That's my goal—to give people memories to treasure. And your family certainly makes it easy… how could anyone *not* throw parties for grandkids as cute as these?"

"They're a whirlwind, aren't they? Kenji, Karen, Hana and now these two!" I still had trouble believing we were helping to care for twins. "Willie and Joe. It's not surprising how Jesse and Miko named them. And Miko still looks so young, like she did the day she and Jesse first came."

Dr. Graham and Rosita made their entrance, loaded down with food to add to the barbecue spread. A minute later, Pearl and her husband arrived, and Mr. Darwin helped everyone unload their offerings. With chef skills no one had realized until recently, he made the barbecue and just filled the ice cream maker with ice to begin churning.

Like Judson, he fixed whatever needed repair around the place and helped Jesse add two more rooms to the carriage house. But he also still worked at his regular job. "He'll probably keep on until he dies in his tracks," Miss M confided the other day. "He asked if it's all right for him to never leave, and of course, I said 'Yes.'"

More tempting smells wafted from the table…rich, tantalizing tamales, as only Rosita could make them. I knew I couldn't resist.

"Another party! And what a day to celebrate!" Magnetized by the babies, Rosita hurried over. "What a busy grandmother you've become, Kin!"

"Yes. I never could have imagined this, not in a million years." And it was true. Nothing in my wildest hopes had prepared me for so much joy.

After the fireworks, with the children sleeping and the adults lethargic, Jesse tended a campfire. Such a comfortable evening, looking back on old times and peering forward to the future. Dr.

Graham spun a tale about the day he met me, leaving out the parts he knew I'd rather keep to myself.

"So you were walking from the ranch? The place where Jesse was born?" Miko's eyes widened.

"Yes. I didn't know where my journey would end, but then Doc came along and gave me a ride. It all seems like a dream now, you know? Back then, he had dark hair and wore no glasses. See how his new ones reflect the fire tonight? Of course, I was a lot younger, too."

Someone else shared about those first days, and then Pearl and her husband, John, made an announcement. Their first baby should be here by Christmas. Everyone congratulated them and Annie.

Things quieted down again, and from the far side where the alley met our neighbor's property, a shadowy figure with a limp approached. Jesse went to meet him and they chatted a bit before he brought the man into our circle.

"This is L'il Wall, everyone! He helped Judson save my life!"

Miss M leaped up to shake his hand. "Judson mentioned working with you, but we've never met."

L'il Wall shrank back from our hugs. "Come t' d'liver a message from Jud. He passed in a minin' accident. Got a big timber off m'leg n' saved m'life. Rescued some other fellers, too, but then come 'nuther crash, n' that was all. Nothin' nobody could do to get 'im out. I'd promised if I ever come back t' let y' know he never fergot y'."

"A quiet hero in so many ways. Just like him to die rescuing others." Doc spoke for all of us.

"Won't you stay a while and have some dessert?" Miss M, hospitable as always.

"No'm. Thank y' kindly, but I gotta git back t' m' own. I'll sleep better knowin' Jud's message got here."

He backed away and turned into the night. As he vanished, Jesse fed the fire and re-told the story of his injuries and amnesia.

"But finally, all of that led you to Miko, and then back to us." Annie's voice quavered. "Back to your mama."

"It did, for sure. At times, I really wondered if anything would ever make sense again, especially after hearing the news about Beau. Tonight would be perfect if he could be here." Jesse drew Miko closer, and I imagined her thinking of her parents and brother. I reached for Annie's hand.

Across the way, Doc put his arm around Rosita, and the flames reflected in his glasses once again. The beginning of the war seemed so long ago, I had almost forgotten we had two Gold Star mothers here.

Someone murmured, "We all wondered if it would ever end, didn't we?"

After a thought-filled silence, Doctor Graham waxed eloquent. "That's war for you. Leads you away, tears at your heart. Then it sends you back home for a brand-new start."

"Why, you're a poet, my dear." Rosita's smile lighted our circle, and crackles from the fire accentuated the cicadas' muted staccato. Cool shadows surrounded us, filled with too many musings to share aloud—mountains of recollections and hopes.

For us, the war still divided past and future, yet with kinship's instinctive comfort. High in the cottonwood, an owl flapped its wings. For a moment, it seemed that Elwyn and Judson joined us too, as evening drew her cloak over our corner of the world.

1.  Where do you think the bottle that Kin found under the tree originated?
2.  What troubled Kin most about Clyde's death?
3.  Why was it so difficult for Kin to forgive herself for sending Jesse away? How can you relate to her feelings?
4.  What characteristics helped Miss M meet Kin's emotional needs?
5.  Have you ever known anyone like Doctor Graham? What do you like about them?
6.  Why was it important for Kin to speak to the sheriff again?
7.  Describe Elwyn's relationship with Judson. What features give Judson a mystical aura?
8.  How does the title relate to the story?
9.  Which literary works mentioned by the characters relate best to *Sunshine Alley*?
10. As Jesse matures and the war wanes, how would you describe the changes in his attitude?
11. What role do self-doubt and confidence play in characters' lives?
12. Consider the significance of the bottles in the story. What ties them all together?

Thanks to all those who have taken time to encourage me in this specific manuscript. Especially, I'd like to thank Shannon for the initial prompt that led to this novel, Gina, Monica, and Jan for help with content and errors, and Lynn for sharing geographical wisdom and her knowledge of Texas history. A big thanks also to Cathy for your never-ending encouragement, and to Liz for your editing skill.

One other person who has been instrumental in my jouney rarely receives the gratitude he deserves. Mike Parker, bless you for your love of words and your steady hand as editor/publisher. I have learned much from you, and truly cannot thank you enough for being so kind, professional, and patient.

*About the Author*

From childhood on, words have comforted and challenged Gail. After instructing expository writing and English as a Second Language, she began writing memoir and fiction.

Intrigued by the World War II era, she creates women's historical fiction and sometimes a cozy mystery. Gail encourages other authors by facilitating writing workshops/retreats. As she and her husband enjoy the beauty of Arizona's Mogollon Rim Country, who knows when another heroine will come to life?

One thing is sure, you can count on Gail's characters to learn from history. Tenaciously, they face hardship by asking honest questions, acting with integrity, and growing in faith.

Visit Gail online at:

www.GailKittleson.com